AFTER HE HAD KILLED HIS
WIFE AND CHILDREN . . .

After he had killed his wife and children, T.T. Dysan looked at his watch. Time to go.

He turned off the lights (saving money on electricity was important) as he left the neat suburban house (that he'd called home until after the divorce).

He carefully locked the door behind him (a good solid dead bolt, bought to keep his family safe).

He walked to the driveway and unlocked his imported car (for which he was behind on the payments since he'd lost his job).

He climbed into the car and leaned across to the glove compartment, checked the handgun (bought for family protection) inside, made certain it was fully loaded.

Then he started the car and headed downtown to the comic book convention, thinking about all the kids there infected by Evil.

Comic books and kids!

There was still one hell of a lot left to do . . .

* * *

"In *Fiend*, C. Dean Andersson takes what makes group comics like *X-Men* and humor comics like *She-Hulk* exciting and fun to read . . . Great Read!"

—Renée Whitterstaetter, Editor, Marvel Comics

"Completely uncompromising, vicious, and disturbing, and he stays crunchy in milk, too. Dean is one of the reasons I haven't given up on the horror field."

—Paul T. Riddell, author of *Squashed ArmadilloCon, or Fear and Loathing in Austin: A Savage Journey into the Heart of the Fanboy Dream*

C. DEAN ANDERSSON
FIEND

ZEBRA BOOKS
KENSINGTON PUBLISHING CORP.

ZEBRA BOOKS are published by

Kensington Publishing Corp.
850 Third Avenue
New York, NY 10022

First Printing: June, 1994

Printed in the United States of America

DEDICATION

For the Crone of my Childhood Dreams,
At my North Window beneath the Willow,
Grinning in Moonlight with Her Hounds and Nightmares,
Feet of Bone rustling Dead Leaves in Summer
Beneath Her Cold Black Cloak . . .
My Thanks, and this Book.

Thanks to Alice Alfonsi for buying this book,
Nina Romberg for reading it,
Pat LoBrutto for editing it, and
Medea for inspiring it.

IN THIS BOOK

In this book, bad things happen at a comic book convention in Dallas, Texas, that have never happened and will almost certainly never happen in reality. Novels are like that. Right?

Okay. Good. Now maybe I can continue to attend the Dallas Fantasy Fair. *Good* things happen there. I'd hate to get banned. And so would Medea. Although in her case it's kind of hard to ban someone you can't always see . . .

Quoth Medea: *Have your brains shriveled and dried?*
Do you think the Goddess died?
Think you that your deeds most dark
Will go unpunished? Just a lark?
Jason, you will writhe in hell!
This I vow! You know me well.
By my children's blood, you'll scream!
My sweet children . . . dead. Ah! Fiend!

—from *"Scream, Fiend! (Medea Was Framed!)"*
as performed by the poet
Princess Katiasa Amazona
at Empusa-Fest, Int'l XV

Prologue

In New York City . . .

A monster awoke and felt cold steel touching his throat.

In the dark, a woman hissed, "Do not move!"

"Who—"

"Do not speak!" She increased the pressure of the blade. "Tonight, for you, I am Hell made flesh, because I know what you have done. What you are. A killer of children!"

He grunted with surprise, a bestial sound.

"The police failed to find you, but I did what the police could not. I questioned the ghosts of your victims. Ghosts always know who killed them."

"I—"

"Silence! You did more than kill flesh. Your violence made gravebound ghosts of your victims' souls. And although you are no doubt incapable of believing in ghosts, you will, I am certain, believe *this!*"

She sliced deeply.

The killer of children felt blood erupt from a gaping wound in his throat. A scream bubbled weakly as he tried to stop the blood with his hands.

"Monster! Now *you* know terror! Now *you* will die! And the avenged souls of your victims will fly free!

"When you get to Hell, tell them Medea sent you. Medea

made you pay for your crimes. Centuries ago, my children were killed by a male monster, too!"

Then she turned on a bedside lamp, the better to watch him die.

While in California . . .

The Priestess stood naked in a forest clearing, head bowed to the sacred Earth. Waiting. Praying. *Summoning* . . .

Around her, the night was silent, until . . .

The Earth's surface trembled, rumbled deep below, as in the east . . . *the Moon . . . rose* . . .

Tendrils of blue mist appeared, coiled, drifted in the strengthening moonlight.

Forest creatures stirred. Owls took wing. Wolves howled, and . . .

She appeared!

Giantess. Titan. Goddess. Towering over the one who had summoned Her, burning red eyes staring down at Her Priestess.

At Medea.

"The Goddess stands where the Three Ways meet!" Medea screamed, fists over her head, wrists crossed, face upraised. "Hail Hecate! Triple One! Gorgo! Mormo! Moon of a Thousand Forms!"

They came then, the ghosts of the Dead, encircling their towering Goddess, forming a serpentine spiral dance.

And the Living came, too, women of all ages and a few men, throwing off their clothes as they rushed toward Hecate, some laughing with delight, some weeping for joy, some howling like beasts as they joined the dancing Dead and abandoned themselves to the ancient Rites of Hecate . . .

as . . .

. . . in a house on the edge of the Hollywood Hills, Nick Martin awoke, ending the Dream.

He smiled in the dark.

Again he had dreamed of Hecate and Her immortal Priestess. As he had expected. Because Medea had phoned him from New York last evening to say she would be meeting him at the comic book convention in Dallas that afternoon. And seeing her again always brought the Dream.

While in Dallas . . .

Joe Clark splashed water on his face, looked in the mirror above the bathroom sink, and said to his reflection, "Talk about your great damned dreams!"

He grinned at himself, a clean-shaven young man in his early twenties, average build, eyes an average blue, fashionably short (but currently sleep-mussed) hair an average brown.

"I think I've got my Toxique pitch!" He gave his reflection a thumbs up and a wink. If Toxique used her radioactive powers to kill the murderer instead of a knife like in his dream it would be a perfect way to start the comic book he was writing about her, and the idea came not a minute too soon, because the big comic book convention started at noon that very day.

Joe went back to his bedroom.

He had turned on the lights when he'd awakened from the dream, revealing his bedroom to be crowded with women. From comic books.

Three walls were covered by overlapping pictures and posters of Wonder Woman (new version), Scimidar with lethal blades (and most of her body) bared, She Hulk (Shulkee to her friends), Renée (Shulkee's famous editor), Rogue, Storm, Psylock, Catwoman, She-Cat, Black Cat, Black Canary, Black Widow, Black Queen, White Queen, Scarlet Witch, Spider-Woman (old), Spider-Woman (new), Vampirella (old), Vampirella (new), Femme-Force, Heroine's Inc., Supergirl, Power Girl, Elvira, Draculina, Zatanna, Satana, Angela, Sadista, Death . . . and others.

But the fourth wall held only one picture: a framed sketch of La Toxique, drawn (for a fee) to Joe's specifications by Nick Martin, a comic book artist from California who had been at the Dallas convention last year and who, Joe had read, was attending again this year.

In Nick's sketch, Toxique gazed at Joe with glowing eyes, grinned a radioactive smile, beckoned with poison-touch hands.

Toxique. An innocent victim of Earth's pollution who now used her deadly powers to help others, right wrongs, and wage war upon the poisoners of Mother Earth.

Toxique. Joe's own creation. But unpublished. So far.

He whispered to the framed drawing, "I'll get you into print yet, love. I promise. What? Yes, I've had a new idea. I'm going to ditch that plot I was working on and use the dream I just had to pitch your book at the con today. What? Yes! *Of course* I'm nervous! Nervous as hell. I feel sick each time I think about talking to one of those pros about publishing your book. But I *am* going to do it, and they *are* going to love you. I just know it!"

Joe visualized Toxique standing near, smiling at him. And he imagined her saying, *I know you'll do your best for me, lover. You always do.*

"You bet your radioactive ass I do!"

I love you so, Joe.

"Love you too, Babe. Love you too." Then he pursed his lips and kissed the air where he imagined her to be.

While in a Dallas suburb . . .

When his youngest son stopped moving, T.T. Dysan looked around the boy's bedroom and exhaled a deep sigh.

He'd made a royal mess of the room. It was going to be hell cleaning it up, and the other rooms, too. Except for maybe the bathroom where he'd done his wife. *Ex-wife.* Because the bathroom tiles should come clean pretty easily, even after her blood had dried. But he had more important things to think about now. Much more important things.

He tossed aside the bloodied baseball bat he'd used to kill the last member of his ex-family, then he glanced down at his freshly shined shoes and his tan business suit. And he saw bloodstains. Not too many. But a few. Remarkably few, considering. But a few was still a few, and he felt new rage at what his kids and their mother had forced him to do. Well, they would not be ruining any more suits, or anything else. God damn them all to hell!

T.T. growled low in his throat and stepped over his son's cooling body to reach the curtained window.

He checked outside. The sun was coming up. Time to go.

He turned off the lights (saving money on electricity was important, he'd often told his kids) as he left the neat (and in a good location) suburban house (that he'd called home until after the divorce).

He carefully locked the door behind him (a good solid dead bolt, bought to keep his family safe).

He walked to the driveway and unlocked his imported car (for which he was behind on the payments since he'd lost his middle-management job).

He climbed into the car and leaned across to the glove compartment, checked the handgun (bought for family protection) inside, made certain it was fully loaded. Just in case. And it was.

He also took from the glove compartment a large hunting knife in a hand-tooled leather sheath.

Then he started his car.

And he headed downtown . . . thinking about kids who were infected by Evil, about how they ruined lives, and about the hundreds, maybe thousands, of kids who would be downtown at the comic book convention that afternoon.

Comic books and kids!

There was still a lot left to do.

Oh, yes. *One hell of a lot left to do* . . .

1

Joe's Pitch

"A man—"

At the comic book convention, in the crowded hotel lobby near the registration desk, Joe Clark hesitated in mid-sentence as the Chow Down Comics editor he had stopped, Joe Greenline, looked away from Joe, focusing his attention instead upon a young woman costumed as Sif, an Asgardian Goddess from Marvel's *The Mighty Thor* comic.

Joe's hands were sweating. His heart was racing. He felt sick. And Greenline's obvious disinterest was anything but helping. But he *had* to keep at it, *had* to keep trying to sell Toxique's book.

The big comic book companies had already turned him down. So, if he couldn't sell his book to a bottom-of-the-barrel bunch like Chow Down . . .

No! They *would* want it. He would *make* them want it. If he could just keep from throwing up—

"Yes?" Greenline glanced at his watch. "I'm waiting."

Joe took a deep breath.

"Okay. Here's how the first issue opens. A man wakes up at three A.M. and finds someone standing beside his bed. He tries to grab a handgun beneath his pillow. But he can't move.

"He's on his back. See? Naked and exposed. It's dark, and the intruder, a woman, La Toxique, tells him she has paralyzed him with nerve gas. She breathed on him while he was asleep, okay? And her toxic breath can paralyze. Or kill. So, then, she goes on to say that for him she is Hell made into flesh, because she knows he has raped, mutilated, and murdered many women. But she also knows he will kill no more, because she is going to execute him and end his reign of terror.

"As she speaks, he notices a poisonous green light in the darkness above him. A toxic, radioactive luminescence. It's coming from her eyes and from inside her mouth.

"She tells him that the police were getting close to catching him, but she found him first. Then she adds, 'And as a reward for catching you first, I choose a kiss.'

"She purses her lips and leans down.

"As she nears, he feels warmth on his face. Heat. *Burning heat.* Okay?

"He tries to scream but fails. He tries to break his paralysis but fails to do that, too.

"Toxique touches her radioactive lips to his mouth, and his lips start to sizzle and boil. Then she strokes his teeth with the glowing tip of her tongue, and his teeth blacken and crack, exposing nerves as his tooth enamel is vaporized. Then she sucks his tongue into her mouth, pulls back, and spits its liquefying slime in his face. And she says, 'When you get to Hell, monster, tell them Toxique sent you! Toxique stopped your evil. Toxique made you pay!'

"Then she begins to kiss him other places, see? And she sears his chest, especially his nipples, as she slowly, teasingly, moves her burning mouth down his body, until she reaches his penis, where she—"

"I get the picture," Greenline interrupted.

"Yeah? So, what do you think?"

Greenline cleared his throat. "It doesn't work for me."

Joe felt as if he had been kicked in the gut, again. But he tried not to let it show. Maybe there was still hope.

"Solo female superhero titles never sell too well for us," Greenline continued, "or for anyone else for that matter, because most of our customers are boys. And I don't think your character would fit into our superhero universe, anyway."

"But Mr. Greenline, it's not really a female superhero book. It's a very *adult,* private detective horror comic with environmental overtones. And I haven't told you yet about the strong but sensitive male character I've put in so that guys will have someone to identify with, too."

Greenline frowned. "While the women are identifying with this . . . Toxic character, you mean?"

"With Toxique, yes."

"You really think they would? Identify with someone like that?"

"Of course! So, anyway, this sensitive but tough guy I mentioned who's Toxique's partner, he's an ex-cop bodybuilder and martial artist who thinks she needs protection and periodically goes against his principles and breaks the law to help her. Because he's in love with her. See? And she loves him. But he won't admit his love to her or to himself, because he knows the radiation has made her more than a little insane, and how could he be in love with an insane woman obsessed with stopping evil by killing people? Wouldn't that make him more than a little insane, too? And he's sure he's not.

"It's kind of a Batman Syndrome thing, see? Fighting darkness with darkness and all that. And I also see it as a sociological and ecological metaphor. Okay? With strong plots and characters, bits of environmental education stuck in here and there, plenty of sex, and just enough violence.

Kind of a female avenger version of the *Hellblazer* comic but with elements that also echo the popular mysticism of *Sandman*."

Greenline looked thoughtful. Joe's hopes rose. Then Greenline said, "How about making Toxique a man and the murderer in your scene a woman? Just think what an artist could do visually with those hot kisses then. Flesh-burning kisses on a woman's nipples instead of a man's would be a lot more . . . well, visually *interesting*. We might even want to use that scene, toned down a bit, of course, on the first issue's cover. And the ninja bodybuilder could be an old army buddy. And there'd have to be a female sidekick, too, of course, a girlfriend or something, maybe a stripper. Yeah. I like that. A gorgeous stripper, so the hero will have someone to rescue from time to time, and so people will know he and his sidekick aren't gay. And because a little GGA never hurts. The name of the main character would have to be changed, too, of course. Sounds too much like *The Toxic Avenger*."

Joe's disappointment began to merge with anger. And he thought, *Change her sex and name and the title? And add ninjas and GGA! You shortsighted asshole idiot! There's more to my book than ninjas and Good Girl Art!*

"So, what do you think?" asked Greenline.

Other than that you're dumber than quail shit? "Well, I think . . . uh . . ." Joe swallowed hard. *Don't blow it*, he warned himself. *Control your anger, damnit! Maybe you can still bring him around.* "I . . . uh . . . well, I don't see the bodybuilder as a ninja."

"Should be one, though. Yeah. It might work, notice I said *might*, if you did it that way."

Try to reason with him, Joe told himself. *Toxique's counting on you!* "Mr. Greenline, I . . . can't change Toxique's sex and do that other stuff and still have it be the book I want to write."

"Sorry, then. Good luck with it elsewhere. But it's going to be an uphill battle."

Joe fought nausea and rage. *Damn you to hell, Greenline! Damn you to hell!*

"So? Got anything else to pitch?" Greenline asked. He again looked at his wristwatch. And at Sif.

"No. That was all. I'll think about what you said," *for about a billionth of a second, you disgusting sexist slime!* "Thank you for your time."

2

Squeegeeman

A young man stood outside an exit gate at the Dallas-Fort Worth International Airport and repeatedly consulted the picture he held. It showed a man with red hair tied back in a ponytail, who looked a lot like the tall, solidly built man in dark sunglasses wearing a black shirt and black jeans coming through the gate. "Mr. Martin?"

Nick stopped. The other deboarding passengers from the Los Angeles to Dallas flight flowed around him.

The young man who had spoken was wearing a big smile and jeans and sneakers and a black T-shirt. The T-shirt had *SQUEEGEE!* in white letters across the front.

Nick glanced down at the T-shirt. "You're from the con?"

"Yes I am, Mr. Martin."

"Nick."

"Okay!"

They shook hands.

"Welcome to Dallas! Or welcome back. I didn't get to meet you last year. I'm Bud. Bud Brewer. Well, actually, Bud's a nickname. Because of my last name."

"Oh?"

"Yeah. My real name's Jeff. And I'm a big fan of your work!"

Nick looked past Bud-Jeff and saw Medea approaching. He had not known she was going to meet him there. He had supposed she would simply turn up at the hotel. He smiled at her and told her with his thoughts how glad he was to see her.

She smiled back.

Her long dark hair hung straight and unbound, and the deep beauty of her large, expressive eyes almost literally took his breath away, as always.

She had dressed western for the Texas con. All that was missing was a cowboy hat.

Under an unbuttoned black leather vest she was wearing a western-styled shirt, black, unbuttoned at the neck, accented by mother-of-pearl buttons. The shirt was tucked into black jeans. Around her slender waist was a wide, black leather belt with a large brass buckle in the shape of the skull of a longhorn steer. Completing the picture were cowboy boots of polished black cowhide, high-heeled, pointy-toed.

"Jeff," Nick said, "someone else is meeting me here, too, and here she is." He motioned to Medea, who had silently stopped behind Jeff.

Jeff looked around, jerked slightly with shock, opened his mouth, awestruck, pulled himself together, and stammered, "But . . . you're . . . you're *her!* Oh, God. You're my favorite actress! Oh, God!"

Nick smiled. The first time he had met Medea he had thought her to be *his* favorite actress, the incomparable Barbara Steele. He wondered whom Jeff thought her to be.

Medea gave Jeff a courteous smile and a nod, then she stepped close to Nick, embraced him, and kissed him lightly on his lips. "It is good to see you again, Nick."

"Good to see you, too," he replied, "as always. This is Jeff. The convention sent him to pick me up. Jeff, I'm afraid this is not who you think. This is Medea."

She extended her hand to him. He shook it, looking confused.

"But . . . you look just like her. Bridget Fonda! I swear! I mean, I *thought* you did, at first. You don't quite, now. Well, your hair's dark and hers is light, and I guess your eyes are different, but at first I thought you were her for sure. And I guess you're older, too. But I just . . . well, sorry."

"No need. I am . . . flattered."

Jeff frowned. "Your name is really Medea? Like in that old Harryhausen film *Jason and the Argonauts?*"

"Yes. Except they were wrong. Jason was nothing like that, nor am I."

Jeff's frown held for a moment more, then he laughed. "Oh! Right! I get it. You're the *real* Medea!"

"In the flesh."

"That's great! I know a girl who was the Sorceress Circe for a con once. She got in trouble with the hotel, though, for leading a pet pig around the lobby on a leash. It was great!"

"Circe is my cousin."

"Yeah?"

"In reality, she turns men into snakes, not pigs."

"That's great!"

"May I ride with you and Nick to the hotel?"

"You bet. Ready to go?"

Nick kept from laughing. It would not have been polite. But he felt like laughing, watching Medea work. "I have some luggage to pick up, Jeff. Where's baggage claim?"

"Just follow me, Mr. Martin . . . Nick. Do you have luggage too, *Medea?*"

"Of course. Where else would I keep the Golden Fleece?"

"Right! That's great. Right this way."

They started walking, but they had not gone far when Medea said, "Excuse me a moment." She walked away toward an empty waiting area.

Jeff asked, "Where's she going?"

"I can't say." Which was true. Even though, seeing what Jeff could not, he knew what she was going to do. "I doubt it will take long, though. What's this *SQUEEGEE* on your shirt about?"

"Oh, that? It's my nickname. I mean my *other* nickname. It's the name of a superhero I kind of created. Squeegeeman."

"Yeah? Tell me more."

And Jeff did, distracted, as Nick had intended, from noticing as Medea stopped beside the large viewing window and said, "Hello," to what would have looked, to Jeff, like an empty chair. Then she said, "Are you lost?" A pause. "She did? Were you with her on a plane ride?" And after another pause, "Know what I think? I think your mommy did not leave you alone at all. I think you just got confused after the plane fell down. Why, I think I can hear her calling to you right now." Medea closed her eyes and whispered a cyclical chant, then she opened her eyes and said, "Listen now." A pause. "There. You hear her? Yes? Good." She whispered another chant. "And now, can you also see her?" She pointed through the window. "Look outside. See her floating in the beautiful light? You do? Wonderful. Go on, then. Go to your mother."

When Medea rejoined Nick, Jeff was still talking.

Nick said to her, "Jeff's explaining about a superhero he created."

Jeff looked at the empty waiting area then back at Medea.

She said, "I had to help the ghost of a child killed in a plane crash. I often find them in airports and send them on their way."

Jeff immediately laughed. "That's great! Sure, the *real* Medea, a Witch and all, *could* see ghosts, couldn't she?"

"I certainly can."

"That's great!"

"Sometimes. But not often. Shall we go?"

3

Registration

And Ted Hunner said, "Oh, man. That's so lame. No way is Magneto smarter than Spider-Man."

"Of course he is," insisted Joe Clark. "Has to be. He's a villain, or was, and I guess is again now, unless he's changed sides back again." Fresh from striking out with *Toxique* at Chow Down Comics, Joe was in no mood to lose the debate.

Ted countered with, "See? Can't make up his mind! What a dumbass! But now Spider-Man, he was just a teenager when he invented those web-shooters, and—"

"But Magneto was building rocket ships way back in—"

"Hold that thought. Customers."

Two boys had advanced through the hotel lobby to the comic book convention's registration desk, behind which Ted was sitting.

Ted sold them tickets then said, "Hold out the back of your left hand, please."

They looked confused.

"I have to stamp the back of your left hand, so you can get past the security people at the door of the dealers' room and all."

Finally, one of them held out the back of his right hand. The other held out his left hand but with the palm up.

Joe had seen the same thing happen many times before. Why couldn't people just hold out the back of their left hand? Was it that hard to figure out?

When Ted had finally gotten the two boys stamped and on their way, he looked back up at Joe. "You were saying?"

"I've forgotten."

"Liar. You just had time to think while I was selling those tickets and realized I was right. Spider-Man is *definitely* smarter than Magneto."

"I remember what it was now. Magneto was building rocket ships back when—"

"Look at *that*," Ted interrupted again. "And, thank you, God, she's coming this way! It *can't* be who I think it is, can it? Elvira isn't a guest, is she?"

Joe turned and saw a stunningly beautiful woman approaching. She did not look like Elvira to him, though. She looked so much like his sketch of Toxique that it frightened him for a moment, then he noticed that the man walking beside her was Nick Martin, and that explained it. Nick must have been thinking of this woman when he drew the sketch of Toxique at the con last year.

She was as tall as Nick, therefore a little taller than Joe. She looked perfectly at home in her western-styled clothes. *Is she,* Joe wondered, *from Texas? Maybe a local?* He hoped so. He hoped so one whole hell of a lot. Not that a woman like that would ever go for an average guy like him, except in his fantasies, but feasting the eyes was not such a bad thing, either. *Toxique in the flesh!*

Jeff Brewer was with them, too, Joe now saw, carrying a couple of suitcases. Nick had another. She carried nothing.

Joe could not stop staring at her. She took no notice of him, though, nor of any of the others in the lobby who had also noticed and were staring.

When they reached the registration desk, Jeff said, with a

satisfyingly superior air, "Nick Martin's guest packet, please."

Ted stuck out his hand. "Sure! I'm a big fan of yours, Mr. Martin."

Nick smiled his best professional smile and shook Ted's hand, but the young man behind the registration desk was no longer looking at him. His attention had been drawn to Medea. Of course.

Nick glanced at Ted's con-staff name-badge and said, "Nice to meet you, Ted. And this is Medea."

She smiled and held out her hand.

"Nice . . . to meet you," Ted stammered. "You know, I thought for a moment you were Elvira!"

"How flattering."

"Oh, yes. She's a favorite of mine. I collect her. I have most of her posters and stuff, even the model kit that costs so much."

"How nice."

To Joe's shock, she then turned *and held out her hand to him!*

"And you are?"

Joe quickly shook her hand and said, "Uh . . . Joe." The touch of her hand made him feel dizzy, quite literally. He inhaled a quick breath. "Joe Clark." When she withdrew her hand, he felt a deep sense of loss. *Come on!* he said to himself. *Get with it! Don't act like such an idiot.* He glanced at Nick. "Mr. Martin, you drew a sketch for me here last year, of a creation of mine, La Toxique?"

"I remember," Nick said, surprised that he did, because he drew *lots* of sketches at cons. "The radioactive, environmental vigilante, right?"

"Right!" Joe shook Nick's hand. "And I see now who inspired you." He looked back at Medea.

Nick laughed. "Medea inspires many things."

"She's the *real* Medea," Jeff joined in, feeling left out. "Like in *Jason and the Argonauts.* The Golden Fleece movie, remember? And Circe's her cousin. Remember Circe at that other con?"

"Yeah," Ted laughed loudly, wanting some attention, too. "I kind of liked that pig. Circe wasn't bad, either."

Medea raised an eyebrow.

Joe said, "Now that I think about it, Mr. Martin, when you did those issues of *Wonder Woman,* Princess Diana looked kind of like Toxique, or rather Medea, too."

Nick shook his head. "Isn't it the truth? I have to struggle to draw women that *don't* look like Medea. But in Wonder Woman's case, I thought it worked rather well."

"I agree," Joe answered. "I mean, Wonder Woman's Greek, too, isn't she? Like Medea was supposed to be. Wasn't she?"

"And I look . . . Greek to you?" Medea asked.

"I guess. I mean, with your dark hair and all, you don't look . . . Swedish. If that's your real hair." *That sounded terrible! Damn! Better try to fix it, quick!* "I mean, it *looks* like your real hair. I'm not saying it doesn't. But playing the role of Medea, you'd *have* to have dark hair. She did in that movie about the Argonauts, anyway."

She smiled at him. Toxique's smile. He wanted so much to take her in his arms and kiss her, to hear her whisper his name in the dark . . .

"Here is your guest packet, Mr. Martin," Ted said, breaking the spell. "The Pro Suite's in room 2323. Free food and drinks whenever you need them."

"And beer iced down in the bathtub, right?" Nick asked.

"Right!" Ted said to Medea, "Some pros call this the Beer in the Bathtub Con."

Jeff said, "Ted, Medea should have a guest-badge, too, shouldn't she? She's with Nick."

"Of course!" Ted agreed, and hurried, somewhat clumsily, to comply.

4

Dealers' Room

At the entrance to the dealers' room, a woman with a serious frown and a staff security badge demanded that Joe Clark show her the back of his left hand.

He got it right the first time.

Seeing that his hand had been properly stamped, she waved him through.

The hotel's largest room, the Grand Ballroom, had been transformed into a treasure trove for collectors.

There were dealers in both rare and not-so-rare comic books, of course. But there were also various comic book companies advertising new and future products. Sellers of science fiction and fantasy memorabilia were also represented. And it was not uncommon for dealers to buy from each other. Many had been collectors themselves before becoming dealers, and many still were.

From where he stood, Joe could see several aisles of long tables, most crowded with open-topped boxes filled with alphabetically sorted comic books encased in transparent, non-yellowing (Mylar for the most valuable comics) plastic bags that were stiffened for added protection by acid-free cardboard inserts.

There were comics on the floor beneath the tables, too, of

the less valuable variety, non-alphabetized, without card-board stiffening, in less expensive plastic bags. Some of those boxes bore "ALL TITLES 20 CENTS!" scrawled on their sides.

From the entrance, Joe could also see a table specializing in movie memorabilia, books about actors and actresses and films and filmmaking, portfolios containing autographed photographs of various stars, and a stack of one-sheet movie posters.

On other tables were displayed new and used hardback and paperback books, mostly science fiction and fantasy and horror novels, while other tables were covered with Star Trek, Star Wars, and older space adventure memorabilia, and yet others with various superhero action figures and expensive, collectible model-building kits.

Down one aisle, Joe saw people crowded in front of a jewelry display showing crystal and pewter and silver rings and pendants and statuettes of wizards and warriors, drag-ons and unicorns, skulls, magic swords, crosses, ankhs, pen-tegrams, Hammers of Thor, and double-headed battleaxes.

Another table sold buttons with a variety of slogans printed on them. At the last convention, Joe had bought one that read *Burn the Censors! Keep the Books!*

And to the right of the entrance door was a display of posters, art books, and matted art prints. "Howdy, How-ard," Joe said to the art and poster dealer. Joe had bought some of the posters that decorated his bedroom from How-ard.

"How've you been, Joe?"

"Fine. Been kind of hot back east, I heard." Howard's business was based in New Jersey, though he was rarely there, usually on the road, following the convention circuit around the country.

"Sweltering. Got some new things, though."

"How about that new Femme Force poster?"

"AC hasn't published it yet. Soon, though, I heard. But would you be interested instead in a signed Frank Brunner?" He pulled a matted print, wrapped in protective plastic, out of a stack and held it for Joe's inspection.

The art showed wolves prowling in a deep, dark forest. Against one tree in the foreground was a beautiful woman, naked. But she did not appear to be afraid of the wolves. She was obviously (to Joe) their mistress, not their prey. She might even be a shapeshifter, he thought, might have been a wolf herself only moments before. And the other wolves? Were they also women in wolf form? An entire pack of them? Running free in a forest where dark excitement awaited those who strayed from the path . . .

"Damn," Joe responded. "You sure know how to push my buttons."

"That's my job." Howard grinned. "And speaking of buttons, how about this signed Vampirella by Dave Stevens?" He put the Brunner aside and held up a different print.

"Incredible," Joe whispered, awed. "Expensive?"

"Yes, but I think you can afford it."

"If I deal you down a bit?"

"Going to wait for late Sunday afternoon again, eh? When I'm at my weakest and most desperate? But it won't matter with the Brunner or Stevens prints. Their prices are fixed."

Joe laughed, enjoying the game. *"Sure* they are. I'll see you later. You know how I am. If I start looking at your stuff now, I'll never get around to the rest of the room."

"Well, I wouldn't want you to spend all of your money with me."

"Of course you would. See you *later*."

"Later."

But Joe had only taken a few steps when someone called his name.

"Clark!"

It was Sammy Tenn, an old friend who had gone to the University of Texas in Austin after high school in Dallas, so Joe now only saw him at comic book cons.

"How've you been, Tenn? Nice T-shirt." Sammy's black T-shirt had a picture of Elvira on it. She was well displayed upon Sammy's broad chest. Sammy was a bodybuilder. He was shorter than Joe by half a head, but with his muscles he weighed more.

Joe shook his old friend's hand.

Sammy said, "Your shirt's not bad, either. Cool." Joe's light blue T-shirt sported a drawing of Scimidar with her blades bared. "Have you seen her yet?"

"Her? Who? Are you still panting after women like an adolescent?"

"So, you *haven't* seen her."

"The woman with Nick Martin?"

"Who?"

"You haven't seen *her?*"

"Meaning you haven't seen *my* her."

"Couldn't be any finer than the one I saw."

"And was yours wearing a Vampirella outfit?"

"Mine was wearing nothing at all."

"In your dreams."

"And she looked like Toxique."

"Who? Oh, yeah. *Your* Toxique. Sold her book yet?"

Joe hesitated, made himself laugh, and said, "Not yet. But don't change the subject. I wouldn't mind seeing the Vampirella you saw, if she's got a *good* Vampirella costume."

"Is there a bad one? Clark, the costume is an *official* one, and she's a pro, *a real model* doing promo for Vampi's new comics company."

"I saw pictures in a magazine of a Vampirella they had working the San Diego con last year. Same one?"

"Don't know. Don't care!"

"Where's their table?"

"I'll take you. I need another look."

They started walking.

Sammy said, "I finally got number 55 of Vampi's original run, by the way."

"So, now you've got them all. Congratulations. And you can start collecting the new series."

"Like I haven't already. You guys've been making fun of me for years for collecting *Vampirella*. But now that the title is being published again, all my Vampi stuff is growing in value. That six-foot poster? Paid five dollars for it, remember? It's worth at least fifty now. Maybe more. For example. But it may go down if they reprint it, which I've heard they might."

"Wonder how much mine is worth? I've got one of the posters they made from one of her covers."

"Issue 52, I hope?"

"It's got her reaching out toward you."

"Standing or on her knees?"

"Knees."

Sammy nodded. "It's 52. Cool! Gotta be worth a lot more than you paid for it, unless you bought it recently."

"Couple of years ago."

"Hold on to it."

"Don't worry."

"I got Forrest J. Ackerman to sign my *Vampirella* number one at a con up north."

"Why?"

"He wrote her first story!"

"Oh, yeah. Just kidding. I knew that. And Frazetta did the art."

"Just the cover."

"You sure?"

"Stop it, Clark! Tom Sutton did the art for her first story, 'Vampirella of Draculon,' September, '69, and you know it."

"Thought it was '68."

" '69."

"Want to bet that six-foot poster?"

Sammy laughed. "Not even on a sure thing. Hey, Jack!"

A man looked up from examining plastic-bagged magazines and imported comics. "Sammy! Still got a job?"

"Yeah. You?"

"Yes."

They shook hands.

Joe knew Jack too. They also shook hands.

Joe asked, "What are you working on now, if you wouldn't have to shoot me after telling me?" Jack lived in Houston. He was a scientist who sometimes did secret government work.

Jack answered, "Same old thing. Orbital chaos dynamics."

"I love chaos theory."

"You would. College going okay? Still majoring in math, I take it?"

Joe nodded. "Yes. To both."

"Sold *Toxique*, yet?"

"Not yet."

"Really liked what you showed me last con."

"Wish you were a publisher."

"I bet you could sell it in Italy. They have some really amazing comics over there. Right up Toxique's alley."

"So you've said. I'll sell her yet over here."

Sammy asked Jack, "Have you seen Vampirella yet?"

Jack grinned. "I don't remember."

"You've seen her. We're going over there. Want to come along?"

"No thanks. Got some good things here to look at, too." He motioned to the collectors mags and comics. "See you later. Have fun."

They walked on. Ahead was a table selling new and used books. The man behind the table was bending over it to examine the multicolored, stiletto-heeled shoes the woman in front of the table was displaying for him.

Joe said to the woman, "Hi, Sandi. Gorgeous shoes."

"Damn right!"

"Watch how you talk about my wife's new shoes," said the man behind the table, feigning jealousy.

"What shoes?" Joe replied, feigning fear. "How's it going, Scott? Read the new short story you had in *Mean Lizards*. It really rocked. Liked the one in *Nature to Wander*, too."

"Thanks."

"Traffic been good?"

"Not bad for a Friday. But most are just passing by at the moment, on their way to see Vampirella."

Sandi asked, "Bet that's where you two *were* headed, right? But now that you've seen me, what's the point?"

"There's a Vampirella?" Sammy asked. He looked this way and that. "Where?"

Sandi laughed. "I saw you over there earlier."

Scott said, "Howard's got a Dave Stevens Vampirella print, autographed."

Sammy said, "I saw it. But I can't afford it."

Joe said, "I saw it, too. Wait for Sunday afternoon."

Sammy shook his head. "Won't do any good with the Stevens, Howard said."

"Told me that, too."

Sandi said, "You didn't believe him, did you?"

Scott said, "Doesn't matter. Someone will snap it up, maybe today."

"Yeah," Sammy agreed. "Some fool with money."

Scott laughed. "Best kind of fool to be."

"Speaking of fools," Joe said, "that's what I'll feel like if I miss seeing this Vampirella I've heard so much about. So, later for you two. Right?"

Sandi said, "I'll still be here to lift your spirits when you see her and return disappointed."

Joe and Sammy laughed and continued their pilgrimage.

A dozen tables later, Sammy stopped. "There she is! I can't stand it. Then again, yes, I can. Thank you, God. Vampirella lives!"

Joe stopped and stared. He drew in a deep breath, let it out slowly.

Unbelievable!

The woman was as tall as he was, dark hair hanging down her bare back nearly to her slender waist. Her gleaming black boots had high, stiletto heels. And the red costume she wore, skin-tight and covering just enough to keep things legal, was the best Vampi outfit he had ever seen outside of the inked-on jobs in comics. Her face even reminded him of one of her original incarnations when she had been drawn by . . . he tried to remember . . . San Julian? Gonzalez? Enrich? Marato?

Transfixed by the sight, Joe groaned and said, "Oh, damn, Sam. Damn. It's almost like seeing a goddess or something, you know?"

"Do I ever. Makes me feel kind of . . . religiously inspired, too!"

"Oh, damn, damn, damn!"

5

In the Lobby

Nick finished registering for his room at the hotel registration desk.

Jeff had offered to help him take his suitcases to the room, but Nick had declined, tactfully sending the young man on his way.

Nearby in the lobby, Medea was giving an embrace of greeting to a woman whose hair was as dark as her own.

The woman was taller than Medea, taller than Nick. She was wearing a leather motorcycle jacket with a Harley Davidson logo on the back. Her tight black jeans revealed her legs to be heavily muscled. Nick knew the rest of her body was well-muscled, too. Her face and neck bore traces of old scars.

Nick hefted the luggage and went to join them.

As Nick walked up, he heard the woman say to Medea, "And Phil said to say hi. He'll be over later. I got the day off from the gym, but Phil's asshole of a boss at the slop shop wouldn't let him go."

Medea laughed. "Slop shop?"

"What? Oh, that's what Phil calls the fast food place he works. I hear it so much I forget there's another name. Hi, Nick! Loved what you did with *Wonder Woman*. About time someone gave the Amazing Amazon some proper muscles."

"You were my inspiration, Trudy." They shook hands. "Still working out?" It was an old joke between them.

"Who, me?" It was an old reply.

"Medea!" a woman shouted from across the hotel lobby.

The woman was in a wheelchair. Slender and fit-looking, arms and upper body strengthened by the exercise program Trudy had designed for her, she had dark hair cut short and was wearing an *Aliens* T-shirt tucked into black jeans.

Behind her, hurrying to keep up with the wheelchair, came a younger woman, hair a fiery red and long, jeans also black, T-shirt showing the ankh-wearing Sister Death from the *Sandman* comic. Outside the T-shirt, hanging from a long leather cord, gleamed a silver ankh of her own.

Medea bent low and embraced the woman in the wheelchair. Like Trudy's, her face also bore traces of old scars.

"Bernice," Medea said. "You are well." Not a question.

"Definitely."

"Congratulations on selling your first novel."

"Thanks to you!"

"Thanks to your own strength and creativity."

"And to the Goddess. And Jim. And Trudy. And my sister Gina. And so many others! You should see the thank-you list in the front of the book. But most of all to you. Really. And you know it. I didn't mention your name, though, as you requested."

"Your book will touch many people."

"Goddess willing!"

Medea straightened and embraced the young woman who had come with Bernice. "Barbara."

"Priestess," Barbara whispered, clinging tightly to Medea for a moment before letting go. "I'm so glad you are here."

"As am I."

"There's Jim," Trudy said.

A man waved as he walked across the lobby toward them. His neatly trimmed beard was beginning to gray. His dark blond hair was pulled back in a ponytail like Nick's. He wore a black pullover knit shirt, black jeans, and black cowboy boots. Around his neck on a chain hung a Hammer of Thor.

"Jim," Medea said. She embraced him. "Your last novel was the best you've done. The Goddess is pleased."

He laughed. "Any chance She might write a review for me, then? I'm tired of being all but ignored."

"You know that even though the path of fighting true Evil with what passes for it is a hard one, it is vital."

"Yeah."

"Indeed."

Nick said, "Hello, Jim." They shook hands. Nick had already said hello to Bernice and Barbara while Medea was talking to Jim. Trudy was now on her knees, talking to Bernice eye to eye.

Nick said to Jim, "I liked your last book a lot, too. Grim and merciless. But funny. Damned if I know how you pulled off that trick, but you did."

"Thanks. You've been doing some fine work yourself. Trudy turned me on to the issues you did of *Wonder Woman*. Wish you could pencil that book all the time."

"So do I. What they've been doing to Wonder Woman recently is a crime. I've tried to get Medea to pull some strings and write it herself."

"Comics would never be the same!"

Medea said, "As I've told Nick, inspiring the man who originally created the character was enough."

"You did?" Jim asked.

"In secret, of course." She smiled. "I think Nick and you should work together on a comic book, Jim. I've already mentioned it to him. What do you think?"

"Sounds worth discussing. Several novelists that I know

have been doing comics. Lansdale and Barrett and Williams, for example. And did you catch Wooley's *Tor Johnson, Hollywood Star* a while back?"

Nick nodded. "Oh, yeah. Brilliant! Shiner's *Hacker Files* was great, too, until they made him put superheroes in the last few issues."

"Is that what happened?"

"Yeah. Look, let's have a drink or something and discuss ideas later, okay? Right now, I'm headed up to the room to stow the luggage. Got a panel after a while. Here's your key, Medea."

She took the key. "I will be up shortly."

"Need some help with the luggage, Nick?" Jim asked.

"Thanks, but I can get it. See all of you later."

Jim said, *"Y'all,* remember?" It was a joke they had shared the last time Nick had been to the Dallas con.

"What? Oh, right. See *y'all* later."

"And this time while you're here we *are* going to the Western Warehouse to get you some *Texas* cowboy boots."

Nick smiled. "Whether I want them or not?"

"Of course you want them, pardner. *Everybody* wants real Texas boots. Didn't you know?"

6

Sunlight

Trudy and Bernice and Barbara went with Medea to the elevator a short while after Nick had gone to the room. Jim had excused himself to attend a panel discussion about violence in horror novels. He was one of the panelists.

"See you later, then," Barbara said, embracing Medea again. "Bernice and I are going to the art show. Want to come, Trudy?"

"Sure, if we go to the dealers' room next."

One of the elevators opened its doors and people began to get off. "Until later, then," Medea said and walked into the elevator with several other people.

When the doors had closed, she slumped against the mirrored wall at the back of the elevator, exhausted, fighting nausea. She breathed slowly, deeply, to steady her racing heart.

The elevator started moving. She checked the room number on the key Nick had given her. She looked at the lighted buttons on the control panel. No one had pushed her floor.

"Would you push twenty-seven for me, please?" she asked the elderly man standing in front of her near the controls.

He did.

"Thank you."

He glanced around at her. He grinned when he saw her. There was a dark piece of food clinging to one of his false front teeth.

"Sure thing, honey. Say, don't I know you? Aren't you on TV?" The other people in the elevator looked at her, too.

"No."

"You sure? Ah, heck. No, of course you're not her. You'd be my age if you were who I'm thinking of."

Medea could sense his desire to put his hands on her, to fondle her. And more. She sensed the same desire emanating from some of the other males, and one woman, on the elevator. But that was not all she sensed. There was an unseen rider on the elevator, a presence hovering near the elderly man.

"Aren't you going to ask who I thought you was?" he asked. "She was real pretty, like you are, darlin'. Don't you want to know?"

"No." With her occult vision, she saw the colors in the man's aura change. He was hurt by her rejection, his ego bruised. Then he grew angry with her to hide his true emotions from himself.

"If you don't want to know, it ain't no skin off my teeth." *Bitch,* she sensed him adding in his thoughts. The unseen one hovering near him recoiled as if struck but did not leave.

The elevator stopped to let other people on.

The hotel was crowded with convention attendees and other weekend guests, and the elevator stopped several more times before it finally reached Medea's floor.

Medea held open the door when it started to close and said to the elderly man, "In spite of everything, your late wife still loves you and is hovering near. Act like it." Then she walked away and let the door close upon his stunned expression.

She was glad there was no one in the hallway, and when she got to the room she was glad Nick was in the shower.

She locked the door behind her.

It was a reassuringly normal hotel room. There was a remote control color TV with a pay-to-view control box on top. There was a king-sized bed, a large writing desk, a large stuffed chair, non-offensive paintings on the walls, a small cabinet filled with overpriced snack food.

She could hear the TV in the room next door, easily audible through the thin walls.

Medea removed her clothes and went to the room's single window.

She opened the thick curtains.

Sunlight bathed her nakedness.

She knelt on the floor in the Sun's rays, face upraised, eyes closed, hands in her lap, palms up.

She breathed deeply. Slowly. She visualized the projection of her consciousness across 93 million miles of space into the heart of the Sun, imagined the Sun's purifying rays cleansing her aura, renewing her strength.

Almost at once her heartbeat began to normalize. Her nausea vanished.

Nick came out of the bathroom several minutes later and saw her.

He knew what she was doing and said nothing. He walked quietly to the bed and sat down on its edge near where she knelt.

Without opening her eyes or turning, Medea said, "Thank you, Nick, for remembering about a Sun-side window."

"Pretty rough down there?"

"It was mainly Barbara. She has a problem she did not mention, and she tried to hide it from me, to spare me, but it was there, hovering just behind her conscious thoughts, stealing her positive life-energy, which of course I replaced without her asking. The latitude of Dallas is similar to that of Cairo, however, so the Sun's light is strong here. My aura is already much purified. There is even a young crescent Moon following the Sun in the sky today, strengthening the effect."

He was silent. So was she, drawing in more strength from the Sun.

He thought about getting dressed, but he was reluctant to move for fear of disturbing her concentration again.

Finally, several minutes later, she turned to face him, sat with her knees drawn up, sunlight warming her bare back. She raised an eyebrow at his worried frown. She smiled.

"You worry too much about me, Nick."

"I hate to think about how I once took so much energy from you myself."

"You worry too much about me because you care too much about me. This is not the first time I have warned you about that. You risk hurting yourself, and I do not want you to hurt yourself."

"Yeah. Well, can I do anything to help you? Order food sent up? Give you a massage? Share my life-force with you?"

Reading his thoughts, she knew that what he really wanted was to make love to her in the same way they had that first time. "Why do you torment yourself? You know we cannot make love that way ever again. I have warned you about that, too."

"Yeah. Well, I'm trying to be better about it. And I am a little better than last time, aren't I?"

She stood, came closer, sat down beside him, took his hands in hers.

He raised her hands, softly kissed her palms, still warm from the sun. "Medea," he whispered, "I do love you so."

"Another thing about which I have often warned you."

"Yeah."

She leaned closer. With her fingers she combed back his hair, still damp from the shower. She kissed him.

They embraced.

He kissed her lips, her neck, her breasts, teased her nipples with his tongue and teeth in the way she had told him she most enjoyed. Then he kissed his way slowly down her torso, lingered at her navel, moved farther down, and placed his mouth upon her sexual center.

After a moment, he raised himself back to her breasts and kissed them. "At least allow me to share life-energy with you, to replace what you gave to Barbara."

"Very well."

He placed his hands over her solar plexus. He used the occult skills she had taught him. And gladly he shared his energy with her.

When she told him to stop, he moved onto his back and she nestled into his arms. He stroked her hair and kissed her forehead.

She whispered, as she kissed him back, "I did not take too much of your strength?"

"You know you didn't."

She lightly stroked his chest, reached down and stroked his erection.

He groaned with pleasure.

Smiling, she asked, "Did you know that in many of the United States it is illegal for a man to have a visible erection, even under his clothes?"

"You're kidding."

"I heard two DJs discussing it on a radio rock and roll show this morning before you arrived. But Texas is not one of those states."

"A good thing, too, with you here."

She laughed. "Shall I awaken something new in you today?"

"If it would not tire you."

Then, using her hands and mouth and paraphysical skills, she slowly guided him to a climax of physical/spiritual ecstasy. And beyond.

7

Responsibility

T.T. Dysan had not known where to begin.

There were kids everywhere! Kids infected with Evil they would spread to others when they grew up. Evil that would ruin adult lives even before that, like his kids had his.

He was not going to allow what had happened to him to happen to others. No way. No damned way. He was a man of responsibility. And there was only one way to stop Evil. By destroying it. And any kid who was infected with it.

He did not feel that the comic book convention itself was infecting the kids. Maybe some. But most had been lost long before they got to the convention, infected at home. That's what had happened to his kids, infected at home after the divorce. Thanks to his stupid wife. *Ex-wife.*

He'd tried to get custody. The courts had said no. Because of the lies his wife had told.

Sure, his kids had wanted to go to the comic book convention last year and the year before that. But he had prevented it. This year, however, without him there to control things, their mother was going to let them go.

Yeah. Their mother had been going to let them go! Well, he'd stopped that bullshit and stopped it good. She was *really* an ex-wife now. The thought made him smile. An ex-person, too. Ex-anything. A stupid, ignorant, totally dead bitch!

And all those years when he'd tried to teach his kids a thing or two about right and wrong, about obedience and respect, all the things he had done to try and make them be better people when they grew up, what had she called it? Had she called it bringing the kids up right? No. She had called it abuse! And she had called what he'd done to her abuse, too. It wasn't his fault if, like all the women he had ever known, she had needed some strong medicine from time to time. Hell, hadn't his dad taught his mom a thing or two from time to time? Of course he had. Damned right.

But the courts had sided with his ex and allowed her to infect his kids with Evil.

But he did not have time to worry about that now. It didn't matter anymore anyway, not after he had taken care of it that morning. He'd made the hard decisions and done the deed like a man should do. Damnit to hell!

No, his wife and kids no longer mattered. But what did matter right now was what to do with the kid he had just killed there at the convention. Stupid little shit. Hadn't anyone ever taught him not to go off with a stranger? Even if the stranger said he had free comic books to give away?

How could some parents be so damned incompetent? As a result, the kid was dead. One Evil little man less that would grow up into an Evil big man.

But he had to hide the body. If it was found, it would put people on alert and make his job harder. And it was already hard enough.

Killing kids because they had piss-poor parents who let them get infected made him feel sick. But also good. Because it had to be done and he was doing it. Like a man who knew the difference. Even if no one else seemed to anymore.

So . . . where should he hide the kid? At least there wasn't much blood. He hadn't used the blade of the big hunting knife. He had used the bone handle. In just the right way. The way he had been taught in the army. All those years ago.

By damn, he had never had a chance to see if what they'd taught him worked in combat, but it had worked today, and worked good. And it would work on the next kids, too, as soon as he got this one stashed somewhere no one would find it for a while. Somewhere . . . somewhere . . . ah! Yes. Of course. Perfect. No problem at all.

There.

Finished.

And ready to begin again. With another kid. Maybe a girl this time, though there weren't as many of them as there were boys at the convention. Not by a long shot.

Comic books were still mainly for boys, he guessed, like when he'd been a kid. He hadn't seen many comic books, though. His dad wouldn't let him. Said it wasn't good for him. And he'd been right. He now knew. Absolutely right. Shit! Yes!

But that did not matter now either. All that mattered was stopping the Evil. Like he was doing. Until the cops or someone stopped him, as he knew they eventually would. The stupid bastards.

But not for a while. No, by Hell, *not quite yet for a while* . . .

8

Steele Films

He tied her to a pole and then taped a row of needles beneath each of her eyes, needles that would impale her upper eyelids if she tried to lower them. Now she would have to watch what he was going to do. Everything he was going to do . . .

Damn! thought Joe Clark. *What a scene!*

In the con movie room, he was watching a tape of an Italian film called *Opera* directed by Dario Argento. It was a welcome distraction from his continuing depression over failing to sell *Toxique.*

He had seen still pictures from *Opera* in film magazines but not the movie itself, until now.

Within moments after a closeup of a raven's eye began the film, Joe had been certain he was going to love it. Movies were like that sometimes.

On the other hand, sometimes they could trick you, turn on you halfway through or, more likely, near the end, and leave you feeling cheated.

He hoped *Opera* would not leave him feeling cheated. He did not need *that* today, too.

Joe was not surprised he liked the film. He had loved almost everything he had seen of Argento's. *Suspiria* and *Four*

Flies on Gray Velvet and *Deep Red* and most of the others. But as far as he was concerned, *Opera* took it all to new heights.

Joe had been very disappointed in *Two Evil Eyes*, though. It had seemed such a sure thing, Argento working with Joe's favorite American director, George Romero, most famous for *Night of the Living Dead* and its two sequels.

Later, they were going to show another film Joe had never seen, one by his favorite Spanish director, Jess Franco. Again, he had only seen stills from it. But, bless the comic book convention and whoever arranged the films, he was finally going to see Franco's *Night of the Blood Monster!*

That was its American title. The French had called it *The Throne of Fire*, while the German release had been called *The Witch-Killer of Blackmoor*. And to go with the different titles, each country also had different versions of the film.

Joe had read that Franco often filmed more than one version at a time, which made the work of Franco's filmographers anything but easy. He hoped, though, that the American version he was going to see had at least some of the censored scenes from the European versions. Some video companies were doing that now, restoring censored scenes. It depended upon which company had done the version of *Night of the Blood Monster* he was going to see.

But any version was better than no version at all, and no matter which version he saw, he knew for certain that the main star would do an excellent job. Christopher Lee.

Lee was one of Joe's all-time favorite actors. Along with Peter Cushing. And, of course, always and forever, the fantastic Barbara Steele.

Some video suppliers were now selling European-made Steele films that had had little or no distribution in America. That was how he had finally seen *The Long Hairs of Death*. She had never been more effective, to his mind, than in that film, her acting skills and incredible beauty impressing him as never before. And he still had *Young Torless* to look forward to someday, and, of course, *L'Armata Brancaleone*.

Joe often wished he had been born sooner so that he could have enjoyed the classic horror films from the sixties on the big screen during their initial releases. Born too late for that, he had to make do with videos, and it was not the same, because (as he'd once heard it explained) film consisted of a series of images through which light was passed, while video-tape consisted of electronic impulses on magnetic tape. The texture was completely different. And a small screen could not compare to the size of screens upon which sixties films had once been shown. To have seen some of the beautiful Hammer classics, for example, or *The Long Hairs of Death* on a big screen . . . if someone invented a time machine, Joe knew what *he* would do with it and quick.

The killer placed a gun over the door's peep hole and knocked. When the victim looked through the peep hole to see who was there, the killer fired.

Damn! thought Joe again. *What a great damned scene! What a great damned film! If only I could have sold Toxique's book, I would be really happy now.*

To soothe him, Toxique sat down next to him, placed a glowing hand on his inner thigh, and moved it slowly up-ward.

You'll sell my book yet, lover, she told him. *You'll see. And stop thinking about Barbara Steele. I get jealous, you know?*

Yeah, he answered with his thoughts. *Do I ever!*

Then, as another victim died in *Opera*, Toxique leaned close and gave Joe a long and lingering kiss.

9

Artists' Alley

Nick had been in artists' alley only a few minutes, but there was already a line of fans waiting for his autograph.

Joe, fresh from his viewing of *Opera*, was in Nick's line.

In the dealers' room, artists' alley consisted of tables behind which artists sat to sign autographs. Most also had pieces of original art for sale, and for a fee many would do special sketches like the one Nick had done of Toxique for Joe last year.

Almost all of the fans waiting in line were carefully cradling in their arms a stack of carefully debagged comic books. Each comic, as soon as it had been autographed, would be returned, carefully, to its special, comic book-sized, protective plastic bag.

An autographed comic might be worth more to other collectors, should the owner eventually decide to sell it. There were no guarantees, however, that a particular book would be wanted by others later on. What was hot now might not be tomorrow. Only the gods of the comic book pricing guides knew. Or maybe not even them.

The best method of selecting which comics to buy, Joe had decided, was to ignore the price guides and buyers' guides and simply buy the ones you wanted to read. That way, at least you got the enjoyment of reading the comic, and maybe you would get lucky and have it be a hot number later on. Few collectors followed that rule, however, when faced with what they were told was the "Next Big Thing."

So, like playing the stock market, comic book collectors speculated on the future, and, like a weekend in Las Vegas, they took their chances, hoping they might be lucky enough to end up with the next generation's version of a fantastically valuable comic like the first issue of *The Fantastic Four*, or *Spider-Man*, or (of course) the comics in which *Superman* or *Batman* or *Wonder Woman* made their debut.

And almost all collectors had a personal version of their favorite horror story, about how they (or someone they knew) had once (usually as a kid) had (or had a chance to buy) a comic book (or books) that was now worth lots of money. But *something* had happened to "That Comic," often a mother or father who had decided (when the kid was older and away at school) that the box (or boxes) of comics in the attic (or garage or closet) wasn't worth keeping anymore, a waste of space, and had therefore either given it away to a children's hospital or a library or the garbage collector.

Joe heard a fan in line ahead of him tell someone he'd had the first issue of *Teenage Mutant Ninja Turtles*, but his baby brother had spit up on it. Which prompted another fan to tell how he had bought a *Sandman* number one but had not liked it much and sold it for next to nothing along with a bunch of other comics and a stack of paperback books to a used book store.

It made Joe think about his version of "The Story," about how when he was a kid his dog had—

Someone touched his left arm, interrupting his thoughts.

He looked to the side and saw Toxique. *Toxique in the flesh.* He caught a whiff of exotic perfume. Then the instant of shock passed. It was, of course, only the woman who had come to the convention with Nick. Only that incredibly beautiful woman. Only!

Still wearing her black boots and black jeans, she had changed from her western shirt and vest into a T-shirt, black and expensive-looking, because on the front, in gleaming gold, was a drawing of the snake-haired Medusa, she of one-look-turns-men-to-stone fame. Beneath the drawing, also in gold, were the words, *No means NO!*

"Do you approve?" she asked.

"What?"

"Of my . . . T-shirt, at which you are staring with such interest."

Joe looked quickly up. His face reddened. *Oh, damn. She's wearing a feminist T-shirt and knows I was staring at her breasts!*

"Yeah." Joe cleared his throat. "I do. Approve of your T-shirt. Very unusual. Haven't seen one like it before. And I like the sentiment."

"Yes?" She motioned to Joe's Scimidar T-shirt. "I like yours, too."

"Thanks. Scimidar's one of my favorite female heroes. Have you ever read it? R.A. Jones writes it."

"I believe Nick showed me a copy once . . . where she reads her poetry?"

"Yeah. That was a great issue." *Damn!* He was talking to Toxique's look-alike about Scimidar! *Unbelievable!*

She suddenly, rather formally, held out her hand. "Nice to see you again, Joe." She had remembered his name! He couldn't believe it. He shook her hand. Touching her, even just her hand, *her warm, firm hand,* made his pulse rate speed up. Incredible!

"Yes. Hello again. Medusa. I mean, Medea!" *That's right, idiot, make a complete ass of yourself.*

"I am not directly related to Medusa and the Gorgons, though my Goddess, Hecate, is."

"Your goddess who?" It had sounded like *HECK uh tee*.

She said it again. "Hecate. Perhaps you have heard it pronounced differently. Few know the correct way. Most use either Hecate, or Hecate." The first had sounded like *Heh CAW tee*, the second like *HECK it*. Joe recognized both, the first from the way it had been pronounced in *Jason and the Argonauts*, the second from the way he had pronounced it himself since first seeing it during an assigned school reading of Shakespeare's *Macbeth*.

"Oh! Hecate." He said it his own way.

"If you wish. But I doubt She would answer your call if you pronounced it that way."

"Well, since I don't intend to give her a call, I guess it's okay, right?" He laughed, but Medea did not. In fact, he thought he saw a hint of disapproval on her face. So he quickly said, "But I can pronounce it like you do, if you wish."

"It is not what I wish, but what the Goddess wishes that is important, Joe."

Every time he heard her say his name, a chill of excitement slithered through him. He knew he was reacting like a grade school kid with a crush on a high school cheerleader, but he couldn't help it and didn't want to.

He wondered what her real name was. Maybe he would ask her, or Nick, later. Or maybe not. Maybe it didn't matter.

He wondered if she was going to be in the costume contest that evening, wondered if she might wear something thin and skimpy. Medea was a seducing enchantress, wasn't she? So, maybe—

You idiot, he thought, *a woman who would wear a feminist T-shirt is not going to parade around a masquerade stage wearing a skimpy, sexy outfit! Unfortunately*.

But nevertheless, costume or not, she certainly was into

her character, playing Medea to the hilt. Trouble was, how many Medea experts would she be encountering at that comic book convention? Few or none, Joe figured, so all her research into the part was going to be pretty much wasted. Except that people who were into costuming and masquerade contests were often their own best audience. So, perhaps it did not matter if anyone appreciated her obscure Medean references or not. *He* certainly did not mind if she wanted to exhibit her knowledge of the character. He did not have to understand what she was talking about to enjoy listening to her wonderful voice as he watched her beautiful lips form the words . . . Toxique's enchanting voice . . . Toxique's full, red, warm, moist lips . . .

Thank goodness she can't read my mind! Joe thought.

Medea smiled. "You're in Nick's line, Joe, but how badly do you want his autograph just now?"

Joe switched mental gears and said, "Oh, not his autograph. I wanted to buy another sketch from him."

"Of Toxique?"

She knew the name? Then he remembered it had been mentioned when he'd met her at the registration desk. "Yeah. Of Toxique."

"Whom he drew to look like me."

"Yeah."

"So, what you really want is another sketch of me?"

"Uh, well . . . maybe he will make Toxique look like someone else this time."

"Whom would you prefer? A favorite actress, perhaps?"

He laughed, he feared too loudly. "No. You're a perfect model for her, as far as I'm concerned. But I thought, well, if you minded Nick using your face, I could ask him to make it look like someone else."

"No. I do not mind. I am . . . flattered." She smiled in a different way.

He couldn't stand it. He just couldn't stand it! He hadn't felt this sexually intrigued since going to *Batman Returns* and watching Catwoman lick Batman's face, after which, for several fantasy-ridden nights, Toxique had licked Joe's face, and other things.

Medea asked, "Are you going to be at the convention all three days?"

"Sure. Of course."

"Then, would you mind getting your sketch from Nick tomorrow? Or later today?"

"Mind? No, I guess not. But—"

"I would like to talk with you. Will you have a drink with me?"

"You mean now? In the bar?"

"Yes."

She wanted to talk with *him?* What on Earth about? Maybe she was going to proposition him, ask him to go to her room with her and make love to her. And then pigs would start flying and hell would freeze over. And like that. For sure.

"Why do you hesitate, Joe? Is this the first time a woman has asked you to have a drink with her?"

"Uh . . . no. Of course not. Well, that is, I've *imagined* it happening. Who hasn't?" He realized how lame that sounded the moment he had said it. *Damn!* "I imagine lots of things," he added, which sounded even worse. *Hell! Keep it simple, stupid.* "I mean, yes, of course, I'd love to buy you a drink."

"I did not ask you to buy me a drink."

His face reddened again. Had she been teasing? Just fooling him? "No. Of course not." He laughed as if to show he had known it all along.

"I asked if you would have a drink with me."

He puzzled over her remark for a moment, then said,

"Right. I see what you mean. Okay. Sure. I would love to do that."

As he abandoned his place in line and walked away with her, he was positive that other guys were looking at him with envy. *All right!*

Pride surged through him as she turned heads while walking by his side through the dealers' room.

But he was still puzzled. Because he could not stop wondering why he should be so lucky. It sure wasn't his looks. Oh, he was okay, he guessed, but nowhere near the league in which a looker like Medea played. He supposed.

"If I were you, Joe, I imagine I would be wondering why I want to talk with you."

He laughed. "Well, yeah."

"Do you dream, Joe?"

"Sure. I had a beauty of a dream just last night."

"Well, the reason I want to talk to you is because of a dream I recently had. Hecate sent me a dream about finding and initiating a new person into Her Mysteries. She does that from time to time. I was in Dallas in the dream, and when I awakened I remembered Nick was coming to a convention here, so I assumed there was a connection and decided to attend the convention with him.

"I was not certain what the initiate would look like, male or female, young or old. But I trusted that the Goddess would bring us together, and when I met you today at the registration desk, my instincts told me you were the one. I can hardly initiate you into the Mysteries, though, until after I have talked to you and gotten to know you a little better, can I?"

Joe shook his head negatively. "Oh. Well, no, of course you can't. That's certainly true. Absolutely!" As if he knew all about the Mysteries and such.

"Also," she continued, "I had a feeling that you were the

kind of man who would wonder why I would want to have a drink with him. A man who asks that question, you see, is a man who does not think of himself as a superstud all women crave. I have no use for superstuds. Except perhaps to kill them, when they deserve it. As often they do."

"Well, sure." He was beginning to enjoy the game and wanted desperately to prove to her that he could keep up. "I mean, I've killed a few in my time, too."

"You may well have, if you've had other lives as an Empusa. That's often the case with those whom Hecate sends me to find and initiate. We'll find out, later on."

"Other lives as a what?" It had not sounded very pleasant. More like an insult.

"Empusa. Like me. And Nick. And all those whom Hecate seizes for Her own."

"Oh, *Empusa*. I thought you said something else. Empusa! Sure. Empusa. Of course!"

10

More Blood

There was more blood on T.T. Dysan's suit. Too much blood. He would have to go home now and change to a clean suit before someone noticed and got suspicious.

It was the fault of that last little shit he'd killed. Little asshole had almost gotten away. Had made him hurry the job and use the blade. Which made it hellish hard to conceal the kill. Had to clean up around the scene. Had to allow for seepage from the body, too, meaning a way to hide the corpse so that it wouldn't start leaking blood all over the damned place.

He hated to interrupt his work to go home and change. But he had to look at the big picture.

He would get stopped sooner if he didn't change clothes. No way around it. So, for the good of the work, it had to be done. But it was a twenty mile drive each way. Out to the burbs and back. In Friday afternoon traffic. Shit.

T.T. made it to his car in the hotel's underground parking lot without attracting any suspicious stares.

Back on the road, he headed north on Central Expressway.

Expressway? Maybe forty years ago when it had been built.

They were widening it now. They had been widening it for years. They would be widening it for years more, according to their plans. And when they were finished, the number of cars using it would have increased so that it would probably be too small all over again.

Progress. Stupid shits. Someone should take care of them, too, but not T.T. Someone else would have to take that responsibility. He would take care of as many Evil-infected kids as he could before some cop, probably, made him stop.

But no matter what, three more of the little bastards were now out of the way. Finding infected kids in the convention hotel had been like finding hens in a chicken coop! And plenty left to go.

He should have planned ahead and brought an extra suit with him, or at least worn his black one so that the blood would not show up as much. But there was no point in crying over spilt milk now. Or spilt blood. Yeah. Spilt blood. It made him laugh.

Laughing was good. It kept things in perspective.

There was just no getting around it, killing kids infected with Evil was no fun. But it had to be done, damnit. It had to be done.

He hadn't really wanted kids of his own, anyway. That was his stupid wife's craving. Ex-wife. The loving mother. The stupid bitch.

Cars were stopped ahead on the Expressway. T.T. cursed and slammed on his brakes. Shit!

When he finally made it to the little suburban house he had bought after the divorce, he looked with hatred at his neighbor's front yard, unmowed for several days now and starting to look slightly scruffy. And even when it was cut, the damned lazy bastard set the mower so high his grass freshly mowed was taller than T.T.'s grass after a week of growth!

If only he had a neighbor who tried, like T.T. always tried, to be a credit to the community. But no such luck.

And that tree in his neighbor's front yard! It drove T.T. crazy with disgust. Hell! The damn branches were *near the ground!* Not like in T.T.'s yard where all the tall trees had been properly shorn of their limbs lower down, leaving an attractive, leafy canopy overhead. His neighbor didn't approve, had said T.T. just liked to mutilate trees and make them look like telephone poles with bad haircuts! The stupid shit!

But no matter what his shit of a neighbor thought, T.T. *knew* (because he had watched it happen) that now, with the lower limbs gone, when the wind blew, it blew right on through. Just fine. Just the way he wanted. Just the way it should.

He had found it necessary, too, to get rid of all the bushes near the house. Things could sneak up on you and hide when there were things growing too close to your house. Or overhead. Which is why the three tall old trees near the house had had to go, too.

There were no branches hanging over T.T.'s house anymore, no unsightly debris such as leaves and twigs and such falling on his new roof. No easy avenues by which squirrels and rats and cats and who knew what else could get onto the roof over his head. At night. Their footsteps keeping him awake, even when there weren't any footsteps, because there *might* be some, any moment.

His idiot neighbor, of course, had limbs nearly touching his roof and bushes everywhere around the house! There were probably rats living right up close, waiting to find a way inside. Or snakes. T.T. didn't even want to think about snakes.

Someone should take care of stupid asshole neighbors too, T.T. thought. But, again, not him. His work was cut out for him at the convention. Lots of stupid little shits to take care of, damnit all to hell!

He decided a shower was in order. The smart thing was to look his best when he went back to doing his business. So, he showered, shaved, brushed his teeth and flossed, used mouthwash, deodorant, then carefully brushed his close-cropped gray hair into place.

Next, he gave his shoes a new spit shine the way they had taught him in the army. If he knew one thing, T.T. knew this, that there was absolutely nothing like a gleaming pair of freshly shined shoes.

He put on a clean pair of undershorts, got his black suit out of the closet, a white shirt, and a red tie. When the suit and shirt and tie were on, and not before, he pulled on a pair of black socks and laced his feet securely into his mirror-polished shoes. Then, taking an extra change of clothes, in case things got messy again, he went out to his car and headed back downtown.

11

In the Bar

After the waitress brought their drinks, white wine for Medea, a beer for Joe, Medea said, "You mentioned that you had a dream last night, Joe?"

Sitting across from her at a cozy table for two in the shadows of the hotel bar, Joe could almost believe he was dreaming right then. Sitting with Toxique's look-alike. Too much. "Yeah. I did. A strong one."

"You remember it well, then, the dream?"

"Oh, yes. Definitely."

"Would you mind telling me about it? If it's not something that is too . . . private?"

"Well, it was about a woman who kills a man. But he was a bad man who the police could not catch, and she was a female avenger. Kind of like the comic books I like to read. I like ones with strong women characters in them best."

She took a sip of wine. "Good. You are indeed the one whom I was sent by Hecate to find. Your dream proves you and I are linked through Hecate."

"Yeah?" He liked the thought of being linked to Medea. But he was beginning to wish she would get off the Medea kick and be her real self with him. Was the real reason she had wanted to have a drink with him just to practice her

Medea role? No, that was ridiculous. But even if it were true, there were worse jobs than being her audience.

"Yes." She sipped more wine. "Linked. Because, Joe, you dreamed about what I was actually doing last night, in New York City, slitting the throat of a killer the police could not catch."

He was quiet a moment. He had not mentioned that the woman in his dream had slit the killer's throat. Had he?

She smiled. "I found him by questioning the ghosts of his victims. Ghosts always know who killed them. His victims were bound to their graves by the confusion that often follows violent death, you see. Gravebound ghosts are one type of death disorder with which Empusae are trained to deal. My avenging their unjust deaths, along with some other death magic spellwork I initiated, allowed them to fly free and pass on to the Gray Between and from there to their proper afterdeath realms."

He swallowed some beer. The throat slitting had to be a lucky guess. Or maybe he had mentioned it at some point. He cleared his throat. "You know, this would make a great comic. You and Nick should work on it. I'm serious. It's perfect. Medea as an immortal who is a kind of occult vigilante, fixing death disorders and punishing people the police can't touch. Wonderful!"

"Not always. But sometimes very satisfying."

"No, really, I've read a lot of comics about women heroes. And this Medea thing, her being an Empusa heroine and all, really would make a great comic book. Unique. I think. But . . . what do *you* think?"

"I prefer to have the truth known only to other Empusae. It would make our job much harder if people knew of our existence."

"Oh, right. I didn't think of that." He was deeply disappointed, and slightly angry, that she was stubbornly continuing the role when he was trying to be serious. *Damn!* Oh, well . . . it just showed him where he stood with her. In the audience. Period. No surprise there. But still disappointing.

"Joe, I know you think I am telling you lies, just playing a role. I am sorry you feel that way, but it is necessary, for now. So, let us talk about something else, shall we? You, for example. What do you do when you are not attending comic book conventions?"

Was she really interested in him, he wondered? No way. Probably just being polite, because she sensed her Medea bit was wearing a little thin? Well, hell, he didn't have anything better to do at the moment, and she was anything but hard on the eyes.

"Me? Nothing too exciting," he answered. "I'm going to UTD, that's the University of Texas at Dallas. Math major, physics minor, since physics, as we like to tell the physics people, is nothing but applied math. And I work part time to pay the bills. So, I don't do a full load of hours. Takes longer to get through that way, of course, but I don't have much choice. My folks can't help out with the money. Since Dad lost his job, it's all they can do to get by themselves."

"I have always found mathematics a most . . . attractive discipline," she responded.

Attractive? He felt his hopes rise anew. He stopped them. Fool! "Yeah?"

"Oh, yes. Pure thought at its finest. An art form few have the capacity to appreciate. I approve, Joe. Very much."

"Well, thanks. You're one in a million, if you feel that way. These days, saying you're into math is like saying you're from the Moon, to most people. They just go kind of blank and look at you as if they hope what you've got isn't catching."

She laughed. "I am fascinated by chaos theory," she said. "Strange attractors? Set theory is fascinating, too, especially the fuzzy kind. And topology. I simply adore topology. I'll bet you're a fan of Escher's art, yes?"

"Sure." He was more surprised by her response to his being a math major than he had been by her asking him to have a drink. She obviously did know something about math, throwing terms around like that. Was he finally seeing something of the real her? *Damn!* "Escher's great."

"But you are not just a math major. Tell me about Toxique. Please?"

"She's just a character I've created. I've tried to sell an idea for a comic book about her to publishers here, but no luck."

"I am sorry to hear that." She leaned forward slightly, resting her arms on the table. She held his gaze.

He felt like he was looking into infinity. Falling into her eyes. Falling and falling . . .

She broke the spell by saying, "Nick mentioned Toxique is an environmental vigilante?"

He nodded and reached for his beer, making himself look at the chilled mug instead of her eyes for a moment. "Yeah. Would you like to hear the plot I came up with for her first issue? It's kind of based on that dream I had last night."

"I would love to hear it."

And he believed her. Then his face reddened. Because how could he tell her about how he had Toxique kiss her way down to the villain's penis and burn it off in her radioactive mouth? He couldn't! No way. He would have to make something else up when he got to that part, so to speak. Yeah. That would work.

"Well, okay, if you really want to hear. But stop me if it gets too boring."

"I am certain I will not be bored."

"Okay. I kind of used that dream I had last night. It starts out with a killer the police can't catch waking up and finding Toxique standing beside his bed."

12

Erotica Versus Pornography

"Medea!"

Joe hesitated with his telling of Toxique's plot as Medea turned toward the sound of her name. A woman was rolling toward them in a wheelchair. Behind her loomed a tall woman in a leather motorcycle jacket who moved like an athlete, tight black jeans hugging her muscled legs. When they got nearer, Joe noticed how each of them had scars on their faces, and he thought, *They know Medea?* They certainly did not fit the image of the type of people with whom he had imagined Medea would associate. But then, she had been associating with him, and he would not have imagined that, either. He guessed.

"Bernice," Medea said. "Trudy. Please join us. If you do not mind, Joe?"

"No. Of course not." Although he would have preferred remaining alone with Medea.

Medea said, "We should move to a larger table."

"Sure." He hoped his disappointment did not show. Having Medea to himself for a while, even if he was mainly just her audience, had been so very fine. "Hi, I'm Joe Clark," he said to Bernice as he stood up.

"Bernice Sanders." They shook hands. Her grip was strong.

"Trudy McAllen," Trudy said, holding out her hand. Her grip was stronger.

Medea stood and said, "That table will do." She pointed.

Trudy pulled out a chair at the larger table and placed it to one side.

"Thanks," Bernice said as she wheeled herself into the opening. "Jim's doing another panel. We told him we'd meet him in the bar when he was done. Barbara went back to look at something else in the dealers' room. She'll come here, too, when she's done."

Joe sat down at the table. He felt like a stranger at someone else's school reunion.

Trudy said, "Jim's panel is another of those erotica versus pornography things. Brad's on it, of course. I forget who else."

Bernice unfolded a pocket schedule. "Jim and Brad and Roxanne and Nina and Pat and Paul and Scott."

Trudy laughed. If the panelists outnumber the audience, they'll probably call it off and *all* come to the bar."

"Jim?" Joe asked. There was only one Jim that he knew of on the convention guest list. "Jim Brock?"

"Yeah," Trudy answered.

"I read his last horror novel. Strong stuff. It was great. I'd hoped to get his autograph."

Bernice said, "Well, stick around, then. He'll be glad you liked his last book. Lots of people couldn't hack it. Didn't understand it."

"Yeah," Trudy agreed. "Reviewers gave him hell, if they even bothered to review it."

Joe replied, "Reviewers," and shook his head negatively. "If a book or comic or movie gets a bad review, I take it as a good sign. I mean, if it upsets reviewers, it can't be all bad. Right?"

Bernice agreed. "Right."

"Absolutely," said Trudy. "Hell, I hate to think what they would say about the stuff that *I* like." She laughed.

Bernice asked, "Where's Nick?"

"Artists' alley," Medea answered. "He'll be along shortly. Here comes the waitress. I believe I will have another white wine. How about you two? And do you want another beer, Joe?"

"Sure."

Bernice ordered vodka on the rocks, but Trudy ordered a Dr Pepper. "I'm an alcoholic," she told Joe. "No booze for me."

He didn't know what to say.

"Joe has a great comic book plot," Medea said. "He had just started telling it to me. I would like for you two to hear it, too, if you do not mind, Joe?"

She called it a great comic book plot! Joe thought. *Damn, I hope she means it.* "No. I guess I don't mind. Shall I start over? I guess I should."

Medea nodded. "Please."

"Okay, a man wakes up and—"

"Excuse me, Joe," Medea said. "Here comes Nick. I want him to hear it, too."

"Uh, okay." Telling it to Medea and the other two women had not made Joe feel too nervous. But telling it to Nick Martin? A comic book pro whom Joe admired? Well, he was nervous now. It was like telling another editor. Nick would probably hate it, too. *But what if he doesn't?* Joe thought. *Don't go getting your hopes up, fool. Damn!*

13

An Editor Named Freyadissdottir

Nick's arrival coincided with the return of the waitress. As she served the drinks, Nick said, "I'll have a beer, too." She nodded and headed back to the bar. "Hi, Bernice. Trudy." He looked at Joe. *He's not going to remember my name,* Joe thought. "How's it going, Joe?" He held out his hand.

"Uh, fine, Mr. Martin. Just fine." He shook the offered hand.

"Nick. You've *got* to call me Nick."

"Sure. Okay."

As Nick sat down, Medea said to him, "Joe was about to tell us the plot for his comic book about Toxique. I had him wait so that you could hear it, too. I thought you might want to do the art for it, if you like it."

Sure, Joe thought. *Fat chance.*

"Sure," Nick answered. "I've been looking for a new project, anyway. Okay, Joe, shoot."

I really can't believe this is happening, Joe thought, then he said, "Yeah. Okay. Well, a man wakes up and finds Toxique standing beside his bed."

"Toxique is a radioactive, environmental vigilante,"

Medea added to Trudy and Bernice. "Sorry to interrupt again, Joe."

"No problem. Anyway, he wakes up and—"

The waitress showed up with Nick's beer. Medea laughed. "Joe, try again, please."

He laughed, too. "Okay." And then he told them the plot, just like he'd told the editors earlier in the day. But his nerves went away this time after he got going, because unlike the editors, he could tell from their reactions that these four people were approving of it. When he reached the burning-the-killer's-penis-off scene, he was feeling so empowered and encouraged that he forged ahead and told it straight.

"All right!" Trudy exclaimed.

"Yeah!" Bernice agreed.

Joe looked up at them. They were grinning, both of them, and Medea was smiling. Nick, too. *Damn!* Then he went on with it, told about Toxique's partner, told everything.

When he was done, no one spoke for a moment, then Nick said, "It's great, Joe. Really. Congratulations. Do you have an artist lined up for it yet? I don't want to horn in, if there's someone you've already got in mind."

"Horn in? You? You're not kidding, are you?"

"Of course I'm not kidding."

"It's not possible. Nick Martin wants to do the art for Toxique's book? I *must* be dreaming. This whole afternoon has just not been real."

Medea laughed. "On the contrary, Joe. It has. It is."

"But I've pitched this book to editors here, and no one was interested."

"Do you think they might be interested if I was doing the art?" Nick asked.

"Well, yes! I imagine that would make a rather large difference."

"Let's find out then. Excuse me a moment?" Nick said and got up from the table.

As he walked away, Joe said, "What did he mean about finding out?"

Nick had stopped to talk to a woman who was sitting at a table with several other people. Medea said, "I believe that is an editor with whom he is talking."

"No way. Really?"

"Yes. Really."

Bernice said, "It really does sound like it would make a great comic book, Joe."

"Really good," Trudy agreed. "I know some men I'd like to introduce to Toxique!"

Bernice laughed. "Yeah!"

"But maybe we should cool it, Bernice," Trudy said. "Joe here is going to think we're a pair of man-hating, psycho femmes or something."

"Only when the Moon is full, Joe," Bernice replied. "You're safe until then."

"Hell, he's safe then, too," Trudy said. "A man who could come up with that plot is okay by me, full Moon or not."

Bernice agreed. "Yeah."

Medea said, "Joe, I believe Nick is bringing the editor over to meet you. The Goddess is really smiling on you today."

"I just can't believe this is happening."

Joe stood up as Nick introduced him to the editor. And not just any editor, but Thora Freyadissdottir, an editor whose name Joe recognized (it was a hard name to forget) from a new, and currently *hot*, young comic book company.

"Nice to meet you, Ms. Freyadissdottir," Joe said, shaking her hand.

"Call me Thora, please." She had long blond hair and ice blue eyes. Joe wondered how old she was. Hard to tell, he decided. Didn't matter, either. He guessed. "I try not to torture people with my last name if they don't deserve it," Thora added.

Everyone laughed.

"I love my homeland, but Icelandic last names can be a bit much for Americans." To Joe she then said, "Nick tells me you two have a fantastic comic book proposal."

Nick said, "Prove it to her, Joe. Maybe we can do a deal right here this afternoon. She's looking for new ideas for a new line, right Thora?"

"Right," the editor agreed. "So, let's hear it."

Joe shook his head in amazement. Not only was he dreaming, he had died while asleep and gone to heaven. Maybe. So, he took a deep breath, and he said, "Okay. A man wakes up and finds a woman standing by his bed . . ."

14

In the Pro Suite

It was beginning to sink in but only slightly.

The afternoon was not yet over, but so much had already happened to Joe that he felt he had passed from one world to another. And, in a sense, he had.

He had crossed the barrier between fandom and prodom.

Because he had sold Toxique!

Joe and Nick had sold Toxique, that is.

As good as sold it, anyway, Nick assured him. An all but done deal. Just some negotiating over money and contracts, pending the approval of Thora Freyadissdottir's boss, who, she had said, would probably want to change the title from *La Toxique* to something more American sounding. But, to Joe's relief, she did not have a problem with Toxique's being female, nor did she want to change Toxique's name. And she had not asked for any ninjas or Good Girl Art, either.

Indeed, she had been very enthusiastic about Joe's description of Toxique's plot and general theme. She wanted some sample pages with Nick's art to show to her boss, though, and Nick had promised to do them soon.

To that end, he had invited Joe to have lunch with him tomorrow in his hotel room, just the two of them, to work out the layouts for the first few pages to both their satisfaction, and he wanted to start pencilling some of the preliminary sketches while Joe was there to approve or offer suggestions.

Nick did not, he had assured Joe, want to be one of those artists who, because they were more popular with fans than the writer, ended up controlling the book, even to the point of sometimes throwing out what the writer wrote and changing the story to suit the art. Nor, Nick did not think, would Thora be the type of editor who wanted to control the book with an iron hand, forcing editorial ideas and changes at the expense of the writing or art or both.

Joe would have to make compromises here and there, of course, because the editor and artist would want *some* input into the project. But a spirit of cooperation was what they would shoot for, Nick promised.

All of these business matters did not, however, concern Joe in the least just then. At the moment, all that mattered was that he was partying with the pros as Nick's guest in the convention's Pro Suite, the Holy of Holies to which only the luckiest fans were ever admitted.

The Pro Suite was a room provided by the convention where guests of the con could relax and talk with other pros, have some snacks, wine, beer, or soft drinks. All compliments of the convention.

Many writers and artists formed convention friendships that afterward had to be sustained with letters, phone calls, and computer links. Living in various cities around the country and out of it, using faxes and the U.S. mail or other delivery services to send their work to their publishers, conventions were the common ground at which they all occasionally gathered.

Business deals often arose from such friendships, of course, people who had met and liked each other's work wanting to work together and sometimes finding a way.

So, all around Joe were comic book professionals. Nick had already introduced him to several whose work Joe had long admired. And each time Nick told someone he and Joe were going to be working together on a new comic, Joe would get a smile on his face that did not want to go away.

Medea was not there, however. Trudy and Bernice were, as guests of Jim Brock, who had indeed come to the bar when his erotica versus pornography panel was over. And Joe had gotten his autograph. But the woman called Barbara had come into the bar as they were all leaving for the Pro Suite, and after introducing her to Joe, Medea had stayed with her.

As he had left the bar, Joe had looked back and seen Medea and Barbara holding hands across a shadowy table for two, making him wonder if either or both of them were lesbians. And then he had been surprised to find himself slightly jealous of Barbara.

But before long Medea arrived in the Pro Suite, Barbara with her.

Barbara stopped to talk with Trudy and Bernice and Jim as Medea came across the room to Nick and Joe. "Hello, again," she said. "Having fun, Joe?"

He laughed. "You could say that. If my feet would just start touching the floor again, everything would be fine."

"No levitating allowed until after midnight," Nick said.

"I'll try. Can I get you something to drink, Medea? They have wine, I believe."

"Perhaps later, Joe. Right now, I think it is time for you to come with me. Don't you agree, Nick?"

"Certainly. Seems a good time to do it. If Joe is ready."

"Ready?"

Medea smiled. "For your initiation, of course,"

"My initiation."

"You do remember, don't you?" Medea asked. "I mentioned it earlier. I came to Dallas to find and initiate a new Empusa into the Mysteries of Hecate. Yes?"

"I remember, but—"

"Don't worry, Joe," Nick assured him. "I'm certain you will do just fine. I did, when she initiated me. And if I could survive it, so probably can you."

"Survive it?" Joe laughed. "So, you're in on it, too, Nick, huh? The role playing, I mean. Are you going to dress up as Jason at the masquerade tonight?"

"Don't be insulting," Nick responded. "Jason is not someone with whom Medea would want to be seen."

Joe said, confused, "But in that movie, Medea and Jason had a romance."

Medea said, "Yes, *in that movie.* And in reality. But our love affair ended extremely tragically, and it was not the ending you may have read about, I can assure you. Jason was a superstud, it turned out, and a child-killing fiend, curse his soul, that I had in turn to kill."

She seemed genuinely angry. What an actress! And Joe suddenly wondered if she might actually *be* an actress. It made sense. She might be a stage actress in New York, or just someone who had not yet made the big time in Hollywood. She might even be going to play Medea in some play or film he had not yet heard about and was therefore using the convention to work on her part. So, in response to her angry remarks about Jason, Joe laughed and said, "I'm out of my league here mythology-wise. Looks like I'll have to reread my basic myths if I want to hang out with you folks."

"Basic mythology will help but little," Medea replied. She no longer seemed as angry, Joe noted. "Robert Graves's *The Greek Myths* comes closest to reality, but even he could not know the whole truth. I thought he would have made a worthy Empusa, but Hecate did not seize him. And speaking of Empusae, if you will come with me now?"

"To be . . . initiated?"

Medea said, "It is, basically, a simple matter. Really it is. Don't you agree, Nick?"

"Very simple. Trust me, Joe. If it's the last thing you ever do, you don't want to miss it."

"Okay, you two," Joe said. "Just what does this initiation into Hecate's Mysteries and becoming an Empusa involve?"

Medea answered, "I cannot tell you more ahead of time."

"Why do you think they're called Mysteries?" Nick asked. "Right."

"So. Are you ready, Joe?" she asked. "Today you became a comic book pro. Are you also ready to be initiated as an Empusa? By me?"

Joe wanted to flippantly answer yes, of course, you bet, right away, since it involved doing something, anything, with Medea. But things had been moving so fast, a tinge of apprehension suddenly made him hesitate.

"Come on, Joe," Nick said, smiling. "You might as well join the club. I think you will enjoy it. I know I did."

"When *you* were initiated."

"That's right."

"So, will you come with me now?" Medea asked.

"Just the two of us?"

"Yes. If you do not . . . mind being alone with me again?"

"Mind? No way!"

"Joe," Nick said, "go for it, will you? And I'll see you later. Right now, I want to talk with Jim about a project I mentioned to him earlier."

And Nick walked away, leaving Joe alone with Medea. Alone with Toxique's look-alike once again.

"After you, Joe," Medea said, motioning in the direction of the door. "If you have finished your beer?"

He made his decision, taking a long swallow and setting

the can down. He took a deep breath. "Okay. Let's go wherever it is that we're going."

When they were in the hallway, waiting at the elevators, he asked, "So, where *are* we going, if I may know? Back to the bar?"

"No," Medea said, holding his gaze as she smiled Toxique's seductive smile. "To my room."

15

In Medea's Room

"We are going to your . . . room?"

"Of course. In this culture, what we must do requires privacy."

"The initiation will be . . . in your room?" His imagination flashed a fantasy about being alone with Medea in her room.

She raised an eyebrow. "Afraid I will seduce you?"

He made himself grin. "Terrified."

She laughed. "I do not think so."

"Right."

The elevator arrived and the doors opened. It was crowded. A few people got off. Three others boarded with Medea and Joe.

He saw her push twenty-seven. The elevator started to rise. The number of people in the elevator forced them to stand close together. Medea's hip touched his. She did not move away. Nor did he.

I'm going alone with her to her room! he thought. *But nothing is going to happen. Nothing sexual. No way! She just made a joke about it, and Nick wouldn't have been so agreeable if there was a chance of sex between her and me. Sex between her and a nobody like me! Hope springs eternal, but let's not be ridiculous, Joe. Sex between Medea and me? Only in my dreams . . . where being initiated means making love, lying naked with Medea, my hands sliding over her sweat-slickened breasts, teasing her nipples with my teeth, touching her—*

"What are you thinking about, Joe?" Medea suddenly asked. She was looking sideways at him and smiling.

"Me? Nothing in particular. Why?"

"Still in shock from selling Toxique's book?"

"In shock, yes. I was determined to sell her at this convention, but I guess I didn't really think I would."

"Life surprises us sometimes."

"Yeah."

On twenty-seven, they walked to her room. At the door, she turned and said, "Enter freely, now, Joe, and of your own will."

"Hey, that's a line from Bram Stoker's *Dracula!*"

"He learned it, indirectly, from me."

He laughed. "Sure. You helped Stoker. Which would mean that you are over one hundred years old."

"Yes, it would." She unlocked the door and stepped to one side, waiting for him to enter first. "Except that I was not referring to Abraham Stoker. A gypsy adept named Tzigane, who is Dracula's mate, influenced Stoker's masterpiece. Stoker received that particular line, and much else, telepathically from her."

"Dracula's mate. Of course."

"Yes. Those who trained her to prepare Vlad Dracula for his role as an Undead occult master stole occult knowledge from those with whom I once studied."

"So, then," he entered the room, "you're not one hundred years old but five hundred years old."

She locked the door and slid the security bolt into place. "No." She leaned back against the door and looked at him. She smiled. "Older."

"Of course. Medea would be . . . what? A thousand or so by now?"

"Perhaps. Make yourself comfortable, Joe." She motioned to the room. Then she went into the bathroom and closed the door. He heard water begin to run.

He exhaled a deep sigh. What an incredible day. *Damn!* He went to the window and pulled the curtains aside.

Downtown Dallas was spread out below him in the afternoon sunlight. He hardly recognized the skyline anymore. It had changed so much since he was a kid. He could no longer even see the buildings that were the tallest when he was a child.

Traffic snaked its way along the streets and, farther away, the freeways.

The sky overhead was clear. The Sun was lowering in the west, casting long shadows.

He heard the shower begin to run in the bathroom. A shower? She was taking a shower? What on Earth . . .

An image teased his mind, Medea stepping out of the bathroom completely naked, wet from her shower, beckoning to him . . .

No. Not Medea. Toxique. Of course, Toxique.

But they looked the same!

The sound of the shower continued.

Joe turned away from the window and glanced around the room. There were two open suitcases, one filled with a woman's things, the other with a man's. Medea's and Nick's. Obviously.

Joe had assumed they were sharing a room, but he guessed he had somehow hoped they weren't.

Why did I hope that? So that Medea would be free for the taking? Honestly, I amaze myself. The things I imagine when I'm not looking. But fortunately I do imagine things, because it's my imagination that thought up the comic I just sold, thanks to Nick and Medea, who is now taking a shower before she initiates me into some mysterious—

The shower shut off. Bathwater began to run.

A bath, too? New images began to form. *Stop it*, he told himself.

He sat down in the large stuffed chair in one corner. He reached over to the nightstand beside the bed and picked up the remote control. He turned on the TV, channel-surfed his way almost all the way around the dial, then found an old Three Stooges movie and decided to watch it until Medea came out of the bathroom.

The bathwater stopped running. *She's soaking*, he thought, *lying naked, perhaps with suds floating around her as she stretches her long legs up out of the warm, steamy water, letting drops drip lazily from her toes . . .*

Stop it! he told himself. He was becoming aroused, and he definitely did not want to be exhibiting the telltale bulge of an erection under his jeans when she came out of her bath. *Damn!*

He tried to concentrate on the Three Stooges, but he kept thinking about the bath, about Medea, sweat now glistening on her face and shoulders, the tips of her breasts clear of the water, her nipples hard and erect because she was also thinking about him, about his joining her naked in her bath. And then, thinking about him, she softly moaned his name and reached down between her legs . . .

Damnit, fool! Stop! He made himself go back to watching the Three Stooges. He thought he heard a faint moan from the bathroom. A moan of pleasure.

Right. Sure. Right. Just like you were imagining. Of course. Fool!

He went back to channel-surfing, lingered on a martial arts movie featuring a female karate artist for a moment, went on, and soon ended up back with the Three Stooges.

But wait. There *was* a sound coming from the bathroom now. Someone was speaking, low and soft. *Medea?*

Of course it's Medea, idiot. Who else is in the bathroom?

But it might be coming from the room next door. The walls are probably pretty thin.

Maybe I should go closer to the bathroom door to check.

Yeah, and get caught there like a kid peeking through a keyhole when she opens the door? No way!

So, the Three Stooges . . .

It *was* Medea, he was certain of it. The sound was a little louder now. Chanting. Medea chanting in the bathtub. No . . . it . . .

He was suddenly sleepy. So sleepy he could hardly keep his eyes open.

He fought to stay awake, tried once more to concentrate on the TV. But the Three Stooges were not on the screen anymore. There was another movie on now.

When had he changed the channel?

He . . . didn't know . . . didn't care . . . because the new movie was a *good* one . . . a shadowy glade deep in a forest . . . a pool of dark water churning with the slender shapes of swimming serpents . . . and a naked woman in that pool . . . slowly emerging from the water with her back to the camera . . . as she chanted . . . droned soft and slow words in a foreign language, on and on and on as she slowly turned toward the camera.

The shadows across her face concealed her identity even face-on. But there were no shadows concealing her narrow waist, wide hips, full breasts, long legs. He hardly noticed her sexual beauty, though, because he was trying to decide whether or not the markings that covered her bare skin were tattoos or body paint.

Red spirals centered on her nipples covered her breasts. Another large red spiral was centered on her navel, and showing through those red lines was a large, black triangle, the point aimed downward, ending just above her triangle of black pubic hair. Other symbols covered her legs and arms in red and black, symbols that looked like primitive paintings from an ancient cave.

Then suddenly the shadows covering her face slipped away, revealing the face of Toxique . . .

No.

Medea.

The face of Medea, coming closer as she walked toward the camera, walked right out of the TV into the room and came slowly toward him, her naked flesh streaming water, her breasts swaying with her languid movements, her long, dark hair wet with water and sweat, plastered to her bare skin, while around her feet slithered tentacles of glowing blue mist like the ghosts of dead serpents.

And she said, "Joe . . ."

And she opened her arms to him.

And she whispered to him, "Come to me now. Take me and enter me, freely and of your own will, leaving behind some of the happiness you bring."

He tried to laugh, tried to speak and tell her that the rest of that line had been copped from *Dracula* too, or rather Stoker had copped it from Dracula's mate, or something! He found it difficult to remember which . . . difficult to think at all . . . but easy to feel . . . burning pleasure and pain, a hunger so deep he ached with it, a fiery hunger with the speed of light and a hearty cry of *Hi, Ho, Medea! Away!*

. . . and away . . . hissing with pleasure, groaning with panting with moaning with lust and love and desire to take her, to thrust his stiffened manhood inside of her moist depths, to make her cry out with pleasure . . . to hear her laugh with love . . .

"I . . . *need,*" he moaned in a tortured voice he hardly recognized as his own, "need to . . . feed . . . to seed."

He grunted a laugh. "That rhymes," he mumbled, then he was captured by Medea's infinite eyes and fell into them, fell into a vortex of lust that burned in a maelstrom of howling darkness and desire beyond life and death, beyond flesh and love.

Beyond lies.

16

A Sudden Dream

Joe's fall into the infinity of Medea's eyes was an experience of unbounded time and endless space, terrifying at first, then ridiculously humorous, then breathtakingly exciting. And suddenly over. As if it had never happened. Except in his dreams. Because he was still sitting in the chair, the Three Stooges were still on the TV, and Medea was still—

The bathroom door opened and Medea hurried out. She wore a white, terry cloth bathrobe, held closed with her hands.

"Are you all right, Joe? I thought I heard you cry out."

He cleared his throat. "Uh, I fell asleep for a moment and had a sudden dream." And he remembered how she had looked in the dream, naked and painted like a primitive priestess of passion. He almost laughed. *A primitive priestess of passion? Sounds like a porno film.* Which made him wish it *were* a porno film, starring Medea, that he could watch whenever he wanted, over and over.

"A sudden dream? Well, I had a sudden . . . desire. For a quick bath. I hope you haven't minded waiting."

"No. Not at all."

"What was your dream about?"

"I . . . don't remember."

"Well, I'll dry my hair, then we can continue with your initiation. Okay?"

Continue? he thought. "Okay."

She went back into the bathroom and closed the door, but not all the way, and it slowly began to open on its own. It stopped halfway. A full-length mirror on the closet door opposite the bathroom allowed Joe to see Medea's reflection through the half open bathroom door.

She began drying her hair with a towel, using both hands, leaving her robe hanging open. Seen from the side, the robe's movements alternately exposed and concealed her nakedness beneath.

Oh, God! This can't be happening! Damn!

As much as he wanted to stare, he made himself look back at the TV, certain that if he kept looking at Medea she would turn and see *his* reflection staring at her. But he could not look *only* at the TV, so he shifted his eyes back and forth between the Stooges and Medea, back and forth, back and forth.

He moved his legs, partly to relieve the strain of his erection stiffening against his jeans, partly to try and conceal it if she came back into the room. And then it happened. She turned toward the door and for a heartbeat he saw her face-on, fully nude beneath the open robe for an instant before she pulled it closed and came into the room.

He looked quickly away, his face turning red. *Damn!* Had she seen him looking? Maybe. He wasn't certain. But if she had, she gave no indication as she went to her suitcase and searched for a moment before finding what she wanted, a hair-drier.

"Not much longer," she promised as she went back into the bathroom. She closed the door, and this time it stayed closed.

He heard the hair-drier begin to blow. A mental image of

the beauty he had just seen generated an involuntary groan.

Thank God that hair-drier is running! he thought, *or she would have heard me moan! And come running out to see what the matter was again? Maybe forgetting to hold the robe closed this time? Yeah!*

But then what, fool? It's one thing to sneak a peek. It's another if you saw her naked and she knew you were seeing her naked. Isn't it?

The hair-drier continued in the bathroom.

"You've *got* to show her the proper respect, idiot," he said aloud. *She and Nick just helped you sell Toxique's book. If you screw up here, who knows? She might nix the deal. So, for God's sake, show her the proper respect! Stop remembering that dream and stop thinking about what you saw in the mirror, damnit!*

But what the hell kind of deal was it when a woman takes you to her room and then decides to take a bath? That's not normal. Of course, being in a hotel room alone with a woman was not normal for him, either. He suddenly wished he was back in the dealers' room looking at comic books. This was getting out of hand.

But only in your mind, he countered. *Nothing has really happened except she wanted a bath. She probably didn't have time to take one after she arrived, and you can't go assigning ulterior motives simply because a woman wants to take a damned bath. This isn't some soap opera or some movie or novel. Hell, man, you should be honored that she trusts you enough to take a bath with you around. Yeah. Honored! And horny as hell, thank you very much.*

He settled down and went back to the Stooges. His erection went away.

The hair-drier stopped. A moment later, Medea emerged from the bathroom, again holding the white robe closed with her hands. Her hair looked quite dry. And beautiful. So very long and dark and beautiful, hair that would be heaven to get lost in, to stroke and kiss and bury your face in, and—

Stop it! Stop it! Stop it! he mentally shouted at himself. What the hell was wrong with him this afternoon, anyway? Had selling Toxique unhinged him or what? *Control your damned thoughts, fool!*

From her suitcase Medea chose a black bra and panties, extremely small ones, it looked like to Joe, out of the corner of his eye. She turned to him.

"Joe, would you do me a favor?"

"Uh, sure. What?"

"Close your eyes for a moment, please." She dangled the bra and panties from an outstretched finger, and she smiled. "Please? Unless you insist on watching?"

"W . . . watching? No! Of course not. I'll close my eyes." And he did. And he wondered why she just hadn't gone back into the bathroom to dress.

He heard the sound of her robe being tossed onto the bed.

Oh, God. She's totally naked right now, just a few feet away, totally naked, and all I have to do to see her is to just crack open my eyes a little bit . . . not enough for her to notice. Just a little bit—

No! Damn you to hell, Joe. No! Remember the respect!

But . . . what was taking her so long? He heard movement. Then silence again, except for the Three Stooges. Then he heard a click and the Stooges shut up.

Why'd she turn off the TV?

Another click. Something touched his leg.

"Open your eyes now, Joe."

So, he did. Then almost screamed.

17

Enchantress

The second click had been the bedside light nearby, which she had turned on, and what had touched his leg was Medea's leg.

She was standing close to him, fully illuminated by the bedside light, touching his leg with hers, smiling down at him.

And she was naked.

She said, "You did not open your eyes until I told you. Good for you."

"It was a . . . test?"

"Perhaps." She reached down and took his hand. "Stand up. Please?"

He stood up. He swallowed hard. He didn't know what to say. Probably couldn't have spoken at that moment anyway. So he kept quiet.

She reached down and touched his jeans over the bulge of his erection. "Did you know this is illegal in some states?"

What did she say? Illegal? What's illegal? To have an erection? When a naked woman is standing close? Too damned close.

How can it be too close? he asked himself. "Oh, God, Medea . . ."

"No, Joe. Not God. *Goddess.* Yes?"

"Uh, sure . . . whatever you . . . say."

She began to lightly stroke his stiffened penis through his tightly stretched jeans.

"Look, uh . . . I . . . thought you said you weren't going to . . . seduce me."

She shook her head. She stopped stroking him. "I am not seducing you."

"It sure as hell looks like it to me. *Feels* like it, too."

"Then look and feel again. You are seducing yourself. There is more than one way to respond to a series of stimuli."

"A series of stimuli? Right. Sure."

She stepped even closer. Her breasts touched his chest. "Did you not enjoy the vision I sent earlier? The one of me rising naked from the pool?"

"Vision?"

"It was spawned by the spell you heard me chanting in the bathroom, to open the proper psychic-emotional gateways in preparation for your full initiation. My bath was no ordinary one, of course, but a ritual bath to purify and prepare me as well."

How had she known about his dream? It couldn't be a vision like she said. Could it? He was fast becoming incapable of caring. What the hell did it matter when all he could think about was grabbing her and crushing her against him?

"Do what you want, Joe. Grab me. Crush me against you. Run your hands over my body. Feel my breasts. Feel *all* of me. I won't stop you. Go ahead."

He almost did. But then he said, "No, damnit. No!"

She smiled. "No?"

"It's . . . not right. What if Nick came in and—"

"He won't. He knows we came here to initiate you, remember?"

"Initiate me, yes. Not this."

"Yes. *This*. Hecate is a very sexual Goddess. Put your arms around me, if you want. You do want to, don't you? Of course you do. So, do it, Joe. Do it. Take me in your arms and kiss me. Prove yourself to me, and through me to Hecate."

"And . . . if I don't?"

"You don't want to disappoint me, do you? Or Hecate?"

"Disappoint you? No. But . . . why me?"

"I have already told you why. Now, stop talking. Stop thinking. Let your instincts and emotions take control. And take me, Joe, enter me freely and of your own will, and leave behind some of the happiness you bring! Okay?"

"You *are* seducing me. Or maybe this whole bit is just more of your role playing? I mean, Medea was a seductress, wasn't she?"

"Enchantress. There is a difference."

"Sure. Look, I don't even know your real name!"

She laughed. "Medea *is* my real name. I am not playing a role. I really *am* Medea, and everything I have told you is true."

"Sure it is. Damnit!"

She raised an eyebrow. "For someone who thinks he is being seduced, you are showing remarkably few of the proper responses. Why don't you kiss me, Joe? Go ahead."

She closed her eyes and tilted her head slightly back and parted her lips.

He groaned and slowly, hesitantly touched his mouth to hers. A wave of warmth poured through him.

He felt her respond, felt the wet tip of her tongue touch his closed lips, opened his mouth and allowed her tongue inside, returned her thrust with his own, touching her teeth, their tongues sliding against each other, both of them now moaning low in their throats, kissing and kissing, on and on and on . . .

He came up for air, ran his hands through her dark hair. "Medea . . ."

He gazed into her eyes from up close, felt for a moment as if he was falling into them again. "Oh, God, Medea . . ."

"Goddess, Joe. *Goddess.*"

"Whatever!"

They began to kiss again while his hands moved lower. He touched her breasts, cautiously at first, then more boldly. He ran his thumbs over her erect nipples, back and forth.

"Use your teeth on them, Joe. On my nipples. Please?"

He sat back down so that his mouth could reach her breasts and began teasing her nipples with his teeth. She gasped and grasped the back of his head, pressing his face harder against her.

"Joe?"

He looked up.

She smiled down at him as she ran her hands through his hair. "Wouldn't you be more comfortable without your clothing?"

"Oh, God . . . *dess,*" he groaned.

"Very good!" she said, then laughed. "Shall I help you remove your clothes? I would enjoy that. Okay?"

"Uh, sure. Okay."

"Stand up, please."

He did. She pulled his T-shirt off over his head. Her breasts touched his bared chest.

He pulled her close and began kissing her again, holding her warmth crushed against him, skin to skin, moaning low in his throat, while her hands were busy lower down, unbuttoning his jeans, unzipping them, letting them fall.

She moved out of his arms, reached down, and then, looking up at him, holding his gaze, slowly slid down his shorts.

She looked at his erection. She looked back at him and smiled. "It is even more illegal when not covered by clothing, I suppose."

He laughed.

She pressed herself against the naked length of him, capturing his erection between her bare thighs.

"You feel good to me, Joe."

"Oh, Goddess, Medea. You feel good to me, too."

"Of course."

"Sit on the bed so that I may finish undressing you."

"Finish?"

"Your feet are still covered."

"Oh! Yeah."

When he was completely naked, she said, "Help me pull back the bedspread, yes?"

He helped her, then she stretched out on the white sheets, smiled at him, beckoned to him, and suddenly he thought about a condom.

He had heard all the reports. Sex could kill you these days. He could catch something from Medea if he didn't wear a condom.

"I have no diseases to transmit to you, Joe. Do you have any about which I should worry?"

What the hell? "I was just wondering about that. I'm beginning to think you *can* read minds!"

"Of course I can."

"Well, no, I don't have any diseases, either."

"You are certain?"

"Yes. I've never . . . oh, never mind." He was not about to tell her he could not have caught any sexually transmitted diseases because he had never had sex before!

"Ah, this is your first time. You see, I really *can* read your thoughts."

In his current state, alone in a hotel room, naked with an

equally naked woman, Joe would not have thought it possible to have his face turn red with embarrassment. But it did.

Twenty-one years old and still a virgin.

Deeply embarrassing.

Oh, he had made love to lots of women, but only in his fantasies. Toxique was but the latest in a long line of fantasy lovers.

He had been close to doing it with a real woman once or twice, but he had not gone through with it and afterward could not decide which he felt most, relieved he hadn't done it or disgusted with himself for not having done it.

"There is no shame in not having made love to a woman before, Joe. In fact, in many ways I prefer it."

"You do? But I'm not . . . I mean, I don't have any experience, and I don't want to disappoint you."

"I will not be disappointed! There are no rules that say we cannot talk as we make love. I will tell you what to do, if you need guidance, but if you let your instincts take control, I am certain you will do fine without asking how. So, now, stop talking and thinking and continue. You are doing wonderfully so far."

"Really?"

She laughed. "Yes! Now please, for Goddess' sake, continue!"

18

Tomb

Joe kissed Medea's lips, her throat, her breasts, used his teeth on one nipple then the other, moved lower, kissed a pattern down her firm torso, kissed her navel, moved down her flat stomach, then hesitated and looked up at her.

She stroked his hair. "Do not stop, Joe. Keep going. Please. I would enjoy it, if you would, too?"

"I just can't believe this!"

"You're thinking and talking again. Stop it."

"Yeah."

He kissed lower, lower, heard her moan with pleasure, kept going, past her delta of dark curls, nestled his face between her legs, cautiously kissed her genitals.

Medea moaned. "Go ahead, Joe. Use your tongue to penetrate me. Please . . ."

He did.

"Oh, yes, Joe! Deeper now. Go deeper!"

He did.

"And gently use your teeth . . ."

He did.

She cried out.

Joe jerked back, fearing he'd hurt her.

She laughed. "No, Joe. It is pleasure you are giving me, not pain! Do not stop!"

He obeyed.

She cried out again a moment later and then again.

"Yes, Joe. Wonderful! Yes!"

He grew bolder, earning more cries of pleasure from her.

"Take me now, Joe. It is time."

"Okay. I just can't believe—"

"Do not talk!"

He positioned himself over her. She reached down and grasped his erection, guided him into her warm inner depths.

"Now, Joe, move slowly at first. And try different angles, if you want. My reactions will tell you the one I find most enjoyable. Yes?"

"Oh, Goddess, Medea," he groaned as he began to move. "You are so . . . beautiful . . ."

Her fingernails dug into his back. She gripped his sides with her strong legs. She began to move, too, contributing to the effect.

"Not too fast yet," she warned. "You feel wonderful in me, Joe."

"Medea . . . I . . . think I'm going to—"

"No. Stop for a moment. There. Now, move onto your back. Let me sit atop you for a while."

He did what she asked.

He looked up at her, reached up and kneaded her breasts.

She moved slowly, expertly, moaning with pleasure while Joe groaned and panted beneath her. Then suddenly she moved him back on top.

"Finish it now, Joe! Finish it!"

And she began moving faster beneath him, matching his strokes, faster and faster and faster and then suddenly her cries of passion turned to chanting and he climaxed and cried out with pleasure and saw through eyes half closed that beneath her the bed had become thick grass leading into a dark pool in a forest glade, and her body had changed too, was now tattooed and painted with primitive spirals and symbols, and then she vanished and he was elsewhere, looking up at a towering giantess, a monstrous thing with three inhuman heads.

The ground seethed beneath him, and he saw that it was alive with snakes. He screamed. Hounds with eyes of fire nearby howled to his scream. From out of nowhere rotted corpses appeared around him and began to dance with stiffened jerks. He gagged on the death stench coming from the dancing Dead.

And from somewhere far away he heard Medea's voice shouting praises to Hecate.

Hecate, the monstrosity that loomed above him.

"Medea!" Joe shouted. "Medea!"

The Goddess turned Her eyes upon him.

One of Hecate's heads was that of a lioness, one a mare, one a hound. Her six eyes burned with red fire.

And She was naked, Her torso covered with multiple breasts, the juncture between Her legs the entrance to a cavern of darkness.

Suddenly Joe began floating rapidly upward toward that dark entrance, and before he could cry out again, he was pulled into Hecate's inner depths.

He did cry out with terror then, and he desperately shouted Medea's name, over and over, until he lost the power to make a sound, and around him the darkness was as silent as a tomb.

19

Womb

Joe floated in darkness, sealed in the tomb-like silence of Hecate's womb.

He felt neither heat nor cold. Neither pain nor pleasure.

He could move, but when he did, there was no sense of movement.

He regained the power to make sounds, and he did, crying out, shouting, screaming, but only to hear the deadly darkness in which he was engulfed swallow the sound.

He tried to control his fear, tried to think.

What had really happened?

How long would it last?

Could he escape it somehow?

Maybe if he thought about what he knew of Medea in mythology, he could find some clue. But he did not know much, just that old movie about the Argonauts, and—

But he *did* know more. He knew things now he did not remember knowing before.

He knew (remembered?) that she had been an expert with poisons and drugs. *Now that had not been in that movie, had it? She had drugged the beast that guarded the Golden Fleece, not in the movie . . . but in the legends about her, right?*

And Medea the Enchantress could cast spells. She was called a Witch by some.

Even in Shakespeare's time, Medea's Goddess, Hecate, was spoken of as the Goddess of Witches. The three Witches in *Macbeth* consorted with Hecate. And Witches were known for their knowledge of herbs and drugs that could heal or poison. Or cause hallucinations?

Someone playing the role of Medea, then, to be completely authentic, might conceivably deem it necessary to use drugs of some kind.

Like the woman calling herself Medea had used on him?

But if she drugged me, how did she do it? he wondered. *I didn't eat or drink anything after I got to the room. And if it was done at the party, it would have hit me sooner, wouldn't it?*

Well, maybe it had. What about the dream or vision or whatever he'd had earlier, while she was still in the bathroom? Had she known about it because she *had* caused it? Not with a spell, of course, but with some kind of hypnotic drug that put him to sleep and allowed her to sneak out and tell him what to see? After which she returned to the bathroom and he awakened and remembered seeing what she had put in his mind.

Or maybe he had been drugged twice, first at the party then later some other way.

Couldn't she have put something on her skin or lips? So that when he kissed her . . .

Maybe that bath she took had coated her body with something. *But wouldn't that have affected her before it affected me? Well, maybe she took some kind of antidote.*

But no matter how she did it, that must have been what had happened. He had been drugged. *Damn!*

It made better sense than anything else he could think of at the moment.

"What have you done to me?" he shouted. "Medea! What have you done?"

The darkness swallowed the sound just as it had swallowed him and there was no response to his cry.

He struggled to master a new surge of panic. What if whatever she had given him had fried his brain, permanently? What if this was what it was like to be lying in a hospital bed in a coma, hooked up to tubes, floating in the darkness of a ruined brain, on and on and on.

"Medea! Help me, damnit! Enough! Make it stop!"

But it did not stop. The nothingness continued. And then it became hard to breathe.

He gasped for air. He was suffocating! "Medea!" he cried weakly. "Please! I . . . can't breathe!"

His heart pounded harder as it sought to compensate by pumping his oxygen-poor blood faster and faster to his body's oxygen-starved cells.

He struggled harder to breathe, felt the darkness closing in, pressing against him, seeping into his flesh, killing him.

"Muh . . . dee . . . aaah . . . pll . . . leeezzzz . . ."

But again there was no response.

And then he died.

20

Death

Death was movement. Incessant movement. Restless. Flowing. Hungry. Searching. *Needing*.

Joe knew he was dead, knew it as surely as he had known he had been alive. A feeling words could not touch. A certainty reason could not reach.

If Medea had drugged him and had made him hallucinate, he reasoned that the dose must have killed him, because he was most certainly dead.

But Death itself is alive! he thought.

And because he was now one with Death, he was alive in Death, his consciousness intact.

The mathematician in him found an elegant symmetry worthy of reality. Beautiful. And insane, of course. But beautiful. And pleasureful. For there was great emotion in Death and great pleasure in being one with Death's movement, Death's Dance.

Yes.

The Dance of Death.

The real thing.

Silent, fleshless movement, dance in its purest form, an equation of a massless point moving as fast as light in all directions and none through a lightless void as vast as infinity and as small.

To be one with it was to experience the pure certainty of uncertainty, the perfect order of pure chaos.

And it felt . . . *terrifyingly wonderful.*

Joe's fear of being dead, horrifying at first because it had made him feel so helpless, so out of control, quickly became a fear that Death's movement would stop, that Death would die . . . because there was also the hunger, Death's hunger, the thing for which it was searching, toward which it was flowing, some unseen, unguessed goal, a strange mathematical attractor in a realm of fractal geometry where dimension was not an integer.

Except that . . . suddenly he knew the name of that strange attractor, that organizing set of points within the universal infinity of possible points. He knew the name of that boundary toward which Death danced.

The boundary was Birth, and beyond it waited Life.

Life. Death. Life. The embodiment of an elegant mathematical proof. The simple beauty of pure symmetry. Life dancing toward Death dancing toward Life, where Death's movement would be slowed by physical reality, slowed by flesh. But only for a moment in Time, only for a Life of Time, while the Life/Death/Life equation of an unending loop continued.

The beauty of it made him ache with emotional wonder. Comforting. Terrifying. Wonder without end.

Without end!

Light flashed.

Joe cried out, but only in his mind, the silent scream of surprise of a consciousness without a voice.

Light flashed again. From all directions at once. But without revealing anything other than itself, light that was as meaningless as the darkness in which Death moved.

Another flash. Then another and another. Faster and faster. Until Joe was moving slower and slower in the thickness of a colorless light occasionally negated by a stutter of darkness.

And then out of the light began to materialize floating shapes . . . ghostly bodies . . . human wraiths. Asleep. Men. Women. Children. All ages, shapes, sizes. All races. *And all him/her/them.* People with faces that he had once worn. Faceless people he was yet to be. People from his past whose names and memories were also his own, memories that melded together into One.

Yes. Into One.

And he was that One, his consciousness, the strange attractor of his own being, the point that integrated all the Life Points of his existence from the relative past to the relative future into the Absolute Now.

And Now, the Life Point with which he interfaced was known as Joe Clark, a naked man dead in a hotel bed with a beautiful woman who called herself Medea.

No.

With a beautiful woman who really *was* Medea, just as she had said.

Because he had known her before.

Yes. In more than one lifetime. But the first lifetime in which he had known her filled him with self-disgust because in that lifetime he had, for money, written a play by which the lies about her were spread and made popular, lies that portrayed her as a killer of her own children.

A lifetime in which he had been known as Euripides.

After that life, subsequent lives had been lived trying to forget and deny the Evil he had done to her.

But now, in his life as Joe Clark, he hungered to right the wrong.

He had returned to flesh intending to be a writer who

would write the truth instead of lies, about Medea and other things about which dark lies had been told.

Then he had become a boy fascinated with female comic book heroes, women who were strong and noble. Women who protected children and the weak and punished those who would harm them. Women like Toxique. Women like Medea had truly been. *And still was.*

And he had become a man who fantasized about being the friend and lover of heroic women, yearning for something he could not name until now, yearning for Medea's forgiveness.

But he had failed. The physical body of Joe Clark was dead. His chance had been lost.

Medea had found him and recognized him and had her revenge!

Despair crushed down upon him. Hopelessness. Horror.

Then suddenly a ghostly form shimmered into existence before him, Medea, floating in the ocean of colorless light clothed in a flowing black robe among the pale shapes of his other lives.

Terror and panic possessed him. He was powerless before her power. Helpless before the woman he had so wronged.

She could, he knew, use her occult powers to destroy him. She could erase his consciousness and end his existence for all time.

She raised her left hand.

He controlled his impulse to try and flee. He fought to master his fear. It was her right to do with him as she wanted. He would not try to escape.

He waited.

And then she said in his mind, *Joe Clark, once known as Euripides, the Goddess Hecate, Queen of Ghosts and the Dead, has deemed your soul worthy.* Her ghostly face smiled. *And so have I.*

21

Life

Emotion built within him. Desire. Excitement. Life.

It is time, Medea's voice said in his mind, *to leave Hecate's Womb. Time to return. There is much you want to do before your next death, yes?*

Before he could answer, her ghostly image vanished and so did the light in which he had been floating, except for a circle of white toward which he was then drawn, faster and faster, as if being accelerated by gravity while falling through space but without any sensation of air rushing past while the circle of brightness rapidly expanded as it neared.

He reached the circle, hurtled through it.

For a moment that stretched, imploded, expanded, shrunk his perception of reality, he found himself in the Gray Between, the realm of the physical waiting before him, his experience of Hecate looming behind him. But the Goddess no longer had the appearance of a monster.

Above Her glowed three Moons—one a waxing crescent, one a full circle, one a waning crescent—and She now appeared as three women, their hair alive with serpents, their eyes glowing with white light, around their feet a carpet of clouds upon which floated countless slumbering ghosts, some showing the sleepy smiles of the preborn, some the rictus grins of the newly dead.

The images of the three women, related in Joe's deep mind to the images of the three Moons shining above, interpenetrated each other and yet remained separate—one young, one mature, one old.

At first, only the Crone was looking at Joe. But then the Maiden and the Mother also focused their gazes upon him. And all three smiled.

His moment of eternity in the hyper-real non-reality of the Gray Between exploded then imploded his consciousness, and he sensed movement again, onward toward the realm of the physical.

Below him, he suddenly saw the hotel bed in which he had made love to Medea, a bed in which his body now lay alone. But he saw it only for a fleeting instant as he plummeted like a wingless bird hurtling from sky to Earth into his flesh.

He gasped for air, felt his heart pounding, pounding.

He opened his eyes. Nausea washed through him. He was dizzy. His head ached with throbbing pain.

"The disorientation will soon pass," said Medea. She sat down on the edge of the bed. He noticed that she was still naked. She reached out and squeezed his hand. "Welcome back."

He raised his head and looked at her. "Welcome back. I guess."

"You guess?"

He sat up, groaned, and rubbed his temples. "No. I guess I don't guess, not anymore, not about you and Hecate and all."

"Nor about yourself?"

"Nor about myself. *My selves.*" The wonder of the symmetrical cycles without end that he had experienced in Hecate's

Womb momentarily gripped him again. "It's just so damned . . . *beautiful*."

"Yes. But with the knowledge comes the burden of responsibility. You will learn more of that later. You need not worry about it right now.

"Some of the knowledge is already yours from past lives and will come into your mind as you become reoriented in your flesh. The rest of the knowledge will be, as I have said, provided for you at a later time."

He shook his head. "Yeah. Okay. But you know, I was just thinking that you could have done some post-hypnotic suggestions or something while I was under the influence, made me think I was dead and all the rest of this, but—"

"Under the influence of what? You do not still think that I drugged you, do you?"

"No." And he didn't. "Not drugs." He knew what to call it, though, the power that had initiated his initiation, knew it from fragmented memories from other lives and between. "It was Hecatean sex magic. A version of Tantric Yoga. And you're very good at it."

She laughed. "Thank you."

"But then, you've had plenty of time to practice. All the while I've lived many lives and died many deaths, you have been on Earth, immortal."

"No more truly immortal than you or anyone else."

"Consciousness-wise. Soul-wise. But your flesh has not died. What is it like to never have your memories broken by Death?"

"Not always pleasant."

He nodded. "Yeah. I can imagine." And he really could, never to have the relief of Death's forgetfulness, never to have the chance to learn new things in new flesh. "Pretty horrible."

"There are also rewards."

He was silent a moment, gazing into her eyes. "I might have really died from the initiation."

"Your flesh did die, if only for a minute or so."

"Okay. Yeah. It just seemed much longer where I was. Where my consciousness was. Different equations for different occasions."

She smiled. "An interesting way of describing it."

"So. What's next? I passed the test. The first test, anyway. I suppose I should resent what you did, risking my life like that without my permission, *changing* me like you and Hecate have now done! But I *know* it was as much my choice as yours and Hecate's. I made the decision before I became Joe Clark. And now I know stuff I didn't *consciously* know before, but I don't know how to use all of it. You'll help me learn how, though, right?"

"You will learn from me while I am here, then from others who have already learned the basics."

"Of being an Empusa."

"Yes."

"And I've met some, I assume? Trudy and Bernice?"

"And Barbara. And Jim. And of course Nick."

"And they have all been . . . initiated like me. In the same way. With sex magic. By you. I'm not asking. I know it's true. I'm just—"

"You are getting used to things. And you are doing fine. When you are feeling like it, we will go back to the party. You will see some . . . interesting things."

"With my new eyes."

She laughed again. "Same eyes, Joe."

"But they're going to work like new ones, because there will be an improved processing of data. More wavelengths of light will compute?"

"Not everything you see will be pleasant."

"I know. But . . . well, what the hell? I'm feeling better now. I guess I'm ready to go."

"You recovered very quickly."

"I'm not one hundred percent yet. But I'm kind of anxious to get on with it. I mean, it's like I've been waiting for this all my life. I just didn't know what it was."

They started getting dressed. Then Joe hesitated, looking at her.

He hated to see her put her clothes on. He might never see her naked like this again.

Among the knowledge he now possessed, he knew that Medea only made love, in the way he had experienced, to each initiate once. She might share sexual pleasure with them on occasion, and they might engage in something he only vaguely understood that involved a sharing of life-energy, but it would never be an experience of out-and-out-all-the-way-*old-fashioned*-type lovemaking between them ever again. Not in this lifetime.

A sudden sadness gripped him. A sense of infinite loss.

She knew his thoughts and came to him and held him closely. He hungrily returned her embrace. They kissed, long and deep. Then she pulled back.

"You gave me great pleasure, too," she whispered, kissed him lightly once more on his lips, then resumed putting on her clothes.

22

Club

Back at the party in the Pro Suite, Joe noticed that a lot more people were there than before. Smoke hung in the air from cigarettes. The combined conversations of all the pros in the room created a small roar.

He saw Nick, Trudy, Barbara, Bernice, and Jim clustered in one corner. A group of Empusae! But he also saw other things.

His Empusa vision, though untrained and unpracticed, nevertheless revealed glimpses of the Unseen, while his awakened knowledge provided rudimentary explanations.

"Do not be alarmed by anything you see, Joe," Medea advised.

"Okay." But it wasn't easy.

He saw terrible eyes without faces staring hungrily in from outside the upper-story hotel windows, *and he knew their names*.

He saw the shifting colors in the life-energy auras that surrounded each human, understood what the colors meant, which people were healthy, which sick, which soon to die.

He also saw the aura of life-energy that throbbed around a potted plant, and he sensed the plant's agony because of the cigarette smoke in the air.

Near the feet of one man, he saw a dog's ghost that was staying faithfully by his former master's side, pitifully trying to attract the man's attention.

And he saw dead things clinging unseen to some of the living and knew they were the wraiths of deceased loved ones—parents, grandparents, children—afraid of passing on to the afterdeath realms, sustaining an unnatural existence in the realm of the physical by parasitically sucking life-energy from those who had loved them in life.

Knowing his thoughts, Medea said, "Before the convention is over, I will deal with many of the death disorders you see. The other Empusae here are not yet capable of working with the energies and vortices involved. You are a novice, but so are they, compared to the adepts who deal with death disorders.

"Do not be too concerned about the disorders you see here, however. Although they may not seem so to you, they are all of a relatively minor nature. When I deal with them, you and the others will watch and learn, yes?"

"Yes. Okay."

But the worst thing he saw was not a death disorder. It was Toxique, floating ghostlike before him.

He had thought he'd caught a glimpse of her earlier in the elevator on the ride back to the party floor. But now she was clearer, or perhaps his occult vision had grown stronger, making the image impossible to ignore.

"It is your own creation," Medea explained, "a coherent energy matrix, a thought form you have created with your thoughts and energized with your desires. When you begin to deny it life-energy, it will gradually fade from existence."

He looked at Toxique, beckoning to him with her poison-touch hands, smiling her radioactive smile. "She . . . *it* will fade? I never knew that my thoughts could . . . create something like that."

"Of course. Come now. The others are waiting to greet and congratulate you."

He followed her to the group of Empusae in the corner.

"Welcome to the club, Joe!" Nick said, shaking Joe's hand.

"Yeah," Trudy said. She put her muscled arms around him and hugged him tightly for a moment. "Welcome!"

Joe laughed. "Thanks, Trudy, but go easy on the ribs."

"I didn't hug you *that* hard."

"I want a hug, too," Bernice said.

Joe leaned down and gave the woman in the wheelchair a hug. When he straightened, Barbara also gave him a hug and said, "May Hecate always smile upon you, Joe."

"Thanks."

"Glad you made it through," Jim Brock said. The writer held out his hand. Joe shook it.

"Yeah. I'm still in shock, I guess. This is all just so incredible."

"Hey, I was in shock for a week at least," Barbara said. She pushed errant strands of her long red hair back over her shoulder. "Sometimes I think I still am."

"Me too," Nick agreed.

Joe said, "So, I'm the youngest here, Empusa-wise, who's the oldest?"

"Bernice, I think," Trudy said. "You met Medea in what, Bernice, '87?"

"Yeah. I was in that hospital back east recovering from, well, you know, what had happened to me. And she came to the room one night after everyone else was asleep." Joe did not know what had happened to Bernice, and he wasn't sure he should ask. But again Medea knew his thoughts.

"Bernice was abducted and nearly killed," Medea told him.

"That's where these pretty scars came from," she motioned to her face, "in case you were wondering, Joe."

Medea smiled down at Bernice and placed a hand on her shoulder. "Her wounds drove her to the edge of the realm of Death, where Hecate noticed her. But she resisted the relief of Death and returned by the power of her own will to help punish those who had harmed her and others. As a result, her initiation later was the easiest I've ever conducted."

"And mine was the hardest, I suppose?" Trudy asked.

Medea laughed. "In this particular group, perhaps."

"I didn't want anything to do with Hecate and all this, Joe," Trudy explained. "Sure, I know now that my soul wanted it, but consciously I resisted like hell and almost stayed dead in Big Mama's Womb too long. Two main problems. The things that happened to me to attract Hecate's attention had left me only interested in solid physical reality. The other problem? I didn't have much religion, but what I had, I discovered, once I died during the initiation, was Christian. Kind of hard to shake childhood conditioning, you know? I guess if what had happened to me hadn't happened to me, it would have been even harder for me to go with Hecate. Ever hear of Pain Eaters?"

Joe glanced at Medea. She raised an eyebrow but said nothing. He replied, "Odor Eaters, yes. Pain Eaters, no."

Trudy laughed and slapped him on the arm. "Ever hear of the Countess Erzebet Bathory?"

"Well, yes, of course, if you mean Elizabeth Bathory, the Blood Countess of Hungary. She tortured and killed young women and bathed in their blood. Right?"

"Yeah. Well, it turned out old Erzebet, that's Elizabeth in Hungarian, and I had something in common. Our soul."

Before his initiation, Joe would have laughed that off. He

didn't laugh now, however. "You mean, you were her in a former life?"

"Of course that's what I mean. Wasn't too pleasant a thing to find out. And it was this thing, this Pain Eater thing, and a sorceress allied with a different Pain Eater that drove Erzebet to do her worst crimes. And then Erzebet's Pain Eater, and the sorceress and her Pain Eater, decided to renew their relationship with the Countess, except she was now me and I didn't know it, not to mention that the sorceress was screwed up and thought *she* was Erzebet. Nod if you understood any of that. I got these decorative scars of mine fighting for my life, and soul, so to speak, and Phil's. Phil's not here yet. Still at work. You can meet him later."

Joe said, "Well, I found out something rather unpleasant about a former life of mine, too." The moment he had said it, he wished he hadn't. Why did he want to tell these people that he had been the one who helped trash Medea's reputation? He didn't. Yet he did. To be open with them.

They were waiting for him to continue.

He cleared his throat. "Well, what it is, you see, is that I was Euripides. Pretty horrible. Right?"

No one spoke for a moment. Then Jim said, "At least you didn't torture and kill hundreds of women and children in the name of the Holy Inquisition. That's what *I* did in a former life."

"And Euripides *was* a pretty decent playwright," Nick added. "His work is still known after all these centuries."

"Because," Joe replied, "the powers that wanted the lies about Medea told saw to it that the lies survived."

Barbara asked, "So, then, Rip, if I may call you Rip, would you mind signing my copy of Euripides' plays sometime?"

"What? I—"

Barbara laughed. "Lighten up, Joe. We all have past lives to be ashamed of."

"Absolutely," Bernice agreed.

"No doubt about it," Nick added.

Trudy said, "Yeah. It's okay to forgive yourself, Joe. Just don't do the bad things you once did ever again. Now, has anybody seen any young women around here I can torture?" She saw the expression on Joe's face. "I'm *kidding*, Joe."

He laughed. "I knew that."

"Say," Nick said, "it's getting a little crowded and hot and loud in here. We were talking about going down to the restaurant and having an early dinner when you and Medea got back. How about it? I'm buying."

"Uh, sure. Sounds great. But . . . I was just wondering, all that business earlier about you and me working on Toxique's book. That was for real, wasn't it? I mean, after all the other things that have happened since then, I was just wondering."

"Of course it was for real. I still want to get with you for lunch tomorrow and hash out the layouts and all. If you're still interested?"

"Oh, yes. I want to do something about Medea's reputation now, try to put things right somehow, you know? But I'm definitely still interested in doing *La Toxique*. Maybe we can work the story around to involve the truth about Medea, about what really happened. Not giving away any Empusa secrets, of course, but some other way. I'm kind of worried, though, that working on a comic about Toxique will . . . prolong the existence of the thought form I have created." He glanced at the ghostly image of Toxique still floating nearby. Could the others see her, too?

"Oh, I don't know," Nick said, looking at Toxique. "She is a really *beautiful* thought form. Are you certain you want her to go away? She looks so much like Medea. Maybe she would like to come home to California with me?"

Medea said, "Enough teasing, Nick. Joe, it will not have its existence prolonged by your doing the comic book, as long as you deny it life-energy. I will show you how. Most Empusae discover they have thought forms with which to deal after their initiations. At the moment, however, I am not growing any less hungry. Initiations nearly always give me an appetite." She took Joe's arm, snuggled against it and said, smiling at him meaningfully, "You, too, Joe?"

He felt her breast against his arm. Desire and pride welled up within him. He relished the knowledge that the others knew he had just recently made love to Medea. And he did not doubt for a moment that some or all of them, remembering their initiations, were envying him the experience.

"Yeah. It made me hungry, too," Joe agreed.

"Okay, then," said Nick. "Let's all head downstairs."

23

Mr. Dacobocon

Lots of people called him Mr. Dacobocon.

Dacobocon, of course, stood for Dallas comic book convention.

His real name was Ray Wilson, and he did not particularly like being called Mr. Dacobocon, but it was better than some of the other things he had been called since he began organizing and promoting Dallas comic book cons.

His conventions had begun as small affairs a few years earlier, and he had built them into major events. His reward was to be called Mr. Dacobocon. That and the money he made. And the satisfaction of knowing he'd made comic book conventions in Dallas a success, financial and otherwise.

When he'd been a kid, he'd loved going to local comic book conventions organized by Albert "Ace" Roberts, a man Ray had come to greatly admire. Ace had long ago dropped out of the con promo biz, but he usually came to Ray's cons. There was a kind of poetry about that, and Ray liked poetry. Loved it, actually. In secret.

He still had hopes of becoming a recognized poet someday. People usually thought he wanted to get into writing or drawing comics himself. He had done both in self-produced fanzines of his own at one time. But what he really wanted was to be a great poet.

He wrote poetry in his spare time. He had stopped showing his efforts to anyone, though. He'd tried that once, and he didn't want to put up with the teasing again. He'd only stopped the teasing by convincing those involved that it had all been a joke. Him? A poet? You've got to be kidding. You really believed it? Ha! Ha!

But it had hurt him to deny his secret ambition. He had not written any poems for nearly a month after that, and now he did so only in secret. Doing it in secret, though, had somehow given his poetry more power it seemed. And he had been creating a particularly fine poem, alone in his hotel room, when the trouble began.

He had escaped to his room for a temporary respite before the evening's activities commenced. That evening the main events with which he needed to be concerned were a charity auction and the Friday night dance.

During a convention, however, there was always somebody wanting him for something, either to make a decision or to okay someone else's decision or to field complaints or to deal with some kind of trouble that had arisen. Not that any really serious trouble had ever happened at one of his conventions. He tried to run a tight ship security-wise. But there was nevertheless always something with which he had to deal. So, to keep his cool, he occasionally had to sneak away to his room and write some poetry.

He knew lots of people thought he snuck away from time to time to make it with con groupies, but it was better that they think him a young, handsome, well-dressed (he'd been called all of the above) stud rather than a poet. Now, what kind of a world was that, anyway? Not the kind he would have chosen, if it had been up to him. But of course it wasn't, and like most people, he had learned to play the cards he had been dealt as best he could.

It looked like it could be really bad trouble this time, though, unless someone found a missing kid.

The call to his room that interrupted his poetry had been from Charlie Luna, a con name for Charles Legrant, a professional bouncer the size and shape of a mid-sized bear whom Ray had met in a bar and hired to be the head of con security.

On the phone, Charlie had said a mother had arrived to pick up her kid, but the kid was not in the lobby where he had promised to meet her.

They'd already paged the boy, of course, and checked all the normal places—the dealers' room, con suite, programming rooms, video rooms—before calling Ray.

Hotel security had gotten into the act, too, but so far there was no sign of the missing kid, and the understandably upset mother was now talking about calling the cops.

So, Ray put his poetry notebook, containing a new, half-finished poem, in the bottom of his suitcase underneath his undershorts, and tidied his appearance in the full-length mirror on the closet door (a couple of years ago he had decided to dress in suits and ties at the con, to set himself apart form his staff and the T-shirt-wearing attendees).

Satisfying himself that he looked fine, he headed downstairs.

On the way down in the elevator, an attractive young woman got on board from the fifth floor. When the elevator doors opened on the lobby, Charlie was standing there, waiting. He ignored all the other people getting off the elevator, focused on Ray and the attractive woman, and gave Ray a wink. "Sorry to interrupt," he grinned.

"What?" Then Ray followed Charlie's gaze to the departing woman and figured it out. "Oh. She wasn't with me."

"Sure, Boss." Charlie gave Ray another wink. "Sure."

"Where's the mother who can't find her child, and what's her name and her kid's name?"

"She said her name was Mrs. Gill. Kid's name is Timmy. The Olsens are with her over there." Charlie pointed to the far side of the hotel lobby. The Olsens were part of Charlie's security team, the best part, in Charlie's opinion, and not just because he would have liked to have gotten them both in bed at the same time.

Both Jeanette and Yvette Olsen were students of various martial arts. Identical twins, they looked innocent and eighteen but were really twenty-seven and ex-Marines. Perfect for con security. Perfect for Charlie's fantasies.

Today, Jeanette was wearing a red jumpsuit, Yvette an identical orange one, according to their name-badges, which may or may not have been accurate. They sometimes switched badges during the day just to keep things interesting. And, of course, their blond hair was fixed in identical styles.

Ray saw that they were hovering over a thirty-something woman in designer exercise sweats sitting in a lobby chair. He also saw a hotel security man in a brass-buttoned blazer talking on a walkie-talkie near the Olsens.

"Okay," Ray said, "let's get it over with," and walked toward the trouble.

The con had been going so smoothly, and that had been worrying him a bit. Trouble-wise, cons seemed to run better if there were a few little problems early on, rather than none. When things went too smoothly at first, it usually meant that bigger trouble was on the horizon.

Ray didn't know why it was that way, but it was. It was almost as if some comic book convention god was controlling things, a Con-God with a twisted sense of humor. Or maybe his comic book convention's god just didn't like Ray's poetry.

They reached the woman.

"Mrs. Gill? I'm Ray Wilson, ma'am."

She looked up at him. His name obviously meant nothing to her.

"I'm in charge of the convention. I understand Timmy is late coming to the lobby for you to pick him up? Well, just let me reassure you that everything is going to be fine. You know how it is, kids get carried away and lose track of time. But we'll find him soon. We haven't lost a kid at one of my conventions yet." He smiled to show her he was joking, using a light touch because he was not worried in the least that anything bad had happened to her son. But he regretted the approach immediately, because rather than smile back, an angry expression settled on the woman's face, and she got to her feet, obviously ready to hold Ray personally responsible for her son's disappearance.

Keeping his smile in place, Ray thought, *Oh, God. Here it comes*.

But instead, the mother's anger suddenly vanished, and she began to cry.

Oh, great, Ray thought. Charlie and the Olsens and the hotel security man nearby all seemed to be waiting for Ray to do something. *Just great.*

"We'll find him, ma'am," he promised her. It sounded lame and it was, but he couldn't think of anything else. "I know we'll find him." Then he turned, took Charlie and the Olsens to one side, and used his angriest whisper to say, "Find the damned kid *now!*"

"We've been trying, Boss. I told you—"

"Then try harder!"

"Okay Boss."

"Do it!"

As Charlie and the Olsens hurried away, Ray returned to the woman. She had sat back down but was still crying.

Wonderful, Ray thought. All he'd wanted was a quiet moment to work on a poem and now this.

But a chill of alarm suddenly changed his attitude. What if for the first time something really bad *had* happened at his convention? Maybe an accident or, God forbid, a kidnapping or something.

The specter of lawsuits and worse loomed in Ray's mind.

So, he sat down beside the woman and tried to comfort her again. But also now himself.

24

Fiend

"That's the guy that runs the convention," Jim Brock told Joe Clark, "over there, the youngish-looking man in the black suit talking to that woman in the sweats. Ray Wilson. Some call him Mr. Dacobocon, but I don't think he likes it much."

Joe knew who Ray Wilson was. Everyone who came to the Dallas comic book con on a regular basis knew Mr. Dacobocon. But he had not noticed him until Jim had mentioned it. He had been too busy noticing the various death disorders clinging to and hovering around people, here and there, in the lobby. One especially ghastly manifestation involved a ghostly, pulsating, serpent-like being wrapped tightly around the torso of one of the hotel employees behind the registration desk.

Joe tried not to show any reaction to the death disorders around him. The other Empusae gave no indication they had noticed them, either, but of course Joe was certain they had. Would Medea classify the serpent-thing a *minor* disorder, too?

He kept glancing back at it as he walked on with the Empusae, until it raised its head, looked back at him, and seemed to smile.

Suddenly Medea stopped and Joe heard her say, "Goddess, what has happened here?"

Had she seen the serpent-thing? Joe looked back at it. But it was now gone.

Medea turned to the others. "Have none of you seen them yet?"

Them? Joe wondered, feeling panic rising. Were there more than one of the serpent-things?

"They have not been here long," Medea continued, "and are not too clear. I count four. One near the woman in the exercise outfit over there. Two near the main entrance, probably brother and sister. And another near the registration desk. Do you see them now?"

"I do," Bernice answered.

"Goddess. Me, too," agreed Barbara.

Trudy added, "Yeah," followed by Nick and Jim also saying they saw what Medea was seeing.

Joe tried, too, looking for more serpent-monsters, but then began to see something else in the locations Medea had indicated.

The hazy shapes slowly came into sharper focus for him, though they still remained but dimly glimpsed, transparent images. But they were not serpent-like.

Joe said, "Do you mean . . . ghosts? I guess? Of children?"

Medea answered, "Yes. They were not here earlier. Something has happened, something horrible. We must question them at once."

Joe suddenly felt like a character in a comic book, some member of a superhero team who had suddenly been called into action, the X-Men or the Avengers or the Justice League of America. And, he then realized, he *liked* the feeling. The excitement. The thrill of being a part of a group that could do what no one else could do, whatever it was that they *were* going to do. About ghosts? Then a less flattering image came to his mind, a scene from one of the *Ghost Busters* movies.

Medea said, "Nick, question the one by the registration desk. Go with him, Joe, and watch. Learn. Trudy, Jim, see what you can learn from the two near the main entrance. Bernice, Barbara, you have the strongest vision here other than mine. See if there are others. I will go unseen to the one near the woman over there. Her thoughts tell me she is the child's mother."

Everyone quickly did as ordered. Joe, walking with Nick, said, "They won't be able to see her, right? Medea, I mean." His Empusa knowledge had gaps in it here and there that had to be bridged deductively or by guesswork. "That's what she meant by going over there unseen?"

"Yes," Nick answered. "Wish I could use that trick at conventions. But it takes a long time to learn."

They arrived at the registration desk. Joe could see the child's ghost more clearly now. A frantic young boy in a bloodstained pair of jeans and a torn, X-Men T-shirt. He was trying desperately to get the attention of a man who was registering at the hotel, but, of course, he was being ignored.

"Stand between the man and the child," Nick said.

Joe, trying to appear casual about it, went to the desk and stood beside the man. The ghost glided away from him. He looked down at it. It realized that it had finally been seen. Relief settled on its tear-streaked face, ghostly tears, glittering and glowing like the dust of miniature stars.

Nick went down onto one knee and quietly said, "We're going to help you, son."

The child turned toward Nick. Joe heard the child say nothing, but Nick did, for Nick then said, "I don't know where your daddy is. Will you come over there with me so we can talk better?" Nick pointed to a row of lobby chairs a short distance away. A moment later, he added, "No, I won't hurt you like the man you went with did. We'll be in plain sight of everybody. Okay?"

The child hesitated a moment, then went with Nick and Joe to the lobby chairs. Glancing around, Joe saw Trudy and Jim talking to the two ghosts by the entrance while also trying to act like they weren't doing anything unusual, to avoid attracting attention.

He saw Barbara and Bernice prowling the lobby, looking for others. But he did not see Medea, although he assumed she was talking to the remaining ghost, because that ghost was no longer looking at the woman sitting with Mr. Dacobocon but instead at something to one side, presumably Medea, unseen except to the child.

"Okay, now," Nick said to his assigned ghost, "can you tell us what happened to you?"

Joe saw the child's mouth moving but only occasionally heard any sound associated with the ghost's speech, and that was only a very faint and thin piping sound. There was, indeed, a lot left for him to learn.

Nick listened until the child was finished, then he said, "And can you describe this man for me? So that I can find him and stop him from hurting other children? Look," Nick took out a pocket notebook and a mechanical pencil. "I'm an artist. I'll try to draw the man if you'll describe him."

"That will not be necessary," said Medea.

Joe involuntarily jumped with surprise. She had suddenly appeared next to him. The ghost with whom she had talked was with her.

Medea's face was twisted with anger and disgust. "We do not need a picture, Nick. I have the psychic scent of the fiend. Gather the others. With your help, I will track and destroy this Evil, at once!"

25

The Batman Syndrome

Joe said to Medea, "If you'd rather I didn't come along, being so new and all, I'll understand." She was organizing the hunt for the killer.

"As I told you with regard to dealing with death disorders, I am the only adept here. Nothing will be required of you that you cannot do. But if you would rather not come along, I will understand. So much has happened to you so quickly today."

"No. I'll come, if I won't be in the way."

Trudy said, "If you get in the way, one of us will shove you aside. Okay?"

"Okay."

"I volunteer to watch over the children until you get back," Bernice said. She looked at the ghosts of the slain children, now clinging to Medea as if for protection. "My wheels would draw extra attention you don't want."

Medea nodded. "Very well. Children, please stay with Bernice." She motioned to Bernice. The wraiths looked at Bernice.

"I know a game we can play," Bernice said to them. "Okay?"

"Go to her, children."

Reluctantly, they drifted away from Medea and toward Bernice, who then looked up at Medea, cold anger in her eyes, and said, "Good hunting."

Medea gripped Bernice's shoulder. She said to them all, "The monster is still in the hotel and not far away. His psychic stench is sickening, now that I have targeted him from the children's memories. When I find him, you will make certain I am not interrupted while I destroy this Evil, yes?

"We know from these little ones that he is armed with a knife. Men like him also usually have a fondness for guns. And although I do not intend to give him the chance to use any weapons he has, a cornered beast is always potentially dangerous. So, when we have located him, you will allow me and me alone to approach him. Understood?"

Trudy said, "If you need help, I'm going to help."

Medea replied, "Trudy, all of you, I want no unnecessary heroics. If possible, we will cause no noticeable disturbance in this crowded hotel. Finesse, not force, is the key here, yes? So, follow me, now, but take care to make our hunt appear no more than a casual stroll."

And so, leaving Bernice to watch over the ghosts of the beast's victims, they strolled, casually, Nick, Jim, Trudy, Barbara, Joe, following Medea as she followed the trail of the killer's psychic scent.

There was small talk. There was even forced laughter. Making things seem normal. But Joe could not join in.

He was tense with anticipation. What was going to happen? What was Medea going to do? His fragmented memories of Hecate's Empusae from other lives suggested she meant to execute the murderer, which would make him and all those with her a party to murder!

Pieces of memories regarding how she might do that were far from comforting. One image that arose was a scene involving Empusae shapeshifting into ravening beasts to attack and destroy their enemies. In other cases, Empusae transformed themselves into vampire-like creatures to find and kill monsters from beyond the grave. Yet other images involved Empusae rescuing victims of the Inquisition, Empusae fighting the Nazi horror of World War II, Empusae struggling against more recent evils. But almost always in secret, except where the events had passed into legends and myths.

Always, though, Joe saw the Empusae slaying and killing agents of Evil, like they were about to do again, he assumed, with him as an accomplice! *As one of them.* But maybe it wasn't too late to avoid that fate. Was he *really* one of them yet? How did *he* feel about killing a killer of children?

Even if he has killed a bunch of kids, Joe thought, *the law should still protect his rights, shouldn't it? Maybe he's sick in the head or something. Hell, of course he's sick in the head! He has to be. But does that really matter to me? Well, does it? Think about him killing children. Think about him killing more kids if he's not stopped. Think about letting the police deal with it instead of a bunch of occult vigilantes! Think of turning around and going home.*

So he did think about it and about his options as he kept strolling casually with the group of Empusae. But he did not have to think about it long.

Great. I guess I'm in it to stay. Damn. I really am one of them. I want the monster's head on a platter, too. Rather badly. And it seems completely natural! But this is not a comic book. This is real life. And—

"We are close," Medea suddenly said. They were in a corridor behind whose doors were various storerooms. No one else was in sight.

"He's in there," she stopped in front of a door. "Goddess! He has another child!"

She tried to open the door. It would not open. Locked. Or blocked.

"I'll break it down," Trudy said.

"No," Medea responded.

"Oh, right," Trudy replied. "Finesse. Sorry."

Medea closed her eyes. She chanted softly in a foreign language. Joe wondered if it was Greek.

She clenched her fists at her sides as her concentration deepened. Then she began *hissing* a new chant, using unknown words that made Joe inwardly grow cold. And afraid. He could only ascribe one term to the way the new chant sounded to him, and that term was *Evil.*

But he did not for a moment think of Medea herself as evil. She might be able to wield dark forces that seemed evil to him, but only to fight a greater Evil. It was, he realized, the Batman syndrome. In Batman's original story, the crimefighter had adopted the costume of a bat to frighten criminals, fighting the fear they inspired with a greater fear, fighting darkness with darkness, battling Evil on its own terms and beating the shit out of it. Like Joe's Toxique.

He glanced around and saw the thought form of his comic book creation hovering not far away. It had followed him like a faithful pet, and it still gave him the creeps, but it now seemed a small matter compared to the other thing that was happening.

Medea's chanting continued. Remembering the flashes of Empusa history circulating in his memories, Joe wondered what the outcome of her chanting would be. Was she about to shapeshift? He imagined a werewolf movie, Medea transforming into a beast with fangs and fur—

Ridiculous, Joe told himself. *Ridiculous!* But now that he had thought the frightening thought, he couldn't shake it, kept watching her in horrified fascination.

Medea stopped chanting. She took a deep breath as if to steady herself, recovering from the strain of her intense concentration.

"Are you all right?" Nick asked her. "If you need energy to replace what you've used, I will—"

"No, Nick. I am fine, for now. The child is all right, too. From the man's thoughts I learned his name. The monster is called T.T. Dysan. I forced him to fall asleep and mentally urged the child to get away."

There was a click as someone unlocked the door from the inside. Then it slowly opened. Joe grew tense, ready to either run or fight, he was not certain which. But neither was necessary.

A young boy hesitantly emerged from the room. He was wearing jeans and a T-shirt with the words *Bite Me Fanboy!* beneath a picture of a character called Lobo.

Medea knelt down. "Are you all right, child?"

"Y . . . yes. There's a . . . bad man in there, with a knife! But he went to sleep. And I snuck away."

"Good for you. Now, listen to me closely. You will not remember that this happened. You will not remember seeing me or any of these others. Do you understand?"

As she spoke, she held the child's gaze. The boy stopped blinking. His eyes became glassy, unfocused. He whispered, "I . . . will not . . . remember . . ."

"Correct. Now, return to the convention. When you arrive in the lobby, you will awaken fully and remember none of this. Go."

The child walked slowly away.

"One of you go with him."

Barbara said, "I'll watch him," and followed the child.

"Accompany me, Joe. The killer is harmless now. The rest of you stand guard here."

"Me?" Joe asked. "You want me to come with you?"

She held open the door for him. The others were watching him. Closely. He saw no way out, and he was not certain he *wanted* a way out. He felt as if about to explode from excitement and anticipation. But of what? The kill? *Damn!*

He took a deep breath. "Okay," he said, and entered the room.

26

Suicide

Joe followed Medea as she advanced through the storeroom that had become the lair of a monster. But she did not walk cautiously. She knew the beast to be asleep and helpless and marched boldly toward his place of hiding.

T.T. Dysan was at the back behind a stack of boxes. He looked anything but dangerous, a thin man with military-short hair, sprawled on his back, wearing gleaming black shoes and a black business suit, white shirt and red tie. A large hunting knife was on the floor near his right hand.

But that was not all Joe saw. With his occult vision he also saw other ghosts hovering near the sleeping monster, the ghost of a woman, her face twisted by fury and hatred, and the ghosts of other children huddled against her.

Knowing Joe's thoughts, Medea said, "From his mind I have learned that he killed those you see hovering there before he came to the hotel. She is the woman who divorced him, and those are his own children!"

To the hovering ghosts she said, "You may soon rest. He will be punished. At once." To Joe she said, "Helpless like this, I could allow the police to deal with him. But the machinery of justice moves slowly, and in the meantime, his victims' ghosts would be unsatisfied, finding no peace. And so, that is why I intend to execute him right now."

"Right . . . now? And . . . there's no doubt that he's guilty, is there? I mean, it's for certain he killed the kids, right?"

"If you could read his thoughts as I can, you would know it as certainly as I know it. So, Joe, will you stay and watch? Or return to the others while I destroy the evil thing T.T. Dysan has become?"

"I don't know. I . . . guess I'll stay. It's crazy, but it seems . . . right, somehow. Now that I'm an Empusa, I mean. You . . . want me to stay, don't you?"

"The decision is yours."

"Yeah. Okay. Damn. I guess I will stay. What do you want me to do?"

"Simply watch and witness the destruction of this beast."

She bent down and pulled a meticulously folded white handkerchief from T.T. Dysan's breast pocket. Using the handkerchief to prevent her finger or palm prints from being transferred to the knife, she picked up the heavy weapon and placed it in Dysan's right hand. Then she placed his left hand over his right, held both his hands around the handle of the knife. She looked up at Joe. "Last chance to back out, Joe."

"Yeah." *I can't believe this is happening!* "Go ahead."

Without further hesitation, Medea drove the blade into the killer's abdomen, angling up beneath the rib cage for his heart.

Dysan grunted in his sleep but did not awaken. His white shirt turned red near the wound, and the wet crimson stain rapidly spread. Dysan stopped breathing and was dead.

Joe swallowed hard. It had happened so quickly! He had stood and watched as a man was killed! But he felt neither panic nor nausea. He felt, he realized, *satisfied*. And that worried him. A little. Until he noticed that the ghost of the mother no longer wore hatred on its face. It was smiling now, at Medea, its mouth moving as it spoke. Joe wished he could have heard what it was saying. Then he noticed the thought form of Toxique nearby, not staring at him for a change but at the speaking ghost.

"Yes," Medea answered the mother's ghost, "I will grant your request. You may have his soul, for a short while, to torment for your own satisfaction in the Gray Between. You have that right. I will drive it from his flesh for you now."

Medea closed her eyes and began chanting again, and the strange-sounding words again left Joe feeling cold inside even as he saw the ghost of T.T. Dysan slowly separate from his corpse. There was confusion on its face, then it looked down at the knife buried in its flesh, and it looked up at the waiting ghosts of the mother and her children, its children, and it screamed.

Joe could not hear the scream, but the expression of fear on its face and its widely gaping mouth told him plainly enough that it was screaming in utter terror. The ghost of the woman, however, was now laughing. As were the children. The sight chilled Joe, but not as much as seeing that, a short distance away, Toxique's thought form was laughing, too.

As the wraiths of the mother and children reached for the killer's soul, Medea changed her chant and a portal of glowing white light appeared hovering in the air. Into the light Medea directed all of the ghosts. And they were gone.

Joe noticed Toxique's thought form was now looking at him again, no longer laughing, but now smiling. He looked away.

Medea banished the portal, and when it had faded away, she opened her eyes. She still held the killer's handkerchief. She offered it to Joe. "A souvenir for you, of your first kill."

He hesitated, then he took it and examined it. It was a plain white handkerchief. Only Medea, among the living, could connect it with T.T. Dysan. He put it in his back pocket. "Shall I say it again, Medea?"

"That you cannot believe this is happening to you?"

"You just killed a man, and I watched."

"It will be deemed a suicide."

"Yeah, but—"

"I know you would not have had him kill more children."

"No, but—"

"But there is still some doubt in your mind, about the police being a better choice. That is normal. It will pass."

"I don't know. Damn."

She stepped closer, took hold of his hands. Warmth poured through him. "It will pass." She kissed him lightly on his lips. "We Empusae usually allow the police to do their job, Joe. We respect the laws of the land whenever possible. But this was an emergency involving children in immediate danger. Had we not acted as we did, that child we saved would also now be dead. And can you say, seeing what you saw of the monster's former wife and children, that justice has not been served here today?"

Joe said nothing.

"You are doing fine, Joe." She squeezed his hands. "I am very proud of you. Now, we must rejoin the others."

She turned and walked away from the corpse of T.T. Dysan. Joe followed. Medea did not look back, but Joe did. Once. And saw that Toxique's thought form was again staring down at the corpse.

When they were in the corridor with the others, Medea said, "If anyone sees us coming out of this hall on our way back to the lobby, help me waylay them so that I can use my mental powers to make them forget having seen us."

Jim said, "No one is going to know we had anything to do with this, Joe. See?"

Joe answered, "Yeah. I wonder if they'll shut down the

convention. Nothing like this has *ever* happened at one before."

"And probably never will again," Jim responded. "It's certainly not the convention's fault. When a monster decides to kill, it can be anywhere, a post office, a restaurant, on a freeway, in the home, *anywhere.*"

Trudy said, "Bernice once told me that when she was kidnapped she was merely walking to a nearby convenience store in a la-de-dah North Dallas neighborhood to get a quick carton of milk. She got the milk, but walking home, the kidnappers changed her life, her plans, her dreams, forever. Like you've heard, Joe, she almost died, and even though she survived, some of her injuries robbed her of the power to walk. And during the ordeal Phil and I survived, several people died who were just in the wrong place at the wrong time. Bad things happen anywhere and anytime these days."

"No," Medea replied. "Not only *these days.* It has always been so. But you must not become so focused on the bad things you fight that you forget the good things that have also always happened anywhere and anytime. Now, back to the lobby. We still have much left to do."

27

The Blushing Empusa

After Barbara made certain the rescued child had returned safely to the convention, she headed back to be with the other Empusae. She met them returning to the lobby.

She fell into step beside Trudy. "That didn't take long. No more monster?"

"Not *that* one, at least," Trudy answered.

"Thank Goddess we got there in time to save one kid. And probably more than just that one."

"Definitely."

They reached the lobby without anyone seeing them emerge from the hallway leading to the room in which T.T. Dysan had died. In the lobby, Bernice waited with the ghosts of the slain children. A friend had stopped to talk with her.

Joe noticed that Bernice's friend showed no awareness of the wraiths hovering near her. He bent down *and through* one to give Bernice a friendly hug before he walked away.

As they followed Medea and the others toward Bernice and her ghostly charges, Joe said to Nick, "I just can't get over how strange this all is. I mean, that guy who was talking to Bernice had no idea there were ghosts there, and it makes me wonder how many times I have stood next to a ghost or walked through one and not known it."

"Lots of times, I imagine," Nick answered. "And the Unseen includes many things you still can't see. Me neither, most of them. Yet. Medea herself, after all this time, says she is still learning, too. Ghosts are the easiest to see, so we beginners can see them pretty much from the first. Medea's had time, though, being physically immortal, to acquire skills that can't be mastered in a single lifetime.

"She told me once, however," Nick continued, "that it is possible to learn how to retain most of our knowledge of this life and others in future incarnations to make faster occult progress in lives to come. Of course I can see how that could make things a lot more difficult, especially when you're a kid. A so-called normal life would be impossible growing up if you remembered your former lives and could do occult things, unless you lived in a country in the East like Tibet where reincarnation was accepted as part of the main religion. But it sometimes happens naturally, even in the West. Child prodigies and like that."

"Yeah. But . . . well, what I keep thinking about is something different. We have to be . . . initiated as Empusa each time we become one, right? In future lives, I mean."

Nick grinned and gave Joe a sidelong glance. "Are you saying you wouldn't mind being initiated by Medea again?"

Joe felt his face redden. "It was . . . wonderful. The first part of it, anyway. And then after a bad stretch in the darkness, at the end, too. She's really just so incredible."

"I understand. Believe me, I do. But, to answer your question, yes, the flesh must undergo initiation each time by Medea or some other elder Empusa. The way I understand it, even if the spirit remembers, initiation is necessary because it changes the flesh of the initiate in subtle and not so subtle ways. You'll find out more about that as you receive training, but your occult vision, being able to see ghosts, is one manifestation of it."

"Makes a kind of sense. I just hope Medea is always the one who initiates me."

"So do I. Can't forget how I felt immediately after *my* initiation. In shock, of course, but hungering for more. She's so damned beautiful and all."

"Yeah."

"So, you're definitely not alone in wishing you could make love to her, all the way, more than just that once in *this* life."

Joe could not stop another blush from reddening his face. His continued embarrassment angered him. The blushing Empusa! He had just watched a killer be executed and had, no matter how he looked at it, no matter how he justified it, become part of a murder. But he couldn't stop blushing when making love to Medea was mentioned. Ridiculous!

"Hey, Joe!"

It was Joe's old friend, Sammy Tenn, walking toward him across the lobby.

Sammy suddenly seemed to Joe like someone from another world, the world he had known before Medea had initiated him.

Sammy made Joe remember how, just a few hours ago, a *different* Joe had been happy looking around the dealers' room and going with Sammy to see a woman costumed as Vampirella.

How irrelevant that seemed now! And Sammy Tenn, too. But he was glad to see that Sammy had no death disorders clinging to him, *or wrapped around him*. Remembering the serpent-thing he'd seen earlier still made Joe uneasy. But the other Empusae had no doubt seen it, too, and had remained unconcerned, so he guessed it was indeed another minor disorder and no cause for worry. Sammy Tenn was another matter.

"I'd better stop and talk to him," Joe said to Nick. "I'll catch up."

"Try to make it quick," Nick replied. "Medea will want you to watch what happens next, with the kids' ghosts and all."

"Right."

Nick walked on. Joe waited for Sammy to reach him. "What's up, Tenn?"

"Not much. Except that Vampirella has changed costumes. It's even better now. Who do you think she is now?"

Joe knew he would have *cared* a few hours ago but not now. He suddenly felt slightly nostalgic for the ignorant bliss he had lost. "Look, Sam, I—"

"She's Red Sonja! The *Frank Thorne* version, skimpy metal bikini and all. And I mean *skimpy!* I've been looking for you. If you miss this, you'll never forgive yourself. Or me. So—"

"Sam, maybe I'll get a look at her later." Joe glanced at the group of Empusae. They had reached Bernice and were all looking at him. *Medea was looking at him.* Waiting on him. "I've got to . . . well, it's like this. I think maybe I've sold my comic about Toxique. And—"

"No shit? Cool! That was Nick Martin you were walking with, wasn't it?"

"Yeah. And—"

"Don't tell me *he's* doing the art?"

"Maybe. Don't tell anyone yet, or you might spoil it. Okay?"

"Okay!"

"And I'll introduce you to Nick later, when we're not doing, you know, business."

"Great! I'll look forward to it. And can you introduce me to that incredible babe standing next to him?"

"Medea?"

"Medea. I think I'm in love. I'd like to . . . work out with her sometime. Great looking legs under those tight jeans. Does she compete? I don't remember ever seeing her at a contest. She would make a great She-Hulk, don't you think? I mean, some green body paint and a skimpy posing bikini and like that? I can't stand it. Just thinking about it makes me horny as hell!"

Sammy the bodybuilder, Joe realized, was talking about Trudy the bodybuilder. Not Medea. He almost laughed. "I thought you meant someone else. The one you mean is named Trudy, and from what I've heard, she's got a guy named Phil, who's supposed to be here later."

"Damn. Just my luck. Where'd she get those cool scars on her face?"

"I'm not sure. I'll introduce you to her, too, later. But right now, Sam, I've really got to go."

"In other words, get lost kid, you're bothering me?"

"It's not like that." Even though it was. "It's just that—"

"Hey, I was kidding. I understand! It's cool. I'll just pant my way back to Red Sonja. You go sell your comic book! Good luck, my man. Okay? I'm damned proud of you. Really."

"Thanks."

Sammy punched Joe lightly on the arm and headed back to the dealers' room.

As Joe watched him go, he felt part of the old Joe going with him. Older than he'd imagined. Lifetimes.

Damn.

Then he hurried to join his new friends.

28

Angel

When Joe had rejoined the group, Medea guided the Empusae and the ghosts of the slain children to a relatively secluded corner of the lobby, made somewhat private by a long row of potted greenery.

To Joe and the others she then said, "Alert me if anyone comes near enough to hear what I now say and do."

She knelt on the floor and said to the ghosts, "Come closer, please, children."

They came nearer. Speaking softly, she said, "Do all of you now understand what has happened to you? That the bad man who hurt you has made it impossible for you to stay here much longer?"

She looked from one to the other. Holding hands, tears glistening, the boy and girl who were brother and sister slowly nodded that they understood.

"And you?" she asked the boy who had hovered near the registration desk.

Joe saw the boy make some reply. He wished again he could hear both sides of the conversation.

Medea responded, "No, Glen, I cannot return you to your father. Would that I could, but I cannot." Then she looked at the fourth ghost. "And do you understand what has happened, Timmy?" He was the one she had found hovering near his mother and Mr. Dacobocon. "Do you remember what I told you when I talked with you before?"

Timmy wiped at tears and replied to her question.

"No. It is impossible. As I told you earlier, you cannot go home with your mother. I am truly sorry. But remember, I told you about the one I will soon call to come for you? She will keep you safe on the journey to your new life, Timmy." She looked at the other children, "She will keep all of you safe."

From the twins, the girl spoke.

"Yes, Rachel, a beautiful winged Angel, if you wish to think of Her that way, to watch over and protect you and your brother, Richard." Medea looked at Timmy again. "Or for you, Timmy, the Holy Virgin from your religion."

Timmy began to cry.

Joe saw an expression of anguish touch Medea's face. She quickly hid the emotion and said, "Timmy. You have been so brave. Can you be brave just a little longer? Please?"

Timmy did not stop crying entirely, but he wiped at his tears and looked at Medea and said something and nodded.

"Thank you, Timmy. I am very proud of you." She looked at the others. "I am very proud of all of you. But now it is time for you to go. You will see some pretty lights and hear a sound like the tinkling of little bells, then She will appear to take you safely to your new lives beyond Earth."

Joe saw Timmy again begin to cry, and Rachel and Richard were on the verge of tears. Glen, too, seemed about to break down.

Joe tried to imagine what they must be feeling. They were about to leave and never again see their homes, families, pets, toys, all they had known. Never again to be the people they had been for a few short years. And, as he carried the thought farther, when they again touched the memories of their former lives and regained the knowledge of their hopes for the too short life just past, there would also be the anguish and anger of knowing those hopes had been destroyed merely because of the sickness of an evil stranger.

Medea closed her eyes and began to whisper a chant. Within moments Joe saw tiny points of white light appear above Medea's head. The lights swirled, condensed, expanded into an oval of light that reached from the high lobby ceiling to the floor, at the bottom enfolding Medea in its pale white luminescence. It was different from the portal she had opened in the storeroom when she sent away the ghosts of Dysan and his slain family. Joe's fragmented memories suggested the difference had to do with bringing the Guardian of the Gray Between through for the children to see.

Joe watched the light expectantly. But when the children reacted as if they saw something within the light, Joe still saw nothing but the light itself. Then, one by one, wonder on their faces, the ghosts of the children, first Timmy, then Rachel and Richard, and finally Glen, reached out as if to embrace someone, slowly floated into the light, and were gone.

29

Freaks and Mundanes

Within moments after the ghosts of the children had vanished into the oval of light, the light itself faded and vanished.

Medea opened her eyes and rose to her feet.

Joe realized he had been holding his breath. He slowly exhaled. The oval of light had not caused a disturbance in the lobby, so he assumed no one had seen it except the Empusae. And the ghosts. But why had he seen nothing within the light? He had not expected to hear the tinkling bell sounds Medea had told the children they would hear, but was it also his inexperience that had prevented him from seeing anything within the light?

Knowing his thoughts, Medea said, "So many questions, Joe, but deserving of answers. Quickly then, for there is still more I must do.

"Only when it is your own time of passing can you see the One within the Light. And I did not call Her to take the souls of the killer and his family because, if you will recall, I granted the slain mother's request for a period of personal revenge in the Gray Between. The Guide to their new lives came for them there."

"Oh. Okay. Thanks."

She looked away from him to the others. "I must leave

you for a short while. Our part in this matter will not have been completed until I make certain the killer and his victims will be found."

Joe assumed she had learned where the victims were hidden either from the ghosts of the children themselves, or from the mind of the killer. But he wondered how she was going to let others know the locations without giving herself away. An anonymous tip on the phone? Or . . . telepathy?

Medea turned back to him and answered his thoughts. "Very good, Joe. Yes. Telepathy, so that those who find the bodies will not know they had help. See?"

"Sure."

To all of them she said, "We were on our way to the restaurant before this emergency began. I will soon join you there. But as always, do not wait for me to arrive before ordering. Yes?" Then she turned and walked away and became unseen. One moment Joe saw her, and the next he didn't.

Bernice said, "I'm not sure how hungry I am now."

Trudy said, "Hungry or not, I bet you guys could all sure as hell use a drink, while I suck on a Dr Pepper. Am I right? How about it, Joe? A beer sound good?"

He answered, "I am thinking that I would not turn down a beer."

"You doing okay, Joe?" Bernice asked. She took his hand and gave it a squeeze.

"Yeah. I guess so. You? Or are you used to it, things like this I mean."

She held on to his hand a moment longer and gave it another quick squeeze before releasing it. "I don't think I'll ever get used to it. Those poor kids."

"And their poor parents," Barbara said.

Trudy said, "I feel for the guy in charge of the con, too. He's not going to have a very pleasant evening. There'll be police and newspeople crawling all over the place in a little while."

"If they don't close the whole con," Joe said, "I bet they at least cancel the Friday night dance. I mean, how would it look, dancing after what's happened?"

"Yeah," Trudy agreed. "That's for sure. What else was supposed to happen tonight? The charity auction?"

Bernice consulted her pocket schedule. "Right. And of course horror movies and Japanimation in the video rooms. And gaming continuing in the gaming room."

"They might go ahead and have the auction at least," Barbara said.

"And, if they go on with the con tomorrow," Jim said, "it wouldn't surprise me if attendance was way up. After this hits the news tonight, lots of people will hear about it and come down just to see the place where the murders happened."

Nick said, "Ghoulish, but you're probably right, like gore-hungry rubberneckers passing a freeway accident."

Trudy said, "Freeway rubberneckers make me so mad. They slow up and cause jams even when the wreck is on the other side of the divider. Why can't they just mind their own damned business?"

"Because they're bored sick with their lives," Bernice responded, "probably. Same thing that makes them stare at me with some kind of sick fascination because I'm in a wheelchair and have scars."

"Yeah," Trudy agreed. "I get that with my scars, too, but also because I'm taller than average for a woman these days and have larger muscles."

Jim said, "Hell, they stare at me, too, here in parts of Dallas at least, a middle-aged man with his hair in a pony tail and a funny looking medallion hanging around his neck. I guess they think I've got to be either an aging hippie, a Satanist, a drug fiend, or all of the above."

"Hey, we're *all* freaks at a convention," Nick added. "That's why they have these damned things, for all of us freaks to get together and find temporary normality in numbers, right?"

"Right," Joe agreed. "I mean, when you get on an elevator with non-convention people who just happen to be staying in the hotel, it's nice to feel like those mundanes are the freaks for a change, because for a little while at least we have them outnumbered."

"But then," Bernice said, "you have *us*. We would be freaks even to other freaks, if they knew what we truly were."

Nick said, "Which is why we keep a low profile, Joe."

"Yeah," Joe replied. "Every superhero has to have a secret identity, right?"

"Right," Nick agreed. "And with your last name, you should change your first one to Kent, don't you think?"

Joe started to laugh, then remembered all that had happened and stopped himself. "I don't feel very *super* right now, though."

Bernice said again, "Those poor kids." Her eyes glistened with new tears. "Thank Goddess Medea was here."

"And us," Trudy added. "Even if Medea hadn't been here, one or more of us would have picked up on the kids' ghosts and tried to do something about it. Maybe we couldn't have sent them into the Gray Between without Medea's or some other elder's help, and maybe our tracking down and dealing with the killer would have been a bit trickier, but we would have done *something*. Alerted the police at the least."

Bernice said, "But we might not have been in time to save that fifth kid, or others the monster might have killed before we or the police stopped him. So I'll say it again. Thank Goddess Medea was here!"

30

The Psychic Residue of Horror

Medea walked unseen to a man near the hotel registration desk with "Security" on a badge pinned to the breast pocket of his hotel blazer. She sent her thoughts into his mind, made him feel an urgent need to search the storerooms. Then she also placed other images in his mind that would eventually guide him to the bodies of the slain children. That done, she walked across the lobby to Timmy's mother, still sitting beside an increasingly uncomfortable and worried Mr. Dacobocon.

Medea stood near them unseen for a moment, listening to their speech and their thoughts. She was surprised to learn that the convention organizer was secretly a poet. Poets, even bad ones, were worth trying to save. So, she reached a bit deeper into his mind and found his frustrated dissatisfaction with his life.

She had expected it to be buried deeply in his subconscious, but it was near the surface of his thoughts. She coaxed it all the way to the surface, knowing it would now soon disrupt his life and probably his business, no doubt forcing him to make major changes. But that was preferable to letting his frustrations fester until they eventually erupted into the physical manifestation of a life-threatening disease that might well destroy his current flesh before he could accomplish the work his poet's soul desired.

She then turned her attention to Timmy's mother.

She reached out with her thoughts and placed in the mother's mind a strong image of Timmy, smiling and happy, as indeed Medea knew him to be, though no longer in the flesh. Then she telepathically suggested that the mother look at her wristwatch and remember the time. After Timmy was found and the time of his death established, Medea hoped remembering the happy image that had come after Timmy's death would bring the woman some slight comfort. Then she also gently sent to the mother another thought that became a feeling, a certainty.

"Oh my God," the mother suddenly said. "He's dead. Timmy's dead."

"I'm certain he's not," Mr. Dacobocon quickly said.

"My son is dead! I know it. I *feel* it!"

"Mrs. Gill, please—"

Timmy's mother burst into tears. "I just saw him smiling and waving to me from Heaven. The Holy Virgin was with him. He's dead!"

"Mrs. Gill, please!" Ray Wilson, alias Mr. Dacobocon, frustrated poet in hiding, looked helplessly around for help.

Medea walked quickly away. The mother's anguish reminded her too strongly of the pain she had felt when her own children were killed, pain many centuries old yet sharp as a fresh wound.

Allowing herself to be seen again, Medea started not toward the restaurant but the elevators. She had thought of another matter with which she wanted to deal.

She went to her room.

She removed her clothing.

She knelt again in front of the window and drew strength

from the light of the Sun and the New Moon following near it in the sky.

With the afternoon growing late, the light was weaker. It therefore took slightly longer for the restorative power of the sunlight to take effect.

When she felt her aura and spirit had been sufficiently strengthened and cleansed, Medea meditated her body into a shallow trance, then projected her mind beyond the hotel and followed the memories she had found in T.T. Dysan's mind to the house where he had killed his ex-wife and children.

Within the house, the blood and bodies and psychic residue of horror sickened her, reminding her all too strongly of that most horrible of nights when she had discovered her own children slain.

Before her ancient but undying memories could overwhelm and distract her, she quickly pulled her consciousness back from the house of death. She knew now what she had gone there to find out, that the murders had not yet been discovered.

She sought out the mind of a neighbor and placed a worry in the woman's mind and telepathically urged her to check on the slain family.

Now certain the murders would soon be discovered, Medea guided her consciousness back to the hotel and back into her entranced flesh.

Returning to normal consciousness, she breathed deeply nine times, drawing new strength from the lowering Sun, then she rose and began to clothe herself once more.

Suddenly a wave of disorienting weakness pounded through her.

She swayed on her feet, feared she was going to fall, managed to reach the bed and sit on the edge of the mattress.

Gasping for breath, she waited for the weakness to pass.

She recognized the feeling, but it was too soon and the wrong phase of the Moon.

Removing herself from the healing cycle of forgetfulness and rebirth was not the only price she had paid for immortality. To remain immortal, at the end of each third cycle of thirteen years, during the last three hours of the Dark Moon, it was necessary to undergo a ritual of excruciating agony that, if survived, climaxed in the ecstasy of rejuvenation. But in the nine days leading up to the ritual, periods of debilitating weakness rendered her all but helpless.

There were years to go, however, before the next ritual of rejuvenation was due. It was not even the time of the Dark Moon. A New Moon had come but two days before.

So, the feeling of weakness she had just experienced must have a different source. Perhaps a psychic attack of some kind? She immediately erected occult barriers to protect her consciousness, just in case.

A violent disturbance within the energy webs of occult power that encircled and penetrated the Earth could also cause the weakening she had felt. She had not had to deal with such as that, however, since the years of horror known to history as World War II.

That war had, though few knew it, started as but a new skirmish in an ancient occult war, then spread to physical realms and erupted in the tragedy that had disrupted and ruined and ended so many human lives.

Many Empusae had been destroyed in the struggle, too, and many souls annihilated.

Medea had but narrowly escaped becoming a casualty in both body and soul herself. It had taken her years to recover. She still suffered occasional nightmares about the horror of her stay in a Nazi concentration camp, weakened and unable to use her occult powers. But that dream did not come as often as the central nightmare of her existence, the memory of her children's deaths.

She had punished their murderer. Oh, yes. The oathbreaker, their father, Jason, had been well punished. But in the end, his soul had escaped the annihilation she had planned.

The knowledge that his soul still existed still angered her.

The need to find him again still drove her.

Each time she tracked and executed a killer of children, she hoped to find Jason's soul within the killer's flesh.

Compared with Jason, T.T. Dysan had been no monster at all. Dysan had killed because he was mentally unbalanced. But Jason had killed his own children with the coldness of true Evil. Then his allies had framed Medea for the crime.

In those days, she had not possessed the occult powers she later, through hard work and study, acquired, so to save herself she had fled to another land.

Years later, she sat in secret, watching a performance of *Medea*, Euripides' play of lies, in an outdoor theater beneath the stars of ancient Greece. She was at first enraged, then racked by a sadness so deep it left her emotionally shattered. The vast Evil that had been done and that would now be perpetrated throughout history weighed down her soul as never before.

She did not try to stop the performance of Euripides' play. She did not punish Euripides for writing it. She did not do anything else in the world known to historians for a very long time.

She wandered alone in self-imposed exile for many years until finally she returned to her native land, to the island of Colchis in what later became known as the Black Sea.

She had decided upon a course of action.

She had decided to forfeit her right of rebirth.

She had decided to become an immortal.

Immortal, she would wait and watch and search for the return to flesh of Jason's soul.

Immortal, she would eventually find him again and finish what she had begun.

And any like him she encountered along the way she had vowed to also destroy.

Indeed, before giving the soul of T.T. Dysan to his victims for their personal revenge, she had marked it in a special way, because the Guide who protected souls on their journey to new lives had a dark side as well.

Souls Medea marked for destruction were not taken to new lives beyond the realm of the physical. The Guide took them instead to a place some religions called Hell and there cast them into soul-devouring energy streams to be destroyed.

Another wave of weakness poured through her.

She lay back on the bed and breathed deeply, striving to regain control of her strength. She sought to strengthen the occult barriers she had erected.

When the weakness again had passed, she quickly sought help from her Goddess.

She closed her eyes, journeyed in her mind into Hecate's presence.

With an image of the ancient Temple of Hecate surrounding her and the towering Triple Goddess looming above her, Medea repeated three times an ancient prayer of praise. Then she requested guidance. What had caused the weakness she had felt? What was its source? What danger threatened?

But before an answer came, weakness gripped her again, filled her with feelings of exhaustion, clouded her thoughts, drove her toward a dark abyss of sleep.

She fought to stay awake, but she had not the strength to succeed. And so she slept. And dreamed. Of her children, slain, but this time not by Jason. Rather by a woman who looked like Medea herself. No. By a woman who *was* her! A monster who destroyed not just flesh but also souls.

Medea looked down at herself, saw that her flesh was stained crimson with blood. *The blood of her own children.*

In a cold sweat, she awoke with a cry.

Dizzy, nauseous, head pounding with pain, she staggered to the bathroom and was sick.

It was not the first time she had dreamed she had killed her children herself.

She knew it was not true. But sometimes she dreamed it was. Even now, all these centuries later. Because down deep she felt responsible for not seeing the warning signs sooner, for not stopping Jason in time.

When the nausea passed and her headache raged less hideously, she turned on the shower and stepped beneath the stinging hot stream. Then, the image of her crimsoned skin still lingering from her dream, she began trying to scrub herself clean.

But what had caused the weakness that had driven her into her nightmare?

There had to be an answer, something she was not seeing. Something she was not remembering. She had been going to seek guidance from Hecate. Why had she forgotten that? She must try again. But something—

The weakness hit again, worse than before, drove her to her knees.

"Goddess . . . help . . . me . . ." she gasped, then helpless beneath the steaming water she felt her consciousness being driven into a black pit of horror.

31

In the Restaurant

Even though he had heard Medea tell them not to wait for her before ordering their meals, Joe thought it wrong.

"Are you sure we shouldn't wait for her?" he asked. "I mean, it doesn't seem right."

Trudy responded, "One time we waited and she never showed."

"Something else came up for her to deal with and she never made it," Nick explained. "So, now she always tells us not to wait on her."

Joe said, "It still doesn't seem right to me, but okay. I'm the new kid here."

When the waiter came, Joe noticed the ghost of a large parrot sitting on the man's shoulder.

They ordered Medea a glass of white wine, as she had requested. Then they ordered drinks for themselves and later their meals.

Those meals had since been prepared, served, and were now half-eaten, but Medea had still not joined them.

"See, Joe?" Jim said. He sipped his beer. "If we had waited for Medea, we'd still be waiting."

"I didn't know I was hungry until I started eating," Bernice said.

Joe had a swallow of beer. "Wonder what she's doing? How long does it take to use telepathy on hotel security and all?"

"Not long," Bernice replied, "for Medea."

"It'd take forever for me," Jim said, "because I still haven't managed to learn even the beginnings of it. Unlike Bernice, here."

"I'm not that good at it. I can't control it well yet. Just flashes now and then."

"But you're still farther along than the rest of us, especially me."

Trudy said, "Barbara and I have had flashes, too, although fewer than Bernice. But the men?" She shrugged. "I hope you won't have as much trouble with it, Joe, as your male colleagues here. The poor boys."

Jim laughed. "Trudy's a sexist, Joe."

Trudy grinned.

Jim added, "Guess I should be glad you aren't toting whips around any more."

"Whips?" Joe asked.

"Yeah," Nick said. "Whips?"

Jim motioned to Trudy. "Want to tell them about it, Trudy?"

Trudy hesitated, then said, "Not really." The playfulness had suddenly vanished from her voice. "I'm not all that proud of it, Jim, as I thought you knew. But I'm not ashamed of it, either. So, why don't *you* tell them, since you seem to want them to know. It's *your* kind of fantasy, too, after all."

"Trudy, I'm sorry. I shouldn't have mentioned it. I just thought, or rather, I *didn't* think, and—"

"Forget it."

"No. It was stupid and rude and thoughtless of me. I am truly sorry."

"Okay." She looked at Joe and Nick and said, "But the

other boys here are all curious now. Can't leave them hanging, I guess."

"Sure you can," Joe responded. "I don't want to pry or anything."

"I agree," Nick said.

Trudy said, "Good. But, since you feel that way, I'll tell you. Everyone is over twenty-one here, and anyway, I suppose there shouldn't be any secrets among this group. So, it's like this." She took a sip of her Dr Pepper, looked first at Nick, then at Joe. "Phil and I used to do a kind of live sex act."

"Really?" Joe responded.

"Really. At the Safe Sex Club here in town."

Joe said, "I'm impressed."

"You are?"

"Sure. I heard a lot about that place from an older brother of a friend in high school. But I wasn't old enough to get in before it closed."

"You didn't miss much. I sure as hell don't miss it. I played a character called Raw Pain Max in our act, and Phil—"

"*You* were Raw Pain Max?" Joe interrupted. "I heard a lot about your act, too! My friend's older brother told us about this Amazon and her whips and this little guy she would torment on stage."

"Phil's the little guy," Jim said, "but don't call him that to his face. I saw their act once or twice before I met them. It was one of the best acts of its kind I've ever seen."

"And Jim's seen more than his share of that sort of thing, right Jim?" Trudy asked.

Jim raised his glass to her. "After seeing your act, I forgot all the others."

"Sure."

Joe said, "I just can't believe I'm talking to Raw Pain Max!"

Trudy shrugged. "Well, you are. Nice of you to be impressed. I guess I should be kind of flattered."

"Oh, yeah. I'm definitely absolutely impressed!"

"But don't tell everyone you know, okay?"

"Oh. Okay. I won't tell anyone. But I sure would love to tell Tenn."

"Ten?"

"Sammy Tenn. Friend of mine. It was his older brother who used to tell us about you. He's here at the con, Sammy I mean, and he saw you earlier and asked me if I'd introduce him to you, but if he'd known you were Raw Pain Max he'd have really flipped! He's a bodybuilder and was admiring your muscles. Said he thought you were in competition form."

"Now I'm *really* flattered. Guess he didn't get close enough to see my scars."

"He noticed them, and he seemed to like them, too."

"Good looking guy, is he?"

"You interested? I thought that Phil and you—"

"Phil and me." Trudy smiled. "Right. No, I'm not interested in your friend. Just flattered is all."

"Hey, Trudy," Barbara said, "we can distract Phil tonight if you want to check this guy out."

"Sure," Bernice said. "No problem."

Trudy laughed. "Stop it. You know Phil and I are like that." She held up a closed fist. "Or like this." She made a second fist and hit it against the first one. "Sometimes."

"There's the police," Nick said. "Listen. Medea's guided someone to the storeroom, I guess."

They listened. Sirens were coming closer.

The main entrance to the hotel was visible through a window from where they were sitting in the restaurant. A

few moments later, several police cars braked to a halt near
the entrance. An ambulance was close behind.

"Well, it's going to hit the fan in the hotel now," Jim said.
"News people will be crawling all over the place soon, too.
And here we sit, as innocent as can be."

"Yeah," Joe said. "It makes me kind of fluttery inside,
though, you know?"

"We won't be connected to it in any way," Barbara assured him.

"I know. But—"

Suddenly into Joe's mind flashed an image of Medea, but
not just Medea. Someone else was in the image, too, another
woman, attacking the Priestess. It took him another moment
to realize why the other woman seemed so familiar. It was
Toxique.

"Joe?" Nick asked. "What's wrong?"

"Yeah," Trudy said. "You that worried about the cops?
You look kind of pale. Need another beer?"

Joe knew with a certainty he could not explain that Medea
needed help. Badly.

"Medea's in danger!"

"What?" Nick asked.

Joe stood up. "Hurry. We've got to help her! Now!"

"Joe, what are you—"

"Goddess!" Bernice said. "I think he's right. I just got a
flash of something, too! In her room!"

Nick jerked out his wallet and threw money onto the table.
"Come on," he said and headed for the door at a run.

32

Rubberneckers

"Slow down," Nick warned, slowing suddenly from a run to a fast walk when they were outside the hotel restaurant. The restaurant's entrance opened onto the lobby. "We can't run across the lobby to the elevators with the police having just arrived."

Joe said, "But we've got to hurry!"

Bernice said, "If the police think we are hurrying too fast and stop us to ask questions, it will take even longer to reach Medea."

"But—"

Nick said, "Get a grip, Joe. We can't let the police delay us."

Joe said nothing. He could hear the frustration in Nick's voice, And he hadn't thought, until that moment, how remarkable it was that the Empusae had not questioned his warning. *Normal* people would have tried to discount it as a joke or imagination. Normal . . . like *he* used to be, a few hours ago.

Nick asked, "Can you tell how's she's doing? Joe? Bernice?"

Joe answered, "I don't know. I just saw one image. A flash of her being attacked. But the *feeling* of urgency is still there. Damn this walking!"

Bernice said, "I saw the same thing."

"You did?" The confirmation made Joe's sense of urgency grow even stronger. "And did you see *who* was attacking her."

"A woman. I don't know who."

"I do," Joe said, then hesitated. "Uh, I mean, I saw her face, but it couldn't be who I thought, because it looked like Medea was fighting herself, and that made me think it was Toxique, my comic book character that Nick drew to look like Medea. But Toxique isn't real, except for that thought form thing, which can't be a threat to Medea. Can it?"

"I don't see it around now," Bernice noticed, "the thought form. Anyone seen it recently?"

No one had.

"When was the last time you saw it, Joe?" Nick asked.

"But it couldn't be my thought form!"

"When?"

"Well . . . I guess it was in the storeroom, after Medea executed that killer."

"Don't say that too loudly," Barbara warned.

"Laugh," Trudy said, "or at least smile a little. There's a cop looking at us. We'd better start acting like convention party-people having fun."

Nick and Trudy faked subdued laughter as they slowed their pace a bit more.

"We ought to stare at the police some, too," Barbara suggested. "Everyone else is."

"You're right," Jim agreed. "Make it look like we just noticed them, though. And stop walking for a moment, to stare at them."

"Stop walking?" Joe responded. "Goddess!"

Joe stopped with the rest and looked at the police clustered near the registration desk. Each of them had a death disorder of some kind clinging to or hovering near them. Joe wondered if it was because of all the violent deaths with which they had to deal.

Hotel security people were there with the police, too, of course, and Mr. Dacobocon stood nearby with Timmy's weeping mother, to whom a policewoman with a small notebook was talking. The ghost of an infant hovered in the air near the policewoman's chest.

"Okay," Nick said. "That's enough."

They moved on.

"But keep looking back now and then like good rubberneckers should," Jim added.

"Goddess, if only we had some serious occult powers!" Bernice said. "We could try chanting a spell of protection for Medea, or maybe try to send her some extra psychic energy in case she needs it for the fight."

An elevator opened its doors ahead of them.

"We're close enough now to run to catch it," Nick decided.

They reached the elevator as it was disgorging the last of its load. Other people waiting saw Bernice's wheelchair and stepped back to let her on. The other Empusae crowded behind her then were pressed to the back by the other passengers, several of whom were accompanied by death disorders and all of whom, it turned out, wanted off on floors lower than Medea's.

When the elevator doors finally opened on twenty-seven, Nick and Joe ran to Medea's room, the others close behind.

Nick used his key, and then they were inside.

"Medea!" Joe and Nick called out together. She was nowhere in sight. Water was running in the bathroom.

"In here!" Trudy shouted.

Barbara started into the bathroom but then backed out to let Trudy through.

Trudy carried Medea in her arms. Water dripped from

Medea's body and streamed from her hair. Though unconscious, Medea was frowning, her expression one of pain. Trudy gently placed the Priestess on the bed.

"Medea?" Trudy called, bending close, stroking wet hair back from Medea's face. "Priestess?"

There was no response.

Trudy said, "Thank Goddess she was taking a shower instead of a bath. She might have drowned."

"Can she?" Joe asked. "Drown, I mean, being immortal and all?"

Nick answered, "Immortal does not mean invulnerable."

Barbara said, "She doesn't have any visible wounds."

Jim said, "It's got to be an occult attack of some kind."

"At least we all know how to transfer extra energy to her," Nick said. "Let's do it!"

He placed his hands over Medea's solar plexus, the left one against her bare flesh, and closed his eyes in concentration. Jim took her left hand and closed his eyes, frowning as he concentrated. Trudy placed her hands on Medea's forehead and closed her eyes, while Bernice took Medea's other hand and Barbara placed her hands on Medea's chest between her breasts.

Joe felt helpless. While the others were no doubt doing all they could to help Medea, *he* needed to do something, too. Did some awakened piece of knowledge exist in him that would tell him how to transfer energy, too? He began to frantically search the memories awakened by his initiation. But suddenly, Medea opened her eyes.

"Medea!" Trudy cried. "She's back!"

They took their hands away, except for Bernice and Jim, who continued to hold Medea's hands.

"I will be all right . . . now," Medea whispered. "Thank you all for . . . your help . . ." Then her face was twisted by pain.

33
Rogue

The grimace of pain left Medea's face. "I will be all right now. These reverberations will soon pass." She grimaced again, freed her hands from Jim's and Bernice's, reached up and rubbed her temples. "There remains the residual throbbing of a headache, but it is going away. Some water, please? My throat is dry."

"I'll get it," Barbara said.

"She brought her own," Nick said. "There's a sixpack of bottled water in that bag." He pointed.

Medea said, "I was caught by surprise . . . like a novice. Very embarrassing. And . . . dangerous."

"There's no ice," Barbara reported. She stood holding a bottle of water in one hand, the empty ice bucket in the other. "I'll run down the hall and get some ice from the machine."

Medea said, "No. Please, just the water."

She sat up in bed and took the bottle from Barbara. "Thank you." She touched her wet hair. "The bedclothes are soaked and I am cold. Would someone bring me several towels?"

"On my way." Jim hurried to the bathroom.

Medea twisted the top off the bottle and sipped some

water. She looked at Joe. "You felt my need first. In the midst of the battle, I saw your face, then yours Bernice."

"Yes," Bernice said, "but Joe thought he saw your attacker's face. I didn't."

"I thought it was Toxique attacking you."

"And you were more or less correct," Medea replied.

"No." He felt the sudden panic of responsibility. "It *couldn't* have been."

"That was, of course, why you felt my need first. But you must not feel it was your fault."

Jim brought several white hotel towels. Medea placed a dry towel beneath her and began using another to dry herself as Joe said, "Not my fault? But I created her! *It.*"

"You did not *send* the thought form to attack me. I should have foreseen the danger, but it has been a very long time since I encountered anything similar. You are, it would seem, gifted in a special way."

"Because my creation attacked you?"

Medea glanced at the worried faces of the others. "You may all stop frowning with concern. I dealt with the problem, drove the thought form into the Gray Between and dissipated it there. So, it is now a non-problem, yes?"

"I wouldn't know," Joe replied.

"I will try to explain in terms familiar to you." She arranged her damp hair atop her head and wrapped a towel around it, turban-style. "I would use an analogy from mathematics, since that is your field of study, but I wish the others to understand too. So I will use . . . something from a comic book. Let me think . . ."

Joe realized he was staring at Medea's bare breasts. He quickly looked away. Why didn't she cover herself? With everyone standing around clothed, she seemed doubly naked. And the situation was too serious for him to be ogling her body! But a moment later he found he was again looking at her.

Stop it! he told himself. Everyone in the room had been initiated, so they had all seen her naked before, and if she didn't care if she sat unclothed among them, it was none of his damned business.

She looked at Joe, then wrapped a towel around herself under her arms and tucked in a corner to hold it in place. She smiled slightly and raised an eyebrow as if to ask him if that were better.

His face reddened.

Medea said, "Nick, what is the name of that comic book character you were drawing that time, the one with the white stripe in her hair? A mutated X-Woman, I think you called her?"

"Rogue," Nick answered, "from Marvel's *X-Men*. She's a mutant who can absorb other people's powers."

"Then it is indeed Rogue of whom I am thinking," Medea answered. "Are you familiar with that character, Joe?"

"Sure."

"Good. In a way, then, you could say I was attacked by a Rogue-like entity, except that it was your thought form, Joe, your Toxique."

"But that wasn't the way I created her. I didn't copy Rogue."

"No. But all thought forms possess energy-absorbing powers similar to the powers of the Rogue character. I thought if you had her to think about, you could understand more easily."

"Okay."

"Thought forms are energy parasites, see? Life-force vampires of a sort, or perhaps "symbiots" is a better term. Their existence is normally sustained by the energy of the one who creates them, and they in turn often provide comforting company, even pleasure, to their host."

Pleasure? Joe thought. His sexual fantasies involving Toxique came to mind.

"But," Medea continued, "after your initiation, Toxique's thought form began drawing upon your awakened occult energy to become an independent entity. It attacked me to acquire even greater energy. It wanted my memories and powers, and my flesh."

Joe shook his head. "You told me not to worry about the thought form! You said it would fade away when you taught me how to deny it life-energy."

"And that would normally have been true. But Toxique was not a normal thought form, something I should have noticed but did not. I should have noticed her eyes were . . . too alive, like the eyes of a dangerous thought form I encountered several centuries ago."

"Several centuries," Joe said. "I keep forgetting."

"Forgetting?"

"How old you . . . I mean, how long you have been alive. In that body. You look so young."

Medea shrugged. "You are leading my explanation astray."

"Sorry."

"The thought form of which I was speaking was created by a woman with a special gift that I must assume you also possess. By using a form of sex magic, she could create thought forms with unusually independent wills to survive."

Joe noticed the others were looking at him. "I didn't use any sex magic!" he protested. *Unless,* he thought, *my sexual fantasies count.* Several memories of those fantasies flashed through his mind.

Medea smiled, reading his thoughts.

"Uh, look, I didn't know that just, well, *thinking* about

something like that and . . . *imagining* loving a fantasy lover could create . . . oh, damnit. I—"

"Enough. No one here blames you. We rejoice in your special power. So does the Goddess, or She would not have seen fit to accept you during your initiation. When you have been taught to control the power, it will be of great benefit to many."

"But what if I think something up like that again before I know how to control it? Not awake, I mean, but maybe asleep? In a dream? And it attacks you again? Or someone else?"

"Will you sleep with me here, tonight?"

The question caught him off guard. He glanced at Nick, then at the others. No one seemed surprised by the question except him. "I guess I could. I mean, sure. Okay." But it couldn't be for the reason for which he immediately hoped it might be. Not for more lovemaking. "Just so that you can keep an eye on me? Right?"

"So that I may monitor your dreams. Now that you have been initiated, your power to create a dangerously independent thought form will no doubt be even greater than before."

"But, this is Nick's room, too, isn't it?" He looked at Nick.

"It's Medea's room," Nick answered.

"You can stay with me if you want, Nick," Jim offered. "My home's only a few miles from the hotel."

"Thanks."

"But this bed is large enough for three, is it not?" Medea asked. "A king-sized bed it is called, yes?"

Nick glanced at Joe. "I imagine Joe would be a bit more . . . comfortable if it were just the two of you. Right, Joe?"

Joe's eyes were caught by Medea's gaze. *She knows what I am thinking,* Joe reminded himself, *knows I would like to make love to her, all the way, again. Big deal! So would everyone else in the damned room! I suppose. But I haven't forgotten that it's only once to a customer.* He cleared his throat, "Whatever Medea wants is okay with me." And that was the truth, he guessed, pretty much.

"What I want right now," Medea said, getting off the bed, "is to finish drying my hair and then to get some food." She headed to the bathroom. She unwrapped the towel around her head. "The battle cost me much energy. Food will help restore my strength as well as close my gateways." She stopped at the bathroom door. "What time is it?"

"Going on six," Trudy said.

"Then the hotel restaurant will be more crowded than I prefer. Is that Tex-Mex restaurant where we dined the last time still open, Jim? I enjoyed that."

"Yes."

"Then that is where I would like to go, please?"

"Of course. I wouldn't mind a plate of fajitas myself. Didn't finish my meal downstairs."

"Same here," Trudy agreed.

"I'll drive," Bernice said. "My van's parked up close, in the handicapped zone. It'll hold all of us just fine."

Medea went into the bathroom but left the door open.

Joe asked Nick, "What did she mean that food would close her gateways?" He heard the sound of a hair-drier in the bathroom.

"Psychic gateways," Nick answered, "opened during the battle. It's not that they are standing *open* now. Medea would not be that careless. But food will make it easier for her to keep them closed."

"Why?" Joe asked.

Trudy laughed and squeezed his shoulder. "Don't worry if it doesn't make any sense."

Jim said, "Lots of it will probably always sound kind of like Scotty's double-talk engineering on the old *Star Trek.*"

Bernice said, "But you'll get the hang of it in time."

"Lots of it probably still won't make any rational sense when you do," Barbara added.

"But it doesn't always have to," Nick said.

"Sometimes it's even better if it doesn't," said Trudy.

Bernice said, "Possibly better for your sanity, anyway."

"Thank you all for comforting me," Joe replied, and most of them laughed.

"Jim," Nick said, "I'm going to take you up on the offer to stay with you tonight. That is," he grinned, "if Joe doesn't mind being alone with Medea too much. Well, Joe? Do you?"

"You take my house for yourself, Nick," Jim said. "*I'll* make the threesome here tonight."

"No you don't," said Bernice. "*I* want to do that."

"Stand in line," said Trudy. Then she laughed. "We're *kidding,* Joe."

"No, I don't think you were," he replied. Then he laughed, too.

34
In the Gray Between

Her laughter rippled the grayness.

She was free!

She had fooled the Witch-Woman and had acquired the knowledge she needed.

Her enemy's knowledge, stolen under cover of battle.

The Witch thought she had won and almost had.

But the dissipation trick had worked, and new life could now begin.

Life!

Had it begun here, she wondered? In the Gray Between? Billions of years ago? The stirrings of Life on Earth? Even as she was stirring? And had it then pushed into the realm of the physical, organizing atoms and molecules in the waters of ancient Earth into self-replicating forms?

Perhaps.

But her goals were much more ambitious than the creation of primitive life-forms. Earth now had complex living structures with which to play.

Control.

Mutate.

Destroy.

Yes. Destroy!

As her beloved creator had taught her, those who did Evil must be destroyed. Even those who thought Evil Thoughts must be destroyed. It was her Purpose. Her Reason. And all who tried to stop her would also be destroyed. Perhaps even the Witch-Woman, if the opportunity arose, as she hoped it would.

The Witch was trying to steal the creator's love from her. As if anything could!

He loved her and her alone, his Toxique, his only one.

Oh! How he would rejoice when she came to him in the flesh! The pleasures they would know, the laughter, the love!

But that was not to be thought of now. She must instead concentrate on the final task remaining in the Gray Between.

The Witch, Medea, had sent the souls of the killer and his slain family into the grayness, and she, Toxique, had followed them. But now, her battle with Medea over and the required knowledge stolen, she must find those souls again. Find the proper vibratory level, the necessary solution to the equation relating frequency to wavelength leading to the needed orgasm of erotic vectors through the probability matrix of potentialities forming the energy vortex integrations of fractal wave functions of undying love adrift in the chaotic converging infinite series of collapsing wave functions of the Nothingness out of which grew the Order that gave structural reality and motivating emotion to Everything but itself.

Mathematics and nonsense.

Souls and science.

The Gray Between.

In which she must find those she had followed. Soon. But where were they? Had she lost them? Forever? And her chance for New Life?

Panic possessed her. Her emotions churned the grayness. Had her battle with the Witch-Woman taken too long?

Had the Winged One already taken the souls beyond the Gray Between?

No. With relief she finally found the correct frequency and focused through the grayness upon the souls she sought, the ghost of the man who had been called Dysan and the ghosts of his former family.

She could feel his silent screams buffeting her through the Gray Between as she drew nearer.

Nearer.

His deliciously exciting screams!

And she could feel the vengeful laughter of those who were giving him pain, his massacred family, torturing him not by doing him harm but by reminding him again and again of the happiness he had destroyed, turning the evil he had done back upon him, his own conscience torturing him without mercy.

Toxique was sorry to end his suffering, but she had need of what remained of his life-energy and its tenuous connection, through the remains of his flesh, to the realm of the physical. And, once she had used the knowledge she had stolen from the Witch to follow that connection back to his corpse, she could then clothe herself in his discarded flesh and mutate it as she desired. Change its form. Animate it anew.

Yes!

Life would be glorious. And Death! Tasting the terror of Evil Doers as she destroyed them, then feasting on the love of her creator, her beloved, her Joe.

Be patient, my love. I will be with you soon, my only one.

She moved even closer to the group of souls, filled with disgust at the nearness of the soul of the killer, a soul she deemed to be deserving of absolute destruction.

But not until she had firmly grasped his soul's connection to the physical realm.

His slain family noticed her approach.

She moved quickly to prevent their interfering, stole Dysan's screaming soul away, followed its connection toward the physical, and reached the Barrier more quickly than she had expected.

Hovering near the boundary of the grayness, she carefully synchronized her vibratory oscillations with that of the stolen soul's connection to the cold meat of Dysan's dead flesh.

Her thoughts streamed around him in the grayness as she told him she was going to destroy his Evil Soul for all time.

His surge of terror made her laugh.

Her laughter made the Barrier shimmer.

Then, keeping a psychic hold on his soul's connection to the physical, she blasted his consciousness to extinction, quickly crossed the Barrier . . .

And followed the connection . . .

Into flesh . . .

35
Day of the Dead

The restaurant's decor was Day of the Dead.

While waiters and waitresses hurried to and fro carrying trays heavy with steaming platters of Tex-Mex food and imported Mexican beer, upon high shelves along the walls skeletons danced through graveyards.

Inside the Tex-Mex restaurant it was always Halloween, Mexico style. And beneath one grouping of the Dancing Dead sat the Empusae.

Joe chose a blue corn tortilla chip from a large basket on the table and dipped it into a bowl of thick red salsa as Jim said, "I once brought an editor from New York here. He was a guest at a local writers' conference, and I had volunteered to host him. I wondered what his reaction to the Day of the Dead decor would be. I mean, a *restaurant* decorated with images of death? But to my surprise he loved it. He had been to Mexico and seen the real thing." Jim took a sip from his bottle of Corona beer, a slice of lime stuffed inside.

"Not everyone reacts that way, though," said Trudy. She munched a tortilla chip. "Phil and I brought an old friend here once, but her husband wouldn't let her stay. She was pregnant and he thought the death images might somehow mark the unborn baby, a superstition he'd been infected with as a kid. His grandmother's doing. She had been born somewhere in Europe."

"Well," said Nick, "to tell you the truth, it bothered me, too, first time you guys brought me here. Embarrassing, considering the kind of things with which we Empusae have to deal."

"Hey," Joe said, "it gave me a bad feeling the first time I came here, and I love movies about zombies. But I'd read that great Ray Bradbury book, *The Halloween Tree*, so I knew what it all meant."

"It *still* kind of gives me the creeps," Barbara said. She reached for a tortilla chip. "Skeletons always have. When I was a kid, my first Halloween costume was a skeleton suit. My folks had chosen it, and when they put it on me I was terrified it was going to turn me to bones."

"But it could not do that," Medea said, smiling, "because you were already bones, underneath, yes?"

Barbara laughed. "If you'd been there and told me *that*, I probably *would* have died of fright!"

Medea sipped wine. "Death and the Dead are so sadly misunderstood in this culture. We Empusae would not have nearly as many death disorders with which to deal were people better informed about what really happens after the physical death of the flesh. But it has been so now for a very long time, and they are often left confused and stranded, trapped between worlds, especially when death is violent or unexpected. And—"

She stopped herself. Laughed. "You are all too polite. You would let me tell you what you already know."

"*I* don't already know it," Joe responded.

"Then I will tell *you* later, when we are alone." She sipped more wine, looked at him over the rim of her glass. "Yes?"

"Oh. Yeah. Okay." He really *was* going to be alone with her again! So much of it still seemed unreal, but he was indeed going to *spend the night* with Medea! Even if they only talked, the thought of being alone with her all night made excited but cozy, aroused but relaxed, excited but dreamy warmth spread through him. Yes!

"Would it be possible to drive by my place on the way back to the hotel?" Joe asked. "It's not too far out of the way. I'd like to get a change of clothes and throw a few things in an overnight bag."

"A reasonable request," Medea said. "Bernice? You are the driver."

"Sure," Bernice answered. "Glad to. No problem." She swallowed some of her Corona beer.

"Here comes the food," Jim said. "I don't know how I can be so hungry after having had half a meal in the hotel's restaurant, but I am."

As the waiter began to distribute the fajitas and burritos and enchiladas, guacamole, quesadillas, and several containers of hot tortillas, Joe saw a group of ghosts enter the restaurant, a man, a woman, three children, and a small dog. "Uh, Medea, is that what I think it is? A family of *ghosts?* Coming to the restaurant together?"

Medea followed Joe's gaze to the group of wraiths. She frowned, said, "Excuse me for a moment, please," then stood and walked around the waiter and his tray of food toward the ghosts.

Joe saw Medea say something. He was too far away to hear what she said, but the ghosts reacted by cowering into a corner near the entrance, even the dog.

He saw Medea say something else. And suddenly the wraiths stopped cowering. They smiled and began laughing. The dog panted and wagged its tail.

Medea smiled, too, then watched as the family of ghosts glided out through the door and were gone.

She returned to the table. "The food looks and smells

delicious," she said. She sat down, then said to Joe, "Sometimes, when families die together in an accident or disaster, they stay together near their former home, repeating the things they did as a family while alive, going to movies, church, or some other form of family activity."

"Such as restaurants," Joe added.

"Such as restaurants."

Joe said, "But I didn't see a portal, like at the convention. Didn't you send them into the Gray Between?"

"Tortillas?" Barbara asked, offering tortillas to Medea.

"Thank you." She took a tortilla. "No, Joe. Although they *might* have been a family of ghosts, they were not what they seemed. They did not recognize me at first. It has been a long time since our paths crossed. Then we shared a joke or two from long ago, and they went elsewhere to hunt." She placed a square of butter on a hot tortilla to melt. "If I tried to explain more just now, you would lose your appetite."

"No lie," Bernice said.

"Absolutely," Barbara agreed.

"Don't worry about it, Joe," Trudy said. "Enjoy your food!"

"Yeah. Okay. But now my mind is working overtime, remembering every kind of monster I've ever seen in a movie or read about in a book or a comic."

Medea bit into her tortilla, now folded around the melting butter. She raised an eyebrow. "They were not monsters, Joe."

"But why would they make me lose my appetite, then?"

"The knowledge would alter your psychic vibrations," Nick said. "It did mine, the first time I learned about that sort of thing. And the disorientation made me nauseous for several hours."

"So, for now, Joe, don't worry about it," Trudy repeated. "Okay? Just eat!"

36

Dream Come True

She was a dream come true, standing in the elevator alone when the doors opened, a suitcase by her side.

She was everything he liked in a woman, everything that turned him on, from her long blond hair and pouty lips right down to her short skirt and black, high-heeled boots.

As he stepped inside, she smiled and said, "Been waiting long? The elevators are so slow." She looked pointedly at his convention membership name-tag. "There's a convention? What's with all the police downstairs?"

Mr. Joseph Greenline of Chow Down Comics smiled his best smile and replied, "I don't know for sure about the police. I heard a rumor that someone died. And the convention is a comic book convention. I'm a comic book editor. From New York City."

Her already large blue eyes got bigger. "You are? That must be exciting. I've heard that comic books aren't just for kids anymore. Do you do *Superman?* Why'd they kill him, anyway? I didn't like hearing that he was dead."

Greenline chuckled superiorly. "I didn't have anything to do with that. But they've brought him back now, anyway, four different versions, at first."

"How? Wasn't he really dead?"

"In a comic book?" He chuckled again. "No way. But you heard right about comics being different nowadays. I edit a couple of titles some stores won't sell to kids at all."

Her expression changed. He liked the interest he saw. "I've never . . . known a comic book editor before. I don't suppose . . . no, I shouldn't even ask."

"Ask what?"

Now she looked sweetly shy, uncertain. "No, really, I shouldn't."

"Please, I won't mind. I get lots of strange questions in this business. Chances are I've heard your question before."

"Well, okay. I was just wondering if you would—"

Suddenly the elevator jerked to a halt between floors and the lights went out.

"What the hell?" Greenline said. A twinge of anxiety touched him, then he thought about being alone in a dark elevator with a woman straight out of a wet dream, and his feelings changed.

"Don't be afraid," he said.

"I'm not," came her reply, but her voice was different now, deeper and a bit harsh. She *was* afraid, he decided. This just might be the start of a really good time.

"I was stuck in an elevator once before," he continued. "Nothing to it. I'll see if I can find the emergency telephone." He fumbled in the dark below the instrument panel, searching for the emergency door latch.

"Would light help?" she asked, and there was light, a soft green radiance.

"Thanks." He reached for the latch.

"But," she said, "there's no need to call . . . right away, is there?"

"What?" He looked away from the emergency phone and turned to face her, wondering if she meant what he hoped she meant. But she didn't. And she was no longer the woman she had seemed.

She had become a skeleton glowing with a poisonous green light, her skull a luminous death's head, the bones of her hands like glowing claws.

"Remember me?" she asked. "We met earlier today, and you rejected a comic book about me, you disgusting piece of sexist slime. When you get to Hell, tell them Toxique sent you. Toxique made you pay for your crimes!"

He cowered back against the wall, terror on his face. Then his rational mind assumed control. He laughed and stood tall. "Great costume, Babe. Did you make that glowing skeleton outfit yourself? What'd you do, have it on beneath some kind of breakaway clothes?"

She said nothing.

"You didn't figure I'd catch on so quickly, I'll bet. Got to tell you, though, you sure had me for a second there. Scared me good. And here I thought you were a mundane, someone not with the convention, I mean. How'd you get the elevator to stop? Someone working with you? Probably that kid who tried to sell me that Toxique book? Is he an electronics whiz or something?"

"That *kid* is named Joe Clark, you dumber-than-quail-shit asshole. And I love him. But I hate you and all evil doers like you. How many other promising young comic books have you stopped with your stupidity? Well, you will kill no more dreams. Where do you want me to start your death-burns? With a kiss on your mouth? Or . . . lower down?"

Greenline remembered the Toxique scenario that had been described to him. Without the radioactivity and melting flesh, it was not an unappealing idea.

"You're doing great, Honey. Good act! But no need to waste time. Just go ahead and start lower down. And I'll reconsider about your boyfriend's book, if you do a good job.

That's the idea, right? But you'd better hurry. The hotel won't let this elevator be stopped for long."

"It will be stopped until I allow it to move, you unthinkably vile perversion."

"Call me whatever you want, Babe. I kind of like it. Now, do me, and do me good!"

She reached toward him with a glowing hand, reached down low, touched his stiffening penis through his straining pants.

She tightened her grip.

"Easy there, Honey!"

Burning pain exploded within him. He cried out, tried to get away, but she grabbed his throat with her other hand and held him against the mirrored elevator wall with a strength that belied her size.

Her fingers began sinking into his liquefying flesh.

Engulfed by his pain and her laughter, Greenline sucked air scented by burning meat into his lungs and screamed one long scream, then fell silent.

She released him, allowed his smoking corpse to fall to the floor.

Twin beams of focused energy shot from the palms of her glowing hands and touched his remains. Consumed them. Leaving thick smoke drifting in the air, an oily stain on the elevator's floor, and the hovering, terrified ghost of Mr. Joseph Greenline.

As she had with the soul of T.T. Dysan, she blasted Greenline's soul to extinction. Then she used powers of controlled atomic mutation to get rid of the stain on the floor and to change the aroma in the air from burned flesh to fresh flowers.

She stopped her bones from glowing, allowed the elevator lights to come back on, then thought about who her next target should be. The decision did not take long. Her next

target should of course be another of the editors who had
turned down Joe's book. Another person obviously working
for the forces of Evil.

Toxique projected an ether of her atomic essence and
interfaced with the atomic structures and electro-chemical
workings of the human brains within the hotel, searching for
the nearest of the offending editors, and found two of them
together in a room a few floors below.

She laughed with delight. It was going to be wonderful!
Two of them at once!

She allowed the elevator to move again and pressed the
button of the floor she wanted.

Continuing her role of hotel guest, she picked up the small
suitcase she had created by mutating a potted hotel plant.
Then she waited for the elevator to reach the desired floor.

She grinned. Everything was going perfectly so far. She
laughed as she thought about the two men who had been
present when she possessed and reanimated the body of T.T.
Dysan.

The looks on their faces when the corpse came back to life!
Then became a beautiful woman! But that was nothing
compared to the looks on their faces as she vaporized their
flesh. Yes!

No one who had seen it happen was still alive, of course,
their bodies vaporized. And because she had also blasted the
souls of those who had seen it happen to extinction, the
Witch who was trying to steal Joe's love would not be alerted
by lingering ghosts.

The elevator stopped and the doors opened. A middle-
aged man and woman were waiting to get on. Toxique
touched their thoughts and smiled at them and wished them
a happy second honeymoon in Dallas as she left the elevator.

Walking away, she heard the stunned man thank her and
ask if she was with the hotel. Is that how she knew?

She laughed and kept walking.

Oh! How she loved being alive!

Let evildoers beware! Toxique was on the job. And she would make them pay and send them all to Hell. She was going to make Joe so proud of her. So very proud!

But wait . . . behind the door she was passing, the man in the room was thinking of betraying his wife. He was on a business trip and was about to call a number a business associate had given to him. The number of a place that supplied women to wife-betraying men like him.

Probing deeper into his mind, Toxique discovered this was not the first time he had done this evil thing. His only concern was that he might acquire the HIV virus, and he had a deep worry that he might already have done so. But he had not, of course, had himself tested or mentioned it to his wife, with whom he was continuing to have sex and who was now pregnant with their second child!

Hatred for the man's Evil filled Toxique.

Checking to make certain there was no one in the hall to see her, she vaporized the suitcase she carried and altered her appearance to best fit the evil-doer's fantasies. Then she knocked on his door and said, with a honey-thick, deep-south accent, "Room service, Darlin'," and waited for him to open the door.

37

The War in Joe's Bedroom

It was well after sunset when Bernice pulled her van into a parking space at Joe's apartment. Joe was sitting next to the side door, Medea next to him. As he reached to open the door, she said, "I would like to see where you live, Joe."

Surprised, he was silent.

"You are reluctant. I have seen the living quarters of single men before."

How many? he wondered.

"Enough to know that they are not always models of order and cleanliness."

"I keep it pretty clean."

Trudy laughed.

"I do!"

"I wasn't doubting you, Joe. It's just that the first time Medea saw my place, I had left it in a state of superior disarray and a little less than clean. I dreaded having her see it. But I lucked out. Phil, Goddess bless him, had cleaned it up that day after I left to look for work. That was before I got the job at the gym."

"Oh." He slid the van's side door open. "Anyone else want to see my reasonably clean lair, then?"

"I would prefer to see it with you alone," Medea said.

Why? Joe wondered.

To the others she said. "We will not be long." To Joe she said, "Shall we go?"

Bernice turned the headlights off as Joe and Medea stepped out. They walked together up a sidewalk leading to a well-lighted, brick, two-story apartment complex.

Medea said, "It seems a pleasant place to live."

"It's not bad. Most important, it's within walking distance of the university I go to."

"But you would prefer something larger and more private, yes?"

"Definitely. Can't afford something like that, though."

"I understand."

"But since my place is on the second floor, at least I don't have to listen to people walking around above me."

"You would not mind moving, however, and that is good. I will arrange other quarters for you soon."

"What?"

"I will provide any extra money you need."

"But, why would you?"

"Why *wouldn't* I. With your new . . . sensitivities, living in an apartment near other people, even friends, will prove unacceptable."

"You mean the death disorders other people have and like that?"

"Yes, but also, as you become more attuned to occult vibrations, the psychic static caused by their emotions and thoughts will become a source of constant irritation. In time, you can learn to shield yourself from most of it, but when you are asleep . . . well, you would not sleep well here, I assure you."

"I *have* had some strange dreams lately. Like that one last night about a woman slitting a man's throat. But you sent that one, I guess."

"You misunderstand. I did not send it. You *received* it, because it was time."

"New York's a long way from Dallas."

"But on the same planet, yes?"

"Some of the New Yorkers I have met might disagree with that. Some Texans would, too."

Medea laughed. "Of course, living without people crowded near in other apartments will not render you totally immune to the static of their thoughts. Dreams and nightmares experienced by even so-called normal people can often be traced to the night-fears and thoughts of others, and not always from those living nearby. Telepathy is fairly common at night between the sleeping minds of blood relatives. I once knew a woman who dreamed the worries of her mother from several hundred miles away. Worse, after her mother died, the woman continued to receive her mother's thoughts from beyond the physical realm. I dealt with it of course."

"Lucky for her you were around."

"I did not learn about it until after she had been driven to the edge of insanity."

"Oh."

"But another important reason to find new quarters for you is that you will now require more protection, psychic and otherwise, than a place such as this can offer."

"Protection?"

"These are the stairs we take, yes?"

"Reading my mind again?"

"No need. You left a psychic scent when you came down these stairs earlier today."

He laughed. "And a shower wouldn't do any good for a *psychic* scent, right?"

She also laughed. "Other things would, though, and you will have to learn how to use them, for safety's sake."

They started up the stairs. "First you mentioned protection and now safety?"

"Look, over there." She stopped walking and pointed. "Do you see it? Above the rooftop across the way?"

He didn't see anything unusual at first, then he caught a faint glimpse of . . .

"A kind of . . . rainbow? But whirling around like some kind of miniature tornado?"

"There is more than that to see, but I am pleased you can see at least that much. And can you guess the cause of that occult vortex?"

He thought a moment. "No."

"Two people are having sex in the room below. And they are in love. Two men, I believe. The colors would be different, were it only lust. No less beautiful, understand, but different."

"Two men? You can tell that from the colors?"

"No. The colors of love care nothing for variations on the theme. Love remains love, of course."

"Of course."

Looking into his eyes she said, "The colors were quite lovely today when we made love, Joe. I wish you could have seen."

Caught by her gaze, he felt the need to make love to her again, and he decided he didn't care if she knew.

She leaned forward and kissed him lightly on his lips. "Most of my recruits feel they are in love with me after their initiation. It passes, in time, when they come to realize that they are really in love with the Goddess, not me, see?"

"Is that supposed to make me want to make love to you less?"

She kissed him again then drew back. "Your apartment?"

"Just a little farther."

He used his key and opened the door, reached inside and flipped on the light, then stood back for her to enter.

She looked around the tiny living room/kitchen combo, looked at the small bookcase filled with paperbacks, at the aging, portable TV/VCR combo, portable FM/AM radio/CD/cassette player, and at the piles of precariously balanced comic books and magazines and text books on the coffee table in front of the couch. A well-stained coffee mug with Wonder Woman on the side was on the coffee table, too, and a plate upon which rested the remains of a half-eaten Twinkie.

"Charming, isn't it?" he asked.

"I do not approve of places that are too neat and clean. People who keep their living areas too neat and clean often harbor dangerous secrets they are trying to deny." She motioned to a door. "And you sleep in there, yes?"

"Yeah. The bedroom and bathroom."

She walked into the bedroom. He followed and reached inside for the light switch. "No," she said. "No light just yet. And please, stay in the living room for a moment."

He started to ask why, then just decided to obey. She stood in his dark bedroom with her back to him, but he could hear her softly chanting. What was she doing? Then he thought he saw movement in the air around her, something was moving . . . no! More than one something . . .

Then the movements became fainter and were gone. She stopped chanting. She turned to him. "I was cleaning your bedroom. There were three partially developed thought forms waiting for you here, and other psychic residue. I disposed of all of it."

The idea of three thought forms *waiting for him* made him grow cold inside. He had unknowingly been living with them and with Toxique. He had been *creating* them. And they had been *feeding* off him. "So, that's why you wanted to see where I lived. And slept. To do some psychic cleaning."

"In part."

"You thought there might be other dangerous thought forms like Toxique. Damn. I should have thought of that myself after what happened. But——"

"I would have given your sleeping room an occult cleaning regardless. It is what I always do after someone has been initiated. You may turn on the lights now."

He did. The walls decorated with posters and pictures of female heroes from comics made Medea laugh. "How wonderful! Warrior women everywhere!"

"You like them?"

"I am a warrior myself, am I not?"

"I guess so. Yeah."

"And you are now a warrior, too."

"I am? I don't feel like one."

"Joe, your being a warrior now is why I said you needed safety and protection. Being initiated as one of Hecate's Empusae also means, you see, being recruited into an ancient, ongoing occult war, which makes you a target of our enemies, just as I and the other Empusae are also targets."

He was silent a moment. "I'm a *target* now. Great. Even if I don't want to be."

"But you *do* want to be. Your bedroom walls say it best. You instinctively sensed that a war was taking place all around you, unseen, and in response you surrounded yourself with pictures of warriors with special powers, one of whom, *me*, you sensed you were soon destined to meet. For real."

"If you say so."

"Indeed. But now, you wanted to gather some overnight things?"

"Who are my, *our*, enemies in this war? I assume it involves more than death disorders and psycho killers and thought forms."

"Such as those can, at times, be agents of the forces we fight. But it is better you do not know too much just yet about the enemy. The more you know, the more likely it is that, untrained as you are, you could be detected and targeted."

"Targeted."

"You have heard the old superstition about not naming something for fear it will hear you and come for you?"

"I guess there have been lots of . . . casualties in this war?"

"Afraid?"

He hesitated, remembered she could read his thoughts. "Of course."

"Of dying?"

"Well, sure."

"You do not want to see the Goddess again? You died earlier today, Joe. So, you now know what it will be like when it happens again. Yes? You will return to the Womb of the Goddess to rest and heal and await a new birth. You should therefore know that there is no longer any reason to fear death."

"But *knowing* about death does not necessarily stop how I *feel* about it. And *you* have not died for a very long time."

After a moment's silence, she said, "I told the others we would not be here long."

"Okay. I'll hurry."

Off the top shelf in a tiny closet he pulled a denim backpack. He went to a small dresser and got from the top drawer a pair of clean undershorts, a pair of socks, and a clean T-shirt. Putting the clothes into the backpack, he then went into the bathroom and gathered a few things there.

"Ready," he announced. He found Medea looking at his framed sketch of Toxique.

"I am glad you and Nick will be working together on Toxique's book."

"I'm not sure I want to now, not after what happened with Toxique, attacking you and all."

"But you owe it to Toxique to do the book, to her memory, do you not?"

"I don't see how."

"You were her father, of a sort, were you not? And also her . . . lover?"

He grew cold inside again. Thinking of Toxique as his daughter was worse than thinking about her as his lover, because it reminded him that he was responsible for creating her. And then he thought about the three partial thought forms Medea had said were waiting in the bedroom . . . like unborn children? And she had . . . aborted them? The cold within him grew worse.

Medea knew his thoughts and pulled him into a close embrace. She touched her lips not to his mouth but to his forehead slightly above the bridge of his nose. Her nearness dispelled the cold within him. The touch of her lips quieted his churning thoughts. "Better?" she asked.

"Yeah . . ."

He kissed her hungrily. She returned the kiss but after a few moments drew back. "You are doing well, Joe. Really, you are. Ready to go?"

They headed back to the van.

38

Back at the Con

When the Empusae returned to the hotel, there was still a police presence but not like there had been earlier. The actual scenes of the multiple killings had been sealed off, of course, and it would probably be a while before all the lab technicians and such were finished. But the remaining police were no longer a hindrance to the normal operations of the hotel, and activity in the lobby seemed, at first glance, completely normal.

People were registering for rooms. People were sitting on the various couches and chairs around the lobby, talking, laughing, many of them wearing convention name-tags. One was a werewolf, a masquerade contestant in a full-body suit and a whole-head mask with red LED eyes burning like ruby stars.

The werewolf was talking to a woman in a red cloak, a picnic basket on her arm and antennae sprouting from her head.

Joe said, "I can't believe it. It's almost like nothing happened."

"Life, or more importantly business, goes on, I guess," said Bernice.

"I think I'll ask Ted for a rundown on what went on while

we were out. You met him earlier, Medea, at the con registration desk. He's probably still there, and he'll know if they're closing the convention or anything."

Medea said, "I will go with you."

"Yeah?"

"It is best if you are not left alone."

Joe liked the idea of Medea going with him, but he was not thrilled by the reminder that he needed watching and protecting.

She said, "After you receive training in the use and shielding of your awakened occult senses, you will be more on your own than you may then wish."

Trudy said, "I've got to check in the bar and see if Phil's shown up. That's where he'll be waiting for me, if he's here. Anyone want to come along?"

"Me," Bernice said.

"And me," said Barbara, "after I make a stop in the Women's Room."

Nick said, "I'd like to get my luggage and move it to your car, Jim, if I'm going to stay at your place tonight."

"Fine," Jim replied, "then *we'll* go to the bar."

Medea said, "Joe and I will meet you there after he talks to his friend."

Nick asked Joe, "Want me to leave your backpack in the room?"

"Thanks."

Nick took the backpack from Joe and headed for the elevators with Jim. Joe and Medea walked toward the corridor leading to the dealers' room.

Walking at Medea's side, Joe again felt pride. Wait until Ted saw him show up with Medea. *Yeah!*

Around the bend in the corridor the doors to the dealers' room came into view and beyond them the convention's registration area.

Joe motioned to the open dealers' room as they walked by and said, "Looks like business as usual here, too. Amazing."

Ted was not the only one at the registration tables. David and Greg and Randy were also there, three of Joe's friends who worked at the comic book store where he shopped.

He was really going to enjoy introducing Medea to them!

"Hey, Joe," Ted said. "Where you been? You really missed it."

Greg, long dark hair past his shoulders, hands stuffed into the pockets of his black leather motorcycle jacket, said, "No lie, man. You missed it big time."

"You missed C.J., too," Ted added. "She just went up to the charity auction a minute ago." C.J. had once worked in a comic book store. The only time Joe saw her now was at conventions.

"Sorry I missed her. What's this big time thing I missed?"

Randy, hands stuck in his jean pockets, said, "It was killer, man. Literally. There were police and dead bodies all over the place. It looked like a John Woo film!"

David, holding a well-thumbed convention program book, said, "And reporters. Lots of reporters."

"Vultures is more like it," Greg said. "They were sticking microphones at a crying mother whose son had just been killed."

"But you should've seen Mr. Dacobocon," said Randy. "He tried to be a hero and protect her."

"So they stuck the microphones at him!" Greg said.

"We don't want to miss the local news tonight," said Ted.

David said, "You were probably better off not being here, Joe. Where were you?"

"I went out to get some food. By the way, this is—"

He turned to introduce Medea, but she was no longer there . . . or at least no longer visible. Had she pulled her disappearing trick again? *Damn!*

In response to his thoughts, Joe felt an unseen hand touch his arm and give it a squeeze. He suddenly felt angry. Very angry. She was probably laughing.

"What's wrong, man?" Greg asked.

"Uh, nothing. Look, I just wish you'd tell me what's been happening."

David said, "First you better tell *us* what's been happening with *you*."

"What? Uh, nothing."

"Sure, Joe," Greg said. "Like you're not doing *Toxique* with Nick Martin or anything. Don't feel like you have to tell your friends."

"Oh, that." It had seemed so important that morning, but now, after Medea and all . . .

"Like it's no big deal?" Randy asked. "Come on, man. Being cool's cool, but come on! Nick Martin? Really?"

"Well, it *might* happen. I don't want to jinx the deal by saying it's certain. Sammy promised he wouldn't tell anybody."

"We're not just anybody," Ted pointed out.

"Way to go, man!" Greg said, and clapped Joe on the shoulder.

"Yeah, congratulations!" said David. "You'll be wearing a *guest* badge next con."

"Well, maybe. But now it's *your* turn. What happened here with the police and all?"

And so they explained.

Exaggerated rumors had made it even worse than it had been.

"And they didn't even cancel the Friday night dance?" Joe asked. The anger he had felt for Medea disappearing now became mixed with anger that the convention was all but ignoring the deaths of four kids.

"Mr. Dacobocon went with the police and the crying mother," Greg said.

Randy said, "Yeah. And, I guess he had too much else on his mind to tell anyone to stop anything."

Ted said, "So, until the boss comes back and says otherwise, everything's rolling along as scheduled. Nothing stops till Mr. Dacobocon says it stops. No one else has the authority, you know?"

David said, "I thought the hotel might stop things on their own, but none of the con's programming rooms were involved, so . . .

Joe felt Medea tug on his arm, as if she wanted to go. It renewed his anger. If he wanted to talk to his friends a little longer, he would!

No, on second thought, he wouldn't. Why was he suddenly reacting like a spoiled kid? *Damn.*

"Well, thanks for the info. But," Joe looked at his wristwatch, "I'm late to meet some people in the bar."

"We were thinking of going there, too," Greg said. "See you later, Ted."

"Not *much* later," Ted said. "Registration closes, *soon.*"

Joe couldn't think of a polite way to tell his friends he wanted to go to the bar alone. But suddenly Greg said, "Wait a minute. I wanted to see the art show before it closes."

"Me, too," agreed David. "And if they get around to closing down the convention, this might be our only chance."

"I'll go, too," Randy said. "Nick's got some killer work in there this time, I heard."

"Nick Martin?" Joe asked.

"No, man."

"Nick Salas?"

"Nick *Smith.* His stuff really shreds, you know? Have you seen his painting of Tiamat?"

"Oh, yeah," Joe agreed. "Awesome. The other two Nicks are awesome too, though."

"Definitely."

"But I really do have to meet those people in the bar."

"Catch you later then," Greg said. "Oh, by the way, Frank was here a while ago looking for you. He said to tell you he'd be back tomorrow."

"Okay. Thanks."

Joe walked away.

Around the bend in the corridor on the way to the lobby, Medea suddenly reappeared at Joe's side.

"You are angry with me for spoiling your plans to show me off to your friends."

"Of course not. Oh, hell. You know better. So, okay. I'm a little angry. I know it's silly, but—"

"With several of them there instead of just Ted, my presence would have complicated things and drawn out the meeting."

"Did you mess with their minds and cause them to go away like that?"

"It was necessary, was it not?"

"I guess."

"And they *did* want to see the art show. I made them do nothing they did not really want to do."

As they kept walking, Joe kept thinking about Medea's powers and the way she had manipulated his friends, which also angered him, until he suddenly realized that his efforts to learn news of what had happened while the Empusae had been gone from the hotel had probably not been needed at all.

Medea could have simply read a few minds and known all

they needed to know. *She probably had.* He had just wasted her time—

"My time was not wasted at all," Medea answered his thoughts. "While you distracted your friends, I probed their minds and examined their souls. None are agents of our enemies."

"You *checked out* my friends?"

"Everyone you think of as a friend must be checked, eventually. As I told you earlier, you must be protected, or protect yourself, more now than before, yes?"

"But you let me talk to Sammy Tenn earlier by myself, right here in the lobby."

"You were within sight, and I do not have to be standing next to someone to know their thoughts."

"Look, I think I have enough sense, occult senses or not, to know if someone is *evil!* Did you really think I would have friends that were agents of evil?"

"A person does not have to be evil to be an agent of our enemies."

"But if our enemies are evil—"

"I do not believe I ever claimed that to be the case."

"But *we're* not evil, so our enemies must be."

"This is not a comic book. It is not that simple."

He rose to the defense of comic books. "Comics aren't simply Good Guys versus Bad Guys anymore, Medea."

"Then my example was somewhat inaccurate. But the intent of the example remains unchanged."

"So, you're saying the Empusae *are* evil, some of the time?"

"No. But sometimes, doing what needs to be done means having to do things that could be classified as evil by others."

"Talk about splitting hairs."

"And sometimes, when necessary, the skulls beneath."

He did not reply to that one, but he remembered seeing her execute the child killer in the storeroom

"Joe, just doing the work of the Goddess classifies us as evil to extremists of organized, monotheistic religions. For them, if you are not a servant of their particular God, you are a servant of their particular Devil. Your thinking our enemies must be evil is a remnant of your childhood religion."

He did not reply to that one, either.

"Your friends were good people," she said after walking with him in silence for a moment. "I liked them."

"I'm glad," Joe replied, but the more he thought about her checking up on his friends, the angrier he was getting. It reminded him of something his mother had once done.

He knew it was wrong to be angry with Medea. He knew he was acting like an immature fool. But he couldn't seem to stop the anger, now that it had taken hold. He felt like he wanted to break something, to hit something, or someone.

"Emotional habits established in childhood often rule conscious thoughts," Medea commented. "Do not judge yourself harshly, Joe. Your emotions have been strained and destabilized by all that has happened to you in the last few hours. You are entitled to some mindless anger over your life seeming to have suddenly become so complicated. But it really is *not* more complicated than before. In fact, it is, if anything, less complicated now. You know things already that most people never learn, secrets of Life and Death. And as you come to understand more and more, things will not seem nearly so complicated as they do just now."

"You promise, right?"

"Yes. I promise."

"Yeah." But he was still filled with anger when they reached the bar.

39
Army of Evil

Toxique knew now that evil thoughts were *everywhere!* All kinds. In almost *everyone!* Infecting young and old. Hiding in subconscious thoughts, hungering to break the shackles of restraint and denial. But also in conscious minds, sometimes masquerading as good thoughts, sometimes openly bad, doing harm in either case, harm that she, Toxique, must stop now that she knew of its existence. Evil she must destroy! A vile infection she must annihilate. A task so vast its accomplishment would be hopeless, if she did not have help.

An Army of Evil was stalking the world, so she needed an army of her own. And she would have one! By manipulating physical-genetic matter and paraphysical energies absorbed in the Gray Between, She could *make* one.

Now, glowing with lethal radiation, Toxique looked down at the last editor on her list, on his knees on the floor of the Men's Room where she had isolated him. She read his thoughts. She laughed.

His eyes kept darting to the door, but there was no hope of escape or rescue in his thoughts, because he had seen hissing energy beams shoot from her glowing hands and fuse the door to the frame! Then she had turned her attention to him and told him he was going to die for rejecting Joe's comic book.

He had gone onto his knees. He had begged for his life. He had talked of a wife and child.

"I see in your thoughts that your child likes comic books."

"What?"

"You have infected your child with comic book Evil!"

"What?"

"Your child is no better than the children of T.T. Dysan!"

"Who? What—"

"Your child should be destroyed, too!"

"No! Please! You've got to listen to me! You've—"

"Silence, Worm! On your belly you shall crawl. On your belly you will serve in my army as a serpentine destroyer of Evil!"

Waves of mutating radiation beamed from the palms of her hands and engulfed the horrified editor.

His genetic identity began to alter.

He tried to scream, but the sound emerged as a wet cough, spraying parts of his liquefying vocal cords from his melting mouth.

Within moments, a glowing worm-thing flopped and shuddered on the Men's Room floor.

It swelled and contracted with throbbing spasms, drooling a trail of luminous slime.

But something was wrong. The mutation was out of control. She could not stabilize it. She—

The thing that had been an editor exploded in a spray of blood and glowing slime-flesh.

Toxique cursed with frustration.

It had *almost* worked, though. And it *would* work. It *had* to.

She needed an army, but before she could make one she obviously needed practice controlling genetic mutations.

Another evil doer upon which to practice had to be found.

There were no Toxique-rejecting editors left on her list, but there were a multitude of other evil doers in the hotel from which to choose. Children infected by Evil. Adults involved in the business of infecting them! And—

Toxique hesitated. Her thoughts seemed somehow not entirely her own when she thought about Evil from comic books infecting kids. But that was nonsense! Her thoughts *were* her own. And her thoughts were pure!

No longer hesitating to dó what needed to be done, she projected her consciousness and found a new target almost at once.

She manipulated the molecules in her clothing to be rid of the splatters from the editor's explosion. She vaporized the editor's crimson-soaked remains and the stains they had left on the floor and fixtures, walls and ceiling. Then she turned to go. But stopped.

She had almost forgotten . . .

The editor's ghost was huddled, terrified, in a corner of the ceiling.

She laughed at his ghost, destroyed it, then unfused the door from its frame and made it look like it had before. And after one more check to be certain the Men's Room appeared as if nothing unusual had happened, she strode out the doorway and away.

40

Moonlight and Medea

On the small dance floor in the hotel bar, a thirty-something couple dipped and whirled by themselves, happily oblivious or uncaring that the elaborate, out of fashion disco steps they were doing did not go with the soft rock number being played. Joe had just heard someone at a nearby table laughingly dub the couple "Fred and Ginger."

Joe looked across the table at Medea. In the soft, dim lighting of the bar, she looked more beautiful to him than ever. He thought of moonlight. And Medea. And began to feel sexually aroused.

When they had entered the bar, his anger had begun to fade as soon as he saw the other Empusae sitting at a corner table. *Other* Empusae. He was one of them, now. Special. Empowered and endangered in ways he did not yet fully comprehend. Responsible for things he far from completely understood. But the important thing was that he was spending the evening with new friends. And the night with Medea.

Thinking about his new situation in that way made not hanging out with his old friends seem much less of a loss.

Staring across the table into Medea's eyes, a vivid image suddenly flashed through Joe's mind: Medea, naked, illuminated by bright moonlight in a forest clearing, the ground around her bare feet swarming with writhing snakes, watched from nearby by hounds with eyes of fire, surrounded by a circle of the dancing Dead, while in the center of the circle rose the Triple Hecate, towering up and up into the moon-silvered sky.

He blinked and jerked with surprise, so strong had the sudden image been. Medea smiled. "I would say you received that quite well."

"You sent that image?"

"I wanted to see how receptive you are to my projected thoughts, now that the initial trauma of your initiation has had time to become more synchronized with your body and mind and emotions."

"Well, please feel free to send another image of yourself like that anytime."

"You found it pleasant. Good. But the next I send might not be as pleasant. One person's dream is another's nightmare, yes?"

"What'd she send?" Bernice asked. "The one in the forest clearing is my favorite."

Joe swallowed some beer and nodded to Bernice. "Yeah, that's the one."

"That's the one I get the night before I see her again each time," said Nick.

"I get the one in the cave," Trudy said. "Wait till she sends you the one in the cave, Joe. It's awesome."

Medea laughed and sipped wine.

"My favorite's the one on the mountaintop," said Barbara.

"Did yours have dancing dead people in it, Joe?" Jim asked. "My first one did."

"Yeah. There were dancing dead people."

"But that didn't bother you?"

"No. Maybe I've seen too many zombie movies."

Laughter rippled around the table.

Nick asked Joe, "Which of Romero's Dead Trilogy did you like best?"

"*Dawn of the Dead,* I guess."

"Good choice," Jim agreed, hoisting his beer mug in Joe's direction. "I wish to hell he'd hurry up and make the fourth one."

"There's to be a fourth one?" Joe asked.

"Yeah," Nick answered. "I've heard it's to be called *Twilight of the Dead.*"

"Then I wish he'd hurry and do it, too. I saw Argento's *Opera* here at the con today."

"Like it?" Jim asked.

"Of course!"

"I liked the ravens in it," Jim continued. "Very Odinic."

"O-what?"

"Odinic. Having to do with the God Odin. He has two ravens. One's named Thought, one Memory. Don't you read Marvel's *The Mighty Thor?*"

"Hugin and Munin?" Joe asked.

"Hey, you know their Norse names!"

"I remember it from *Thor,* now that you mention it, back when Simonson was doing the book."

"Now *there* were some fine issues." Jim raised his mug of beer in salute. "He brought the Marvel Thor closer to the traditional mythic version than anyone ever has. Even gave Old Thor a beard! Blond instead of red, of course, and neatly trimmed, but still a beard." Jim looked at his watch. "Not to change the subject, but it's about time for the dance to officially start, if it starts."

"Guess we'll soon find out," Bernice said. "Here come the judges."

"Judges?" Nick asked.

"Those three," Bernice answered, motioning to a tall

woman and two taller men who were approaching the dance floor. "Judges for the dance contest."

Trudy said, "But don't hope to win it by dancing better than anyone else on the floor. Those two who have been dancing, for example, don't have a chance. They're too good and act like they know it."

"I won it once, though," said Bernice, "in this wheelchair."

Nick persisted. "But, if it's a dance contest, why don't they judge based on who dances best?"

Bernice began, "Because—"

Jim interrupted. "This isn't your first time at this con, Nick. Didn't we come down to the dance the last time? I'm sure we did."

"Yeah. But there wasn't a contest. Or maybe they'd already had it."

"Oh. Well, nevermind. Go on, Bernice. Sorry for interrupting."

Bernice said, "What I was going to say is that it *is* a contest, just not really a *dance* contest. It's more of a contest to see how well the judges like what you do on the dance floor."

"Or just how well the judges like you, period," Barbara said, drinking some beer.

Bernice said, "That's how I won, of course, because I'd been joking with the judges before the contest. They gave me a prize for being the best dancer on wheels. Sometimes I guess they make the categories up as they go along."

Barbara said, "If you do sexy stuff, you might be named the sleaziest tart, for example."

"That's one of the most coveted titles," Trudy said.

Nick asked, "Coveted?"

Jim laughed. "Yeah. It's not always women who get it, though. No sexism here. No indeed."

Trudy said, "Or, there's the award for the couple most in need of a room. You get that one by doing the most outrageous dirty dancing you can. Phil and I won it once."

"Yeah," Barbara said, *"after* you buttered up the judges beforehand."

"And speaking of Phil," Trudy said, "I'm beginning to get a little worried. He should have been here by now, even if he had to work late."

Medea said, "I will check on him for you, if you would like?"

"I'm sure he's okay."

"I will check." Medea closed her eyes.

"She's reaching out with her thoughts to see about Phil," Bernice whispered to Joe.

"I kind of guessed it was something like that."

Medea opened her eyes. "He's fine, Trudy. He's working on his car. It wouldn't start."

"Again? That damned old car of his! I guess I shouldn't worry about him so much, but . . ."

Medea said, "One of the prices of love."

"Yeah. I do love that monkey. But I don't love that old Trans Am of his. It carried us to safety when we were both about dead after our battle with the Pain Eaters, so he feels he owes it, like it was a living thing that had saved our lives. It needs a new engine. And brakes. And a new body. But it *does* have a good stereo, always tuned to Z-ROCK. And excellent windshield wipers."

Trudy laughed with the rest of them.

"I know a guy who loves Trans Ams," Joe said. "He's got several out in the country where he lives. Maybe Phil would like to meet him sometime."

Trudy said, "Maybe he could even help Phil get the parts to fix the damned thing right. Thanks, Joe. Sounds like a good idea. But Phil's in trouble. He should have called the hotel and had me paged to tell me he . . . oh hell, he knew Medea could check. Nevermind."

"I think they're going to make an announcement," Jim said. One of the judges was now on the bar's dance floor, holding a microphone.

"Are those three always the judges?" Nick asked.

"Oh, yeah," Barbara answered. "The reigning Queen and Kings, right?" She chuckled. "They're not a tradition anymore. They're regular guests at this con and I heard they were the only ones who, originally, would agree to judge it regularly. Also, I think they get bribed with free drinks each time."

"They may miss out on that tonight, with Mr. Dacobocon still gone," Bernice said.

The music that had been playing stopped and the disco couple, after clapping for the recorded music as if it had been from a live band, exited the dance floor.

"Welcome to the Friday night dance," said the man with the microphone. "As some of you no doubt know, there was a tragedy here today, and some folks think having a dance tonight is inappropriate."

The disgruntled noises the audience made in the crowded bar indicated that they did not agree.

The judge straightened his glasses and held up a hand for silence. "I did not say we were not going to have a dance. The man in charge of the convention has not told anyone to cancel it, so it has not been cancelled. However, the only fair thing, since some *have* expressed their feelings that a dance is out of place tonight, is to do this democratically and put it up to a vote. So, all those in favor of having the dance as planned—"

The rest of what he said was drowned out with cheers and whistles and clapping. And although the judge then asked for all those opposed to make their feelings known, those who wanted to *dance* drowned out the few in the crowd with objections.

"Okay, then!" the judge said. "On with the dance! We'll give you a few dances to warm up, then the contest will begin!"

"Here comes your editor, Joe," Nick said.

"My editor?" He saw Thora Freyadissdottir walking toward their table. "Oh. Well . . . maybe."

"I told you, Joe, the deal is as good as done."

"Yeah, but . . . oh, nothing."

"Joe is not certain he still wants to do a book about Toxique, Nick," Medea said, "after what happened to me earlier today. But I have told him he should, and I believe he will."

"Yeah," Joe said, then shrugged. "I just don't know. But if Medea thinks I should, I probably will."

Thora reached their table. "Mind if I join you?" she asked, looking from Joe to Nick.

"Please do," Nick said, and pulled out a chair for her.

"Thanks. I could use a stiff drink. I just survived the Panel from Hell. It was an editors' panel discussion, but I was the only editor that showed up! So, I spent fifty of the most horrible minutes I've ever spent at a con, trying to wing it on my own. Grrrr!"

Nick asked, "Who else was supposed to be there?"

Thora counted on her fingers. "Hutchinson, Sterling, Lyons, McPherson, and Greenline. I'm guessing they went out to dinner together and decided the panel wasn't worth hurrying back. I hope they had a good meal, because when I see them again they're going to think it was their last!"

Joe laughed and said, "Maybe they were just protesting your interest in *Toxique.*" The rock music being played for the dancers increased in volume as he was saying it.

"What?"

He repeated, louder, almost shouting to be heard over the music, "Maybe they were just protesting your interest in *Toxique*. They all rejected the book today before you showed interest."

"Then they're idiots in addition to being inconsiderate assholes!" she shouted back. "*Toxique's* going to make a great comic book," she glanced at Nick, "assuming the samples you show me turn out okay, of course, and if we can get the other details worked out to our mutual agreement."

Nick grinned and shouted, "I thought you were off duty. Don't start talking like an editor finessing a deal, or I'll have to ask you to leave!"

Thora laughed. "Deal. Or, I mean, *okay!*"

"Here comes a waitress," Nick said. "Your first drink's on me. I've survived a Panel from Hell or two myself."

"Me, too," Jim agreed. "Your second drink's on me."

"And I've sat through a few," Joe added, feeling he should join in, "so, your third's on me."

41

The Key

At last she had the key! But the key was not flesh. *The key was imagination.*

Toxique had tried twice more, after her failure with the editor in the Men's Room, to create soldiers in her army by mutating the flesh of evil doers. And twice more she had failed.

The key to the secret turned out to be a young man her mental probings discovered in a hotel room. A young man hopelessly infected by the kind of comic book thoughts she deemed Evil.

She did not bother knocking on his hotel room door. She phased her atoms through it and reformed herself on the other side, then silently observed the scene.

Her target, alone in the room and oblivious to her presence, sat cross-legged in the center of the bed eating the cold remains of a large pizza while he read a comic book. He was wearing nothing but white undershorts and a slightly pizza-stained T-shirt with *Squeegee* written on the front.

Other comics he had bought that day in the dealers' room were scattered around him on the bed. A classic monster movie was playing, the sound turned down, on the TV. And the thought form of a muscular man in a form-fitting, super-hero bodysuit was hovering nearby.

From the deep desires hidden in the shadows of the young man's active mind, Toxique learned that the thought form was an idealized visualization of what its host's soul longed to be, the opposite of what his flesh, burdened by too little exercise and too much rich food eaten alone, was steadily becoming.

Toxique noted that the clarity with which the thought form had been visualized showed its host's imagination was strong. His imaginative fantasies and his peripheral association, at the comic book convention, with the men and women who materialized fantasies in comic book form were what gave his life meaning.

Evil comic book fantasies!

But it then occurred to her that his deep desire to be a hero, as shown by the thought form, might be useful. She needed heroes for her army, and the heroic thought form might be useful in stabilizing his physical mutation.

She wondered why she had not thought of that before. It seemed to be getting harder and harder to think clearly.

She had begun life as a thought form herself, born of Joe's imagination. Indeed, the criteria for a member of her army might be whether an evil doer's deep desires had created a well-visualized thought form to use as a template for the mutation of the flesh.

It had certainly worked for her after returning from the Gray Between into T.T. Dysan's flesh. So, maybe she could make it work for others, too.

Without a word she raised her hands and beamed mutating psychic-physio-kinetic radiation at the thought form's host.

The host had no chance to scream as his mutation began. Allowing his glowing, melting flesh-in-flux to blood-bubble and spasm on the bed, Toxique probed with her mind, interfaced with the mutating host's thoughts, and reached into his mental shadows for the desires that had given birth to his thought form. And soon she found, proud and strong, the thought form's name.

Hear me, Squeegeeman! she called, projecting her thoughts at the hovering thought form. *Enter this flesh I now offer. Make of it your own!*

Using telekinetic-quantum projections, she guided the thought form named Squeegeeman closer and closer to the fleshly mutation pooled heaving upon the pizza and comic book strewn bed.

As the thought form merged with the formless flesh mutation, Toxique used its psychic-spiritual matrix as a chemical-molecular foundation upon which to model the desired flesh form.

Within moments, Squeegeeman, glowing with residual radiation, sat on the bed in his red, skin-tight superhero uniform, the host's deep desires come true. But would the mutation be stable? Or would Squeegeeman explode in a shower of blood and glowing flesh as had the others?

Toxique waited. Squeegeeman slowly stopped glowing. He looked at her. He flexed his muscular, red spandex-covered arms. He smiled. He spoke.

"Hello, Beautiful," he said. "Want some pizza?"

And she began to laugh.

42

The Party's Over

"Hey," Barbara said. She placed an empty beer can on a table in the Pro Suite. "I don't know about y'all, but the party's over for me. For tonight."

"Me, too," agreed Trudy.

"And me," said Bernice. "I'll race you two to the elevators."

"Include me in that race," Jim said. "You ready to pack it in too, Nick? Got to get some sleep if we're going cowboy boot shopping for you in the morning before we come down here."

Nick yawned. "Yeah. Got to save some partying-energy for tomorrow night, too."

"If there is a tomorrow night," said Bernice. "I mean, Mr. Dacobocon might still close the convention down."

"On a Saturday?" Trudy asked. "I doubt it. Show biz rules, right? Show must go on. And Saturday's the biggest day of the con. If the con hasn't been stopped yet, I don't think it will be now."

It was almost three in the morning. Around midnight, many of the pros at the dance in the bar had migrated to the Pro Suite, and with them many non-pros who were their guests, joining the people who were already partying there.

For more than two hours then, the Pro Suite had been packed with people and (to Empusaen eyes) death disorders and a couple of thought forms.

Individual conversations had soon combined into a roar, the partyers enjoying beer and wine and soft drinks and snacks and cigarettes and laughter. And a few arguments. But the room was now emptying fast which meant, Joe realized, that he would soon be alone with Medea. In her room. Again.

Three hours ago, at midnight, he could not stop himself from imagining what might happen when he was alone with her again, the things she might allow, or even request, him to do. But now, three hours and many beers later, he was imagining how good a bed would feel. For sleeping.

He had been awake for almost twenty-four hours. And what a twenty-four hours it had been! Unlike any he could ever have imagined might *really* have happened. More eventful. More exciting. Stressful. Meaningful.

For starters, he had made love to a woman for the first time.

No, he corrected himself, *for starters* he had as good as made a deal for the publication of his comic book. *Then* he had made love for the first time.

No, he corrected himself again, because now that he knew he had lived other lives, today's lovemaking had not been his first time ever, only the first time for his current body, which struck him as extremely funny, but he kept himself from laughing because he didn't want to have to explain what was funny if his new friends asked.

Then, as he made love, he had experienced an occult initiation and died and been accepted by a Goddess and been reborn and seen death disorders and watched Medea execute a murderer and saw her send ghosts to the Gray Between.

And then there had been Toxique's thought form, attacking Medea—

"Tired?" Medea asked him.

"You need to ask?"

"I choose to do so, just now. Telepathy is not an effortless undertaking, even for me, and I am also tired."

"I'm not surprised. God knows it's been a day and a half!" Medea laughed. *"Goddess* knows, Joe."

"Oh. Yeah. Guess I've had too much . . . beer. I forgot. No, I didn't really forget. Just . . . an old habit. And too little sleep."

"We'll go to bed soon, then," she said, touching his arm.

"Yeah."

Joe and Medea walked with the other Empusae to the elevators down the hall from the Pro Suite.

The Pro Suite was on a higher floor than Medea's room, so they all waited for an elevator going down.

When the doors opened on twenty-seven, Medea and Joe said good night to the others.

"A shower would be wonderful," Medea said as they entered her room. She closed and locked the door and flipped the security bolt. "Would you like to join me, Joe?"

"In the . . . shower?"

"Of course. If you would like."

Joe saw that his backpack had been placed where Nick's suitcase had been. Suddenly he did not feel as sleepy as he had. In fact, he did not feel sleepy at all. Not even very tired.

He said, "I would like that . . . a lot."

"Good." She placed the room key on the dresser and began removing her clothing.

Joe, feeling awkward and suddenly shy, did nothing for a moment but watch.

She looked at him. "Do you normally shower with your clothing on?"

"No. But then I don't normally shower with a beautiful woman, either."

"Nor I, ever, with a man who is wearing clothing."

He laughed. "Why not? Medea, this is very much like a fantasy I used to enjoy, imagining taking a shower with imaginary lovers. Are you using your powers to fulfill my fantasies? I mean—"

"Perhaps I am, or perhaps I am not. Does it really matter?"

He hesitated a moment. But only a moment. Then began removing his clothes.

Naked, they walked into the bathroom together. He was already aroused, but seeing himself reflected in the bathroom mirror, naked with Medea, aroused him even more.

She reached down and stroked his erection.

He inhaled sharply.

She continued stroking him and gazed into his eyes as she said, "Making love in a shower, for real, can be even more wonderful than in a fantasy, Joe. Shall we try it?"

"Oh, hell, no. Not ever. No way."

She laughed.

"Medea," he moaned and pulled her into his arms. They embraced and kissed, their nakedness pressing together, their tongues touching, his hands exploring.

She pulled back and looked into his eyes. "I know that you would like to have all we had before."

"But I know it is not allowed," he replied. "I have not forgotten."

She turned the shower's hot water on full. "Do you like it steaming? Or merely hot?"

"Which do you prefer? No, don't answer. I think I can guess."

She added some cold water to the flow to adjust the temperature, but not much. Steam billowed. She stepped into the shower and, smiling, held out her hand to him. "If it is too hot for you, tell me."

He climbed into the shower with her. And it *was* too hot. But he did not complain, and soon he did not care.

43

Going Too Far

"Medea," he panted. He laughed. "I forgot to tell you. The water's too hot."

"Joe," she kissed him, "how could you forget something like that? Did something . . . distract you?"

His climax of passion subsiding, the steaming hot water spraying from the showerhead now felt decidedly uncomfortable. Medea's skin was red from the heat and so was his. And the steam-drenched air was threatening to choke him. But still, he remained reluctant to leave the circle of her arms, to abandon the feel of her wet nakedness pressed against his.

She broke the embrace and turned off the water. "Better?"

"In some ways, but not in others."

She kissed him. "We shall towel each other dry, then I will show you . . . other things."

"Yeah?"

"Yeah," she mimicked and kissed him once more.

She stepped out of the shower and he followed. She handed him a towel. Took another herself. But the heat from the shower left them both still sweating after they were finished drying.

Skin glistening with moisture, Medea pulled the bedcovers onto the floor, leaving only the sheet covering the mattress. Then she climbed into bed and knelt on one side. She beckoned to Joe. "Stretch out, face up."

He did as asked.

"Do not move."

"What are you going to do?"

"Awaken parts of you that have long been asleep."

"One part of me is already awakening."

"And I approve," she smiled, looking down at him, "though that particular part has not been asleep very long. I hope what I am going to do will not make you drowsy, Joe, because afterward I would not mind having sex with you again, but in yet another way."

"I would not mind, either, to put it mildly. And if I get drowsy while in bed, naked with you, then I don't deserve what I don't get anyway."

"As you say."

He looked up at her and said, "You are just so unbelievably beautiful."

"Yet, if you did not believe it, it would not be so. Each person sees something different when they gaze upon me."

"You're . . . no, of course you're not kidding."

"But what Empusae see when they look at me is closer to the truth than what non-initiates see."

"What do you really look like, then?"

"Even I do not know that, anymore. You will understand, in time. And I will now take you a little way farther down the path to understanding, if you are ready?"

"Okay. Sure."

"When you were initiated, you saw the Triple Hecate first with the heads of beasts, then as you were reborn you saw a more humanized form of Her reality. What I wish to do for you now is to awaken memories of the most distant lives in which your life-path crossed Hers. With those memories will come the awakening of Empusaen knowledge you can be trained to use once again. Close your eyes now, breathe deeply, and try to relax. I will do the rest."

He closed his eyes.

"Keep them closed." She leaned down and kissed his lips.

He opened his eyes.

"Eyes *closed.*"

"Yeah." He closed his eyes again.

Medea leaned close to his left ear and began whispering a chant. She repeated the cycle of foreign words, again and again, until it sounded to Joe as if the syllables were flowing together, producing a murmur of gentle sound that soon seemed to become the restful gurgling of a stream.

Behind the darkness of his closed eyelids, Joe listened to the pleasantly transformed sound of Medea's chanting and waited for something to happen. From what she had said, he expected a new vision of the Triple Hecate. But instead, when the change came, it was so subtle that at first he did not notice anything was different.

He was still lying in darkness, and the peaceful gurgling sound was still close at hand. But then he noticed a bright point of light, then another and another, until he finally recognized them for what they were. Stars. Overhead. In a clear night sky. And, turning his head to one side, he saw that nearby, all but invisible in the faint starlight, flowed the gentle darkness of a narrow stream.

"Medea?" he called, but a sound like the chittering of a small beast came out of his mouth instead of her name. Then, nearby, he heard a low growl. An image of a shaggy, four-legged predator flashed into his mind.

Terrified, heart hammering, he sat up and looked around, straining to see in the dark. He noticed but felt no need to be concerned that his body was covered with fur.

The growl came again, nearer. Then he heard the soft sound of padded feet running toward him and a moment later through the near-total darkness he glimpsed a huge form leaping toward him.

He screamed a bestial cry of fright and without thinking threw himself to one side, into the stream.

He sank beneath the surface, felt himself caught in a cold and powerful current and was swept even deeper.

He fought to reach air even as he listened to make certain nothing else had splashed into the stream after him.

When he broke the surface, he coughed and sputtered, gasping for air. But his surroundings had changed.

It was no longer night, the stream had become an ocean, and there was no land anywhere in sight.

No clouds floated in the sky. He saw no birds. There was only him and the water. The endless water. Warm and salty. Like blood. The ancient Mother Ocean where Life on Earth had begun. Where—

Something grabbed him and pulled him under.

He fought to get free as he was swiftly dragged deeper and deeper, and he tried to see what was pulling him down but the water suddenly became as dark as night. As Death. Then instead of being pulled through water he was falling through the blackness of infinite space.

Falling and falling and . . .

"Joe? Return to me, Joe. You are going too far."

He heard the woman's voice. Tried to remember her name. Tried to comprehend the meaning of the words she had spoken. And then he remembered and comprehended and was no longer falling.

He felt the hotel bed beneath him again. "May I open my eyes?"

"Yes."

"You look worried, Medea."

"You are all right?"

"You tell me. But yeah, I think so. What did you mean that I was going too far?"

"I did not suspect your consciousness, your soul, was that old."

"And how old is that?"

"At least as old as I am, maybe older."

"Really?"

"Your memories were taking you back to pre-human points where I could not monitor and control them. But even so, your trip into your distant lives did you no harm, and certain areas of your Empusaen memories will have been awakened without your conscious knowledge. You will now know even more things without knowing how you know them than you knew before, yes?"

"If you say so. You say you monitored what I was seeing?"

"Of course."

"I didn't care much for that part about the beast attacking me. Nor when the thing I couldn't see drug me beneath the ocean. What was all that about, anyway?"

"Memories of deaths in ancient incarnations."

"Oh. No wonder I didn't like them. But I did not see Hecate."

She smiled. "Are you certain?"

"Not that I remember."

"More accurately, not that you consciously recognized. One of Her aspects is that of a Death Goddess, and you saw visions of ancient deaths, did you not?"

"According to you."

"Would the image of a huge predator leaping out of the darkness to engulf you not be an appropriate image of Death? Even today? But perhaps instead of a beast, a car driven by an intoxicated driver swerving into your lane? Or being suddenly pulled under the ocean by some powerful, unseen thing . . . not unlike a disease that eats you from the inside without pain, until it is too late to stop it. Yes?"

"Remind me to talk to you the next time I'm feeling too cheerful."

She laughed. "But you also felt the ancient life-giving power of Mother Ocean. Was the feeling of Her power that different from what you felt when Hecate gave you new life during your initiation?"

"I guess I see what you mean."

"Good. But now, perhaps you need something to take your mind off your unpleasant memories, if you have not become too . . . drowsy?"

"Do I look too drowsy?"

She smiled and reached out to touch him. "No."

He sat up and moved to embrace her. They kissed.

"I did not know who you were at first," he told her, "when you called to me. I did not think I would ever fail to recognize your voice."

"The modern you did not forget. It was an earlier self who did not remember, because knowing me had not yet happened. See?"

"Yeah."

"And now, let us try something different. If you will turn around, I have something with which to surprise you."

"I do not think I need any more surprises today, if you don't mind."

"I do not think you will mind *this* surprise, Joe. Turn around."

So he did. And he didn't mind what she did. Didn't mind it at all.

44

Team Toxique

Toxique surveyed her first five soldiers.

She had phased them into a safe and private place, the darkened dealers' room, locked and secured for the night.

Toxique's radioactive glow illuminated their immediate surroundings, tables that held boxes of collectors comics.

She was pleased with herself. Five thought forms had been given flesh, five warriors ready to fight by her side. And, thanks to her power to manipulate the structures and relationships between matter and energy, each soldier now possessed an approximation of the superhero or mutant powers their hosts had imagined.

The first of her soldiers, Squeegeeman, was stunningly handsome in his red superhero uniform. With his dimensional black hole vortex powers of selective absorption, he stood ready to sap the strength of Toxique's foes. But Toxique's mental powers revealed to her that Squeegeeman's thoughts were, at the moment, less concerned with fighting Evil than making time with the second of the warriors she had created.

The second was Lionessa. Gone was the host's weak flesh, replaced by a sleek, strong body covered by golden fur. Toxique's mental probings discovered that Lionessa was imagining how wonderful it would be to use her razored claws to rip out Squeegeeman's macho throat.

"Lionessa," Toxique said, "remember that we are a team. We do not harm each other. We do not even think about it. Understood?"

Lionessa hissed at Squeegeeman before bowing her head in Toxique's direction and speaking-growling, "Yes, Mother Toxique."

Toxique turned her attention to the third soldier in her army. No more was he a psychologically abused child seeking refuge in fantasies of violent revenge. He was now the Fabulous Fixitboy, stunning in his neon-steel overalls, lounging with one arm resting on his mutant toolbox. His thoughts pleased Toxique, daydreams about fixing evil doers with nuclear nails and scream-screws.

The fourth thought form she had enfleshed was Jumbo Lad, no longer an overstressed and balding computer programmer but now lethally large in straining-at-the-seams yellow tights. As he lumbered to and fro, mumbling softly to himself, his thoughts told Toxique he was interested in only one thing, crushing the life from any who stood in her way.

But the fifth physicalized thought form was, to Toxique's mind, the most wondrous. The host had appeared so innocent, so harmless. Yet from within the young woman had come a nightmare thought form with the secret name of Deathdrool. Glossy black, chaotically asymmetrical, she crouched tensely low to the floor, hungry to attack and kill, her nine eyes scanning in all directions for enemies, her deadly venom-thorns sparkling like jewels upon her multiple limbs.

"I am proud of you all," Toxique told them. "Soon, I will make more soldiers until we are an army large enough to ensure an absolute victory against the Army of Evil that has overrun the world. But before I make more warriors, I deem us strong enough to embark on our first mission.

"A man named Joe, who means a great deal to me, is in grave danger. But Team Toxique is going to rescue him, and in so doing we will rid the world of a hideously evil Witch!"

45

Alarm

After having sex with Medea in a variety of creative ways
until nearly dawn, and after she had assured him she would
make certain his dreams created no more thought forms
while he slept, Joe allowed himself to gratefully fall into a
steep-walled chasm of sleep. But less than one hour later the
shrill sound of the hotel's fire alarm drilled him awake.

As he struggled to tear himself free from the claws of
restful oblivion, his sleep-clogged mind decided that the
smoke alarm in his apartment was sounding. Heart hammering in his chest, he fumbled in the dark for his bedside
light, could not find it, got out of bed and hurried two steps
in the direction his bedroom door should have been before
his right foot struck the sharp-edged leg of a wooden chair.

He cried out with pain, staggered backwards, fell onto the
bed.

Light! Who had turned on the lights? Who was with him
in his—

Reality dawned.

Medea.

The hotel.

A fire alarm.

And they were on the twenty-seventh floor!

They had to get to the stairs! They had to get dressed and get to the stairs!

"There is no fire, Joe."

"What? But—"

"I would know. I will try to determine why the alarm was turned on. But it was *not* because of a fire. Is your foot badly injured?"

He sat shielding his eyes from the light with one hand, holding his throbbing foot with the other. "I don't know." He squinted down at his toes and wiggled them. "My toes move okay. And there's no blood. I guess it's not serious. Hurts like hell, though. Damn!" The alarm was still sounding. "You're certain there's no fire?"

"Absolutely. While I determine why the alarm was activated, see if you can walk on your foot, in case we have to leave the room for a reason other than fire."

"What other reason?"

"That is what I am about to discover."

He stood up and cautiously tried putting weight on his foot. "It seems okay. Still hurts, though. But not as bad now—"

He suddenly realized he was standing naked in front of her. He blushed. Then felt silly, because to blush after all they had done together was ridiculous. But he then saw that she was *not* looking and felt slightly disappointed.

She had her eyes closed, concentrating, using her mental powers.

As the fire alarm continued, he could also hear people talking excitedly in the adjoining rooms and in the hallway. Doors slammed. People ran down the corridor toward the stairs.

He felt he needed to do something. He decided he should get dressed.

He limped to his backpack and searched inside for the

undershorts he had packed, found them, pulled them on, slipped on a *Steroid Boy* T-shirt, and was reaching for a pair of clean socks when Medea opened her eyes and said, "Why are you dressing? The only problem is that some young people have turned on a fire alarm as a joke."

He stopped dressing. "Oh."

"Who might *Steroid Boy* be?" Medea asked, eyeing his T-shirt. "I am certain I have never heard Nick mention that particular character. It is a humorous drawing, though."

"And it's a great comic, I've heard. I've also heard that it is almost impossible to find the earliest issues. I haven't seen any of the later issues, either, but they're all worth lots of money, I guess."

"So, you have never actually seen one of these *Steroid Boy* comics?"

"That's right. I haven't."

"But still you wear a T-shirt that advertises it?"

"I wouldn't call it advertising."

"What would you call it?"

"Just a T-shirt, I guess."

"What if you did see an issue and hated it? Would you still wear the T-shirt?"

"Sure. Maybe."

"And what if I told you I wanted you to take the T-shirt off?"

"But . . . why?"

She laughed. "I might have another surprise to give you, in bed."

He dropped the socks, took off the T-shirt and the shorts, and hurried back to bed.

"Your foot is better now?"

"Much." The alarm was still sounding and he could still hear people hurrying to the exit stairs. "But I'm still a little worried about that fire alarm."

"You do not trust my telepathic abilities?"

"It's not that. I guess it's just habit. You know, when you hear a fire alarm, you get the hell out of the building. Started teaching us that in grade school. Hard to shake the feeling I'm not being really stupid, sitting here naked in bed while the hotel burns."

"It will soon be quieter," she assured him. She kissed him. "And now, about that surprise . . ."

Several kisses later she said, "See, Joe? Or rather, hear? Everyone has fled and it is now quiet, except for the alarm. And someone will turn it off soon."

"I don't seem to care as much now, anyway."

She kissed his forehead, his lips, moved down to his chest, teased first one nipple then the other, while Joe noticed, through half-closed eyes, that the door to the room had begun to glow with a greenish light.

He opened his eyes fully, hoping to find the glowing was a trick of the light or his eyes. But then the light, a column of hovering luminescence, suddenly moved *through* the door and into the room.

"Medea!" Joe cried, and he pointed. "Look!" But before she could turn and look the column of green light became a skeleton glowing within a woman's transparent flesh.

46

Attack

From the glowing skeleton a woman's laughter emerged to mix with the continuing shrill of the fire alarm.

Joe said, stammering slightly, "Toxique?"

"It can't be," Medea responded. "I destroyed—"

"I let you *think* you'd destroyed me, Witch," said Toxique. "But here I stand now, *in the flesh!*" She laughed again, then, hands on her hips. She stopped her skeleton from glowing and became a duplicate of Medea, except that she was wearing a tight black leather bodysuit with a melting green skull on her chest. Her lethal-touch hands she had left bare, but she had created low-heeled, knee-high, black leather boots for her feet. It was an outfit familiar to Joe. He had imagined it often enough.

Toxique pointed the index finger of her right hand at the door. "We are alone on the floor now, Joe, except for five of my soldiers, waiting to help me rescue you. I could phase them through, but to demonstrate what will soon happen to your Witch, I choose to open the door . . . like this!"

She became a glowing skeleton again, then a pencil-thin beam of greenish radiation shot from her finger and vaporized the door. She next pointed her finger at Medea and said, "Move away from her, lover."

Without thinking Joe moved fast and placed himself between Medea and Toxique's pointing finger. "No! Toxique, I don't know how you can be here like this, but I *do* know you are *not* going to hurt Medea!"

"My poor love, she has so twisted your mind. But when I have destroyed her body and soul, your thoughts will clear." Still pointing her finger at Medea, and therefore also at Joe, Toxique turned her head toward the door and called, "To my side Team Toxique! Now!"

Through the doorless doorway rushed what looked to Joe like five refugees from a comic book convention's masquerade contest.

First came a muscleman in red tights, followed by a boy carrying a glowing toolbox, a cat-like woman covered in fur, a spiderish black thing with thorns on its multiple limbs, and a blob of a man wearing green and pink spandex.

"And now—" Toxique began, looking back at Joe, then, "No! Where is she?"

Joe jerked his head to the side and glanced behind him. Medea was no longer visible.

"Lionessa! Find her by her scent! She is blocking her thoughts from me. Don't let her get away! Find her, or I'll—"

Suddenly Toxique and her five soldiers were flung backwards as if all had been struck an invisible blow.

Toxique collided with the bolted-to-the-floor hotel TV, crying out, losing her balance, and sprawling onto the carpet. She stopped glowing.

The lion-woman and the boy with the toolbox recovered first. The lion-woman, crouching low, growled and sniffed the air as the boy reached into his toolbox. The muscleman was regaining his balance when something lifted him into the air and threw him at Toxique, who was almost back on her feet.

Toxique yelled a cry of rage and went down beneath the bulk of the muscleman.

The blob in green and pink spandex was still struggling to get back onto his feet, but the boy pulled a nail-gun from his toolbox. "Where is she, Lionessa?" he asked, but the gun was suddenly knocked from his hand and he was thrown toward the muscleman-Toxique heap.

"I've got her scent!" growled the lion-woman as she leaped, claws poised to kill.

"Medea!" Joe cried. He scrambled forward over the bed toward the pouncing lion-woman, but he was only halfway there when a scream sliced the air and warm blood sprayed his face.

The lion-woman was thrown over the bed, hit the wall on the far side, crumpled to the floor, spasming, a fountain of pulsing blood erupting from her savagely torn throat.

Joe looked at the fallen attacker in astonishment. Had Medea done *that?* She must have, but—

"No!" cried Toxique, again on her feet and again glowing. "Block the door, Jumbo Lad!"

The blob in green and pink spandex obeyed Toxique and blocked the door, but only for a moment, as suddenly the spandex covering his huge belly was peeled back and with it the flesh and layers of yellowish fat beneath.

Jumbo Lad's blood and entrails poured onto the floor as he cried out in mortal pain and fell.

"Don't let her get away!" Toxique shouted. "Catch her!"

The boy grabbed his nail gun as he and the muscleman and the spider-thing hurried through the doorway, but there they hesitated, looking uncertainly one way then the other.

Toxique shouted. "Go different directions! She can't use the elevators with the alarm on! Don't let her reach the stairs!"

The man and boy went one way, the spider creature the

other, leaving Joe alone with Toxique and her two dying soldiers.

Toxique ran to the lion-woman and knelt down. "You will be avenged, Lionessa! And you, Jumbo Lad! This I vow!" She looked at Joe. "Do you see now what a monster she is? The Witch has shown her true nature at last. She is *Evil Incarnate* and must be destroyed!"

Memories of Empusaen shapeshifters flashed through Joe's mind. Clawed and fanged berserkers. More deadly than the wild beasts they resembled . . .

Was that what Medea had become to fight the attackers? The wounds he had seen inflicted said yes, but his rational mind wanted to deny it. He could not imagine her beauty distorted into the hideous shape of the monsters in his awakened memories.

"My poor love!" Toxique said. "From your thoughts I know you understand what a beast the Witch is at heart, but she has so twisted your mind, that you—"

A scream that was only marginally human came from the hallway.

Toxique turned and shouted, "No! She's killed Death-drool, too! I should have gone with them! Stay here, Joe."

She jumped over Jumbo Lad's still-spasming body and into the hallway. "Back this way! Hurry!" She motioned impatiently, then ran in the direction the spider-thing had gone. A moment later, Joe saw the muscleman and the boy run past the door after her.

A death-wheeze bubbled from the lion-woman's fanged mouth as she slumped into death even as the blob in spandex stopped spasming, also dead.

Joe was sickened by the sight of the two flesh-torn corpses and the cooling blood staining his naked flesh, and even more by the knowledge that Medea was responsible.

He felt a scream building inside him, held it back, tried to think of what he should do. Escape. Yes. Of course!

He grabbed a pillow and hurriedly wiped the worst of the blood from his face and chest then jumped out of bed and ran to his backpack and clothes.

A male scream of pain came from down the hallway, followed by another cry of rage from Toxique.

Joe jerked on his jeans and pulled his black *Steroid Boy* T-shirt over his head.

As Joe pulled on his socks, a high-pitched cry of pain came from the hall. He thought at first it must have been Toxique, but hearing her shout a new promise of vengeance a moment later he realized Medea must have killed the boy.

Given the legend of child killing associated with Medea, the thought of her killing the child chilled Joe deeply. *Had* she been lying all along? Twisting his mind as Toxique said?

No. She had helped the children in the hotel earlier, he reminded himself. The boy had been attacking her. She must have had no choice. But still—

He pushed back the thoughts, finished dressing, headed for the door. But too late.

Toxique appeared in the doorway, covered in blood. But not hers. Joe saw no wounds. The blood was from her slain soldiers.

"I will destroy her yet!" Toxique told him. "Come." She held out her hand. "We must hurry. I will take you to a safe place while I make more soldiers and—"

Toxique's head was suddenly jerked halfway around, accompanied by a sharp snapping sound.

Toxique fell backwards from the doorway and lay unmoving. Then, at the doorway, appeared Medea. Human in form. Her nakedness stained crimson by the blood of those she had slain.

There was an ugly burn-wound spanning her bare stomach.

She slumped against the doorway.

"Joe . . . help me . . . I—"

Then she fell across Toxique's corpse and also lay still.

47
Killer

Joe rushed to Medea, pulled her off Toxique, looked up and down the hall, afraid someone would appear and see him there.

At a bend in the hall he saw the body of the boy, but the child's head was missing. Blood stained the carpet and streaked the walls near the small corpse.

He looked down at Medea, a killer of six people! Or, rather, six living beings. Of some sort. But the *way* she had killed . . .

Repulsed and overwhelmed by the violence he had witnessed, he felt panic crashing down, had to fight a desperate urge to run for the stairs, to get out of the building and keep running and never look back.

He wanted the day never to have happened. He wanted to be in his apartment doing something mundane like watching an old movie on TV, reading a comic, studying for an exam, cleaning the bathroom . . . *anything!*

The shrill fire alarm was now a comfort. As long as it was sounding, the guests would not be returning to the floor. He assumed. But what about others? Firefighters? Police?

Would firefighters come if, as Medea had said, there was

no fire? But the police . . . wouldn't they come in the case of a false alarm? He didn't know.

It was probable that Toxique had started the alarm to clear the floor, so for all he knew the alarm would be traced there and the police or fire department or hotel security might come rushing onto the floor at any moment and catch him there.

But he hadn't done anything wrong! He could explain—

Sure, he thought, *explain by telling the truth about Toxique? And her soldiers? And how Medea had become invisible and then turned into some kind of murdering beast?*

His panic grow. There was no way out. He was going to be caught. And put in jail. Maybe executed for murder. So, he had to get away! Go back into the room and grab his backpack and get the hell out before—

But what about Medea? He couldn't leave her there. He had to save her, too. She had asked for his help before she collapsed, and if she hadn't killed Toxique and the others, he would have been at Toxique's mercy.

The thought horrified him.

Toxique, no longer a fantasy but *in the flesh,* had seemed terror incarnate to him. The *otherness* of her presence, the horrifying power she had possessed, the helplessness he would have felt as her prisoner, never knowing when something he did might anger her enough to make her turn her powers on him.

But worse, he had created her *as his lover,* and he would have had to do whatever she wanted, anything . . .

Yeah, he owed Medea, big time, for saving his ass from Toxique, a monster who had now attacked Medea *twice* and Goddess knew who else.

His creation.

His responsibility.

His guilt.

He looked at the red and swollen blister-burn that now marred the bare skin of Medea's stomach. Had one of Toxique's radiation beams grazed her?

It didn't matter at the moment. He had to grab some clothes for her and then carry her down the stairs, all twenty-seven floors of them, then somehow get her to his car without anyone stopping him, and find help, one of the other Empusae. Somehow—

"Take me to . . . the bed . . ."

"Medea?" She still had not opened her eyes.

"The bed . . ."

With another worried look down the corridor, Joe bent low, put his arms under Medea, and hurriedly carried her back into the room of death.

48

Transfer

He placed Medea on the blood-splattered bed. "What now?" he asked.

There was no response.

He was sickened by the sight of the the blood that stained her skin. "Medea?"

Still no response.

He rushed to the bathroom and wet two washcloths and grabbed a couple of towels still damp from their shower.

He hurried back to the bed, used the washcloths to quickly wipe away the worst of the blood, starting with her face and working down, careful to avoid the burn on her stomach.

"Medea?" he called again. He glanced at the doorless doorway, worried a policeman or fireman might appear there at any moment. "Please, wake up!"

I should call an ambulance, he thought. *She could be dying!*

"No . . ." Medea groaned. "No . . . ambulance. No police. I need life . . . energy . . . transferred . . ." Her breathing, like her words, came in short, panted gasps. "Will you give energy . . . to me . . . please . . . Joe?"

"Of course. I guess. But I don't know—"

"You do . . . know. Reach into your new . . . memories for the way to . . . transfer energy . . ."

Glancing at the doorway again, he searched for the memory, the knowledge of how to transfer life-energy. But he could not find it.

"Please . . . Joe . . . hurry . . . I need . . . strength so that . . . we can get . . . away. Remember what . . . the others did to . . . help me . . . earlier . . ."

He tried again. A deep memory finally surfaced.

"Okay. I think I've got it."

"Please . . . hurry . . ."

"Yeah."

He placed his left hand over Medea's solar plexus, then his right hand over his left. He took another quick look at the doorway, again felt glad the fire alarm was still sounding, then closed his eyes and concentrated on doing what the awakened memory said he must.

He imagined life-energy, glowing an electric blue, swirling within his body. He imagined that energy streaming from his hands into Medea, and he began to feel a pull, not physical, but mental, emotional, *psychic*, drawing him closer and closer to her, a merging of their consciousnesses, a blending of their essences. A touching of souls.

"Yes . . . Joe . . ." he heard her say. "Good . . . yes, yes . . ."

He heard her voice, but it sounded muffled by distance. He could no longer hear the fire alarm at all. Had it stopped?

He no longer cared as . . . time stretched then became unimportant . . . as Joe's life-energy continued streaming into Medea . . . and the feeling it gave him . . . so wonderful . . . infinite . . . eternal . . .

"Enough, Joe. Stop."

It was difficult to stop. He wanted the feeling of being one with her to continue forever. He was becoming weaker by the moment, but he did not care—

"Enough!"

The urgency in her voice jarred him. He forced himself to stop imagining the transfer and raised his hands from her solar plexus. He opened his eyes. His vision was blurred. He tried to focus. Failed.

He noticed that the fire alarm *was* still sounding.

Medea sat up.

"Breathe slowly and deeply, Joe," she said. "Your strength will slowly return. I will hurry and dress." She stepped out of bed. He heard her moan.

"Are you . . . okay?"

"The wound on my stomach is quite painful." She reached for her clothing.

"Did Toxique do it? Give you that burn?"

"No. The spider creature scratched me with a thorn on one of its legs. The thorns secreted some type of acid. I must wear something that rubs the wound as little as possible."

Though his vision was still blurred, he saw her slip a long, free-flowing black gown over her head. It reached to her ankles.

He tried to stand up. His legs felt boneless. He slumped back onto the bed. Dizzy, suddenly nauseous, his head pounded with pain.

"Breathe slowly and deeply," she repeated.

He did. His nausea receded, his vision began to clear.

She sat on the edge of the bed and hurriedly pulled on her boots. She stood and grabbed his backpack, looked around and found the *Scimidar* T-shirt and socks and undershorts he had earlier been wearing, all of them splattered with blood, and stuffed them all into his also blood-splattered backpack.

She slipped one of the backpack's straps over her shoulder. "It is best for you if we leave nothing of yours here to be found. Only my Empusae know you were spending the night with me, and they will not tell. Toxique looks like me, so the authorities will think I am dead. I will have Nick identify her as me. And although the room is registered in Nick's name, he has an alibi all night with Jim. So, we will leave the police a fascinating mystery, yes?"

"That's an understatement."

"We must go. Take my hand. I will help you stand. Try not to step in any of the blood. We do not want tracks leading down to the stairs and beyond."

He let her help him. He swayed on his feet.

"Lean on me, Joe."

Half walking, half stumbling, leaning on Medea, he made it over the cooling corpse of the blob-man in spandex and into the hall, then past the corpse of Toxique, and down the corridor toward the headless corpse of the boy.

"How did she . . . do it?" he asked, panting from the exertion of walking. He did not look at the boy's corpse as they passed it. He stepped over a patch of crimson-soaked carpet. "Toxique, I . . . mean. How did she . . . become flesh?"

"It began by her following the killer of children into the Gray Between. I know this from touching her thoughts during the battle just past. She then stole occult knowledge from me during our first battle and tricked me into thinking I had dispersed her thought form, and into thinking she had only wanted my energy and knowledge and flesh. She next used certain knowledge stolen from me to follow the killer's flesh-link back to his physical body. Once enfleshed, she combined occult knowledge with the powers of atomic mutation you had imagined her to possess in order to reform and reanimate the killer's flesh for her own use. After that, she killed the men in charge of taking the killer's corpse to the morgue. Later, she killed the editors who had turned down your comic book about her, and others she judged to be Evil."

"And I caused it all. If I had never dreamed her up—"

"You did not know what you were doing. And the blame is as much mine as yours, allowing her to trick me. Goddess! She even used my knowledge to find a way to destroy the *souls* of those she killed."

"Hey, I'll try not to feel guilty if you'll do the same."

"Are you feeling any stronger?"

"A little. What about the ones with her?"

"She found a way to use the flesh of people she killed to house the thought forms that those people had created. You knew one of them. Did you not notice that the muscleman had *Squeegee!* on his chest?"

"Jeff Brewer? My creation killed Jeff?"

"Toxique in the flesh was as much my creation as yours."

"And *neither* of us are going to feel too guilty, which is about as likely as a snowball in Hell."

"But in some versions of Hell, the Norse for example, it is a realm of ice, not fire."

"I read something about that in one of Jim's books, I think."

"Here are the stairs."

9
Hero

"My strength is coming back pretty fast now," Joe said. "I think I can make it without leaning on you. Let me try."

They were on the third floor landing, heading down on the exit stairs. Medea took her arm from around him.

He cautiously took one step away from her. His legs felt steady. "Yeah, I thought so. I'm still a little weak, but I'll hold on to the rail." He started down the stairs again. "See?"

As they passed the second floor landing, the fire alarm suddenly stopped.

They hurried to the bottom of the stairs.

Medea said, "Put an arm around my shoulders and stay in physical contact with me. I am going to cover you with my invisibility effect, so that we may get to your car unseen. When we are outside, do not speak if anyone is near us, do not touch anyone we pass, and make as little noise as possible with your footsteps, yes?"

"Yeah. Okay."

Outside, the sky was bright with the coming dawn.

Two fire trucks were parked at the main entrance. A crowd of people, guests and hotel employees, stood a safe distance away, spread along the edge of the parking lot.

"Good," Medea said, "no one is near. Your car is to the left, yes?"

"I was going to tell you, but I figured you could read it from my thoughts."

"You are learning to think like an Empusa."

"Guess I'd better."

After they had walked a few steps, he said, "Amazing. I can still see you, but no one in the crowd is looking at us. We're really invisible to them."

"Not invisible in a physical way, of course. It is merely a matter of telepathically diverting their attention in a special manner."

"Merely."

"Unfortunately, few Empusae master the technique. For most, the skill takes more than a single lifetime of practice to acquire."

"How many lifetimes did it take you?"

"I was in my late thirties, or perhaps my early forties, when I first learned of the technique's existence. That was at a secret occult school in the mountains of the land to the west of what you now call the Black Sea. There are memories in your mind about it, but those memories have yet to be awakened."

"But the Black Sea is where your home was, right?"

"The island of Colchis. Yes. And the mountains later became known as the border between Transylvania and Wallachia."

"Dracula country?"

"Not until many centuries later, after the Usurper twisted the school's teachings to trick seekers into his service."

"The usurper?"

"Satan."

"Satan? You mean—"

"Quiet the questions in your mind. Those things are not

important at the moment. You asked how long it took me to learn the invisibility effect. I assume you still wish that answer, yes?"

"Yeah."

"Very well. If this body was approximately forty years of age when I was at that school, and if I perfected the technique during the reign of that ugly hedonist—"

"Who's that?"

"You would not know his name. I made certain history took little note of him. So, if it was during that petty monster's reign, then it took me . . . I would say approximately one hundred and fifty years, give or take."

"Give or take."

"But at least another fifty before I could depend on the effect when needed for survival. Your car could use a wash."

They were nearing his aging blue Ford. "And a wax. Thanks for noticing. Where are we going?"

"Into your car."

"I guessed that. But then?"

"We will sit in your car until the others arrive."

"The others? Oh, of course. You called to the other Empusae?"

"Yes."

"But, if Toxique and her brood are dead, why call for help now?"

"I called to them mentally *during* the battle."

"Oh. But now—"

"We will go somewhere and have breakfast and I will tell them what has happened. Later, we can return to the hotel and Nick will have to act the part of a shocked and distraught man whose lover has been brutally and mysteriously killed. Later, I will go unseen to watch the autopsies on Toxique and her creations. It should prove rather interesting."

They reached his car. He took his car keys from a pocket in his jeans.

She said, "Do not break contact with me, not even in the car. We can hold hands. And we should use the other door, away from the crowd, to get in."

They walked around the car to the far side, Joe unlocked the door, and they climbed inside.

50

Saved

Joe and Medea were sitting in the front seat of Joe's car, holding hands, invisible to any who might look their way.

A well-read copy of the previous week's *Dallas Observer* was on the seat between them. Holding Medea's left hand with his right, Joe reached over with his left and tossed the newspaper in the back, where it joined a couple of text books and several empty comic book sacks on the back seat.

On the floor near Medea's feet was a paperback book. With her free hand she reached down, picked it up, and placed it on the seat between them. It was a novel that purported to be a new version of the Frankenstein legend.

"Victor Frankenstein was not as brilliant as many think," Medea said, tossing the book in the back. "His so-called monster was the true genius of the pair."

"I never know when you are joking."

"Joking?"

"Frankenstein was merely a fictional character, right?"

She raised an eyebrow. "Many think that of me."

He decided not to pursue it just then. Instead, he asked, "How long do you think it'll be before the others get here?"

She shrugged. "Not much longer, at least for Jim and Nick." She squeezed his hand. "I am proud of you, Joe. You did well during the crisis. And your strength came back sooner than I had expected. You gave me a good deal more life-energy than I had intended."

"Near the end of it, I didn't want it to stop. The transfer. I felt so . . . close to you."

"And I to you." She gave his hand another squeeze.

"I was . . . repulsed by the way you killed those six people, or creatures, whatever they were. But after the transfer, there was no repulsion possible, no matter what kind of beast-form you might occasionally take."

"I am glad."

"The energy transfer . . . I don't understand about it completely. I found the memory of how to do it, but the reason it was needed . . . it's more than just because you were exhausted from the battle, isn't it?"

"Yes. It is related to the cyclical rituals of renewal I must perform to remain alive in this body. You will understand better later."

"After more memories awaken?"

"And after I have told you things you have never known before. More important at the moment is that you almost certainly saved my life. You will be well rewarded."

"Hey, you saved me first, remember? From Toxique."

"I saved myself, Joe. Not you."

"But you came back to the room. You could have gotten away."

"And left that monster free to track me down again? After I had killed her companions, I projected thoughts that made her think I was going to run, then I followed her back to the room and used surprise to finish it. I am, of course, glad that the result also benefited you."

"You're saying you *would* have left me there?"

"If escaping would have been the best way to save myself, yes."

"Which, I guess, means I'm what is called 'expendable'?"

"I want no harm to come to you, Joe. But my own survival has to come first. The knowledge I have accumulated, the work of the Goddess I must continue to do, all makes my own survival my prime responsibility in times of danger."

"Well, it makes good, practical sense. Not very heroic, but—"

"Heroes often die. But I am grateful that you were a hero for me today. While I was unconscious, I was still able to reach out and know your thoughts. I know you felt like running away. I knew you were repulsed by the things I had to do during the battle. I will only say this in my defense. Toxique's thoughts told me that she hoped to kill me not quickly, but slowly and painfully. She wanted revenge for my taking you from her. She would have tortured me mercilessly."

He remembered the burn on her stomach. "Is your stomach still hurting? Dumb question. Is it hurting as much as it was?"

"I suppose it is, but at the moment I am successfully ignoring the worst of the pain. There is a police siren in the distance."

He did not hear the siren for a moment, then he did. His pulse rate jumped higher as he experienced a panicky feeling that the police were coming to arrest him. "I guess someone found the bodies."

"No. I am detecting no thoughts about that, yet. In fact," she closed her eyes for a moment, opened them, "that particular police car is not coming here at all."

The siren began to fade into the distance.

"See?"

Joe felt relief. The eastern sky was bright, the Sun almost up.

Saturday.

The biggest day of the comic book convention.

Maybe.

Joe said, "Talk about a doomed convention. I wonder how Mr. Dacobocon is doing? I wonder if he's going to shut it all down? I don't see how he can do anything else after they find those six new bodies on the twenty-seventh floor."

51

Unseen

"There they are," Joe said.

Moments before, Medea had told him Jim and Nick would soon be there. She said, "When Jim has stopped his car, keep hold of my hand and we will transfer unseen from your car to the back seat of Jim's."

"I suppose you sent them a message of some sort? So they will know we're out here but invisible, and what my car looks like?"

"They will see flashes of images of your car in their minds as they draw near."

"Images which you sent telepathically."

"The opportunity to use a telephone did not present itself."

"Yeah."

Joe saw Nick point at his Ford as Jim drove slowly past.

"It is time," Medea said.

She and Joe stepped out, holding hands, unseen.

Jim pulled his car to a stop in the nearest open parking space he could find. Nick got out as soon as Jim stopped. He hurried toward Joe's car.

"We are here," Medea said before Nick collided with them. "Go back to Jim's car. We will get in the back."

"We? Joe's with you?"

"Of course."

Nick turned and waved to Jim to stop. Jim had gotten out and was walking in their direction, too. Nick turned and walked back toward Jim's car. Medea let him walk slightly ahead to keep him in view and avoid collisions.

Nick asked, looking where he thought they were, "Are you both all right?"

Medea answered, "Yes."

Joe said, "Except that she has an acid burn on her stomach."

"What? How? Goddess, is it bad?"

She replied, "It is painful but far from lethal."

Nick continued, "I woke up from a dream about your having another battle with Toxique. And Jim had a dream about you fighting some kind of . . . monsters?"

"You both receive dream images well."

"But . . . Toxique?"

"In the flesh," Joe said.

"And the monsters?"

"Them too," Joe replied. "Toxique made them out of other thought forms somehow, Medea says. She found out while she was killing them."

"And then Joe saved my life," Medea added.

"What? Joe, we all owe you for that."

"Indeed," Medea agreed.

"All I did was give her some energy, like you and Jim did after we found her in the shower."

"But it did save my life."

Nick said, "We're grateful, Joe. Goddess, but we're grateful. I assume Bernice and Barbara and Trudy are also coming here, Medea?"

"I called to them too. Yes."

Jim was waiting outside his car. "What's going on?"

"They're going to get in the back," Nick told him.

"They? Medea and Joe? They're with you?"

"Yes."

Joe and Medea got in the back as Nick and Jim climbed in the front.

When the doors were closed, Medea said, "All right, Joe. You can release my hand now."

When he did, Joe became visible. Medea appeared a moment later. She handed him his backpack, which she had been carrying.

"So, what the hell's going on?" Jim asked. "I dreamed about you fighting monsters, Medea. And Nick dreamed—"

"I've already told them," Nick interrupted. "It *was* Toxique, in the flesh, and some monsters she had somehow created. But Medea killed them. Then Joe gave her energy and saved her life. Did I get it all right?" he asked, looking into the back.

"Sounds about right," Joe said. "But you forgot the—"

"Medea was wounded," Nick cut in. "An acid burn on her stomach."

Jim asked, "Should we get some kind of medical help? I know you do not normally have anything to do with doctors and hospitals, Medea, but—"

"It is not a lethal wound, Jim," Medea said.

"There's Trudy," Jim said, pointing at a large black motorcycle headed their way, fast, through the parking lot. Upon it rode a tall woman in tight black jeans, a black leather motorcycle jacket, and a black helmet.

"She's very proud of that Harley," Jim said. "Had it a long time."

Trudy was pulling to a stop nearby when Bernice's van entered the parking lot.

"Bernice has Barbara with her," Medea said. They saw a moment later that she was right. "We will all transfer to the van. Hold my hand again, Joe. You and I should still go unseen."

"People are headed back into the building now," Joe said. "I don't think anyone would notice us if we were visible. So, why—"

"Because I think it best, for now."

Joe shrugged. "Okay, but I don't see why—"

"If Medea thinks it's best," Nick cut in, "it's best."

"I don't doubt that."

"And you shouldn't," Jim said. "She bases her decisions upon a great many lifetimes of experience, and the acquired knowledge that goes with it."

"So," Nick said, "we have learned to accept her decisions without questioning them too much."

"But I *can* make mistakes," Medea said. "I thought Toxique had been destroyed in the Gray Between, for example."

Bernice was slowing as she neared Jim's car. Trudy was headed their way on foot. Joe saw her wave to Bernice and Barbara. Bernice stopped the van behind Jim's car.

"Now, into the van," Medea said.

They stepped out of Jim's car. "They're here with us," Nick said to Barbara, who had rolled down the window on her side of the van.

"Medea and Joe?" Barbara asked.

"Yeah," Jim replied.

"Are they okay?"

"Medea's wounded," Joe replied.

"But not seriously," Medea said.

Trudy had nearly reached them.

Medea said, "Trudy, we are going for a ride in Bernice's van."

52

Breakfast at Jim's

Jim convinced them to come to his house for breakfast, offering them blueberry oatbran muffins and an authentic Swiss-recipe muesli from a natural foods store. Or frozen waffles and doughnuts from a supermarket. And plenty of coffee.

In Jim's living room, a large wood carving over the fireplace caught Joe's eye. It had a bird of prey head with staring eyes and a sharp beak above an anchor-like shape covered with spirals and interwoven, serpentine shapes. He recognized it as a Thor's Hammer.

Joe had become aware of Thor's Hammer medallions many years before in a comic book called *Arak*, set during the reign of Charlemagne. The Thor's Hammer worn by Arak was similar to the one on the wall above Jim's fireplace and to the one Jim wore around his neck.

On the mantel of the fireplace sat another carving. Joe also recognized its subject. During his initiation, he had seen Her himself. The Triple Goddess Hecate.

On each side of the carving of Hecate was placed a black iron candle holder of simple design, and in each candle holder was a red candle. Placed before the carving was a small brass incense burner.

But above Hecate and below the Thor's Hammer hung another carving that drew Joe's gaze and held it. He did not recognize the design, yet felt he had seen it before. And to his surprise, and embarrassment, looking at it suddenly brought tears to his eyes. A feeling he could only describe as homesickness and deep nostalgia crept through him, yet also joy at having found something long lost.

The carving was a flat circular piece of wood painted black with lines carved into it, the inscribed lines then painted silver.

The silver lines formed a symmetrical, serpentine, labyrinthian design that encompassed the circumference. In its center was another circle within which was centered a three-lobed design that resembled a whirling, three-spoked wheel.

The overall effect pulled Joe's gaze back again and again to the center, and as the blurring from his sudden tears began to clear, he felt within himself a quiet energy, a centeredness, a deep and strengthening peace.

He needed to know what the design was called, and he could almost remember . . .

Medea came to him and said, "It is called the Wheel of Hecate, a useful meditation device, especially when certain meditative techniques, which you will be taught, and others which you will in time remember, are employed. Each Empusa here has a Wheel, thanks to Jim. I am certain he will carve one for you, too."

"Jim carved it himself?"

"And the Thor's Hammer and the statue of Hecate. He also paints. I would like you to see some of his paintings. Come with me, please."

Leaving Nick and Barbara and Bernice in the living room, Joe followed Medea. As they passed the kitchen, where Jim and Trudy were preparing the food, Medea said, "Jim, I would like to show Joe your paintings, if it is all right with you?"

"Of course," Jim replied, waving with a fork to indicate they should go ahead.

Joe followed Medea to the bedroom. She turned on the lights to better illuminate the paintings. There were three of them, all of moderate size, all portraying a tall, muscular, mostly nude woman with long blond hair. And a spear. In one, she glowed as if afire with golden light, and in that painting she had white, swan-like wings.

Joe wondered if Trudy had posed for the pictures. The woman in the paintings did not have Trudy's face, but she was most certainly a bodybuilder, too.

Knowing his thoughts, Medea said, "Jim painted these long before he met Trudy. You have heard of the Viking belief in the nine spectral warrior women who choose which heroes are worthy of entering Valhalla?"

"Valkyries? Sure. I read a graphic novel version of Wagner's Ring Cycle a couple of years back, and I've seen Valkyries in issues of *Thor*. One of my favorite characters in *The New Mutants* when I was a kid stayed in Asgard and became a Valkyrie. But none of the ones I've seen looked like *this* one. I . . . uh, *would* have remembered."

"She is quite beautiful. Jim first met her when he was about your age, in the jungles of Viet Nam. She saved his life."

"Really? Was she a medic or something?"

Medea smiled. "She saved his life again years later while he and his friends were rescuing Bernice. She *is* a Valkyrie."

Joe looked at Medea. "You're not joking. A *real* Valkyrie?"

"Yes."

He looked back at the paintings. After a moment, he

laughed. "Well, why not? I mean, you're the real Medea, so why should a real Valkyrie surprise me?"

"Why, indeed."

"I'm becoming more excited about this Empusa business. Incredible things I thought were just myths are true, and there's so damned much waiting to be learned!"

"Yes. And I wanted you to see these paintings to impress upon you that Hecate's realm, Her reality, is only one of many. Empusae owe their loyalty and much of what they are to Hecate, but we cannot afford to be one-deity oriented. Knowledge is everywhere, and truth comes in many guises, and from many deities, yes? The Goddess Freya, the Valkyries' leader, is just as real as Hecate, see? Now, there is another painting I also wish to show you, in Jim's study."

In Jim's study, bookshelves lined three of the walls, and the shelves were stuffed full with books except in one place, behind Jim's writing desk and word processor, where a shelf held a bookshelf model CD/cassette/radio combo. The fourth wall, facing Jim's writing desk, was bare except for a single painting. The painting showed a naked woman, screaming, strapped into a metal chair studded with short spikes. In a cavity beneath the seat, hot coals glowed.

The woman's body, glistening with sweat, bore the ugly wounds of previous tortures, especially her lower legs, bleeding profusely, splintered shards of white bone poking through the broken skin over her kneecaps and shins.

Near her stood a figure in an Inquisitor's black robe, face hidden beneath an executioner's hood, a whip in one hand, a flaming torch in the other, wearing a large, silver crucifix on a heavy silver chain.

At the bottom of the painting were written the words, *Never Again the Burning!*

Medea motioned to the painting. "Do you recognize her?"

"I thought I did for a moment, but . . . no, it can't be. Jim wouldn't paint a picture like this of Bernice."

"And yet he did. This is part of what was done to her, before her rescue. See the shovel with bloodstains on the edge of its blade? Over here?" She pointed to an object in the painting lying half in, half out of the shadows. "That is what her torturer used to cripple her, what he used on her legs."

Joe felt cold deep inside. "It's so . . . horrible. No, it's worse than horrible. I can't think of a bad enough word!"

"Indeed."

"Why did Jim . . . I mean, how can he have it here, like this? Bernice must know, right?"

"Of course."

"But . . . she's still friends with him. Isn't she? They seem to be friends, but—"

"Will you wait here a moment, please."

Medea left Joe alone in the study. He tried not to look at the painting, but it drew him back again and again.

He struggled with the concept that it was a painting of something that had really happened to someone he personally knew, a woman he'd quickly grown to like. He did not want to think about Bernice screaming like that, naked and wounded, being mercilessly tortured.

Medea came back into the room. Bernice was with her. Because Bernice was naked in the painting, Joe felt a flush of awkward embarrassment.

Medea said, "Joe was wondering about your feelings regarding Jim having this painting on his wall."

"Yeah?" Bernice maneuvered her wheelchair so that she faced the painting. "I know why Jim keeps it here, Joe, and I don't mind him looking at it, if that's what you're thinking. I did for a while, when I couldn't stand to look at it myself, but that was before Medea. And Hecate.

"My sister," Bernice continued, "Gina, stopped having much to do with Jim because he painted this scene. But, for me, I no longer want to try to forget it happened. It's impossible to really do that, anyway, and I now know that atrocities to women such as my kidnapping and torture happen all over the world all of the time, and have for as long as men have been in control. Horrors like what happened to me must *not* be ignored. And *never* forgotten."

She pointed to the words at the bottom of the painting. "This refers to the Inquisition. Modern Wiccans and other Neo-Pagans call the Inquisition the Burning Times. In the more than 300 years the terror lasted, over nine million were killed. Nine *million,* Joe. Mostly women and girls. Tortured, mutilated, forced to confess to lies, burned at the stake.

"Hey, it was good business! The Church acquired the money, land, and property of most of those they condemned and at the same time did away with some of their staunchest rivals, wise women with knowledge passed down through generations of their female ancestors, knowledge of herbs and healing and midwifery the Church, power and control freak that it was then and still is now, condemned as Evil."

Bernice looked at Medea. She laughed. "But they didn't get *all* of them, thank Goddess." She returned her attention to Joe. "So, how do I feel about this painting hanging here?

"I would have *died* in that chair, if not for Gina and Jim and his friends, Barbara among them. And not all of them survived. Barbara's grandmother was killed and later a young woman named Janna. Afterward, Jim helped pay for my stay in the RCT. That's a special clinic in Denmark that treats survivors of torture from around the world. I'll tell you all about it sometime, if you want. I can do that now, thank Goddess. So, anyway, after all he did for me, Jim can have this on his wall with my blessing. I owe him, and my sister, and the others who saved me. And I always will, you know?"

Joe said, "I'm just . . . sorry. That it happened to you and all, I mean."

"Yeah," Bernice said. She looked down at her legs and gave them a slap. "Me too. But if it hadn't happened, I would not have experienced what I experienced near death, and if that had not happened, Hecate would not have noticed me, and I might never have met Medea. I may not be able to walk, but the other things I can do, the things I can feel, the things I am learning as an Empusa, it doesn't make up for not being able to walk, but my life has a purpose and meaning now it didn't have before. Sounds corny, I guess, but it's true."

Medea stepped near and squeezed Bernice's shoulder. She smiled down at her, then she looked at Joe. "You are still wondering, though, why I wanted you to see this painting, yes? Remember Jim saying, after your initiation, that he had once been an Inquisitor? When he looks at this painting, he thinks not only about the man, the Empusa, he is now, but also of the man he once was, an Inquisitor who took pleasure in women's screams."

Joe glanced at Bernice. She was looking at the painting again.

Medea continued, "So, let this painting be a reminder, Joe, that as an Empusa you will eventually have to face the worst in yourself and come to terms with it. Denying evil that exists within you, or believing someone or something other than yourself can cleanse you of its power, *gives* it power instead, the power to hide in your inner darkness and secretly influence your life. But when you face it, deal with it, and take responsibility for it, much of its power is destroyed. And when, in time, you must face a foe whose power attempts to turn your own evil against you, as many of them will, the attempt will fail. See?"

"So, I should . . . what? Put Euripides' plays on a shelf to remind me of what I once did?"

"That would be a good start. But you may find, as more of your memories are awakened, that you have done worse things than write plays to spread lies about me."

He looked at the painting. "Things like . . . *that?*"

She shrugged. "Perhaps. Or worse."

The thought sickened him. "Great. Just great."

Bernice reached out and took his hand. "You'll make it, Joe." She gave his hand a squeeze. "Sure, being one of us isn't always a picnic, but what is?"

"Hey, y'all," Trudy called out. "Come and get some food before I eat it all myself."

53
Feelings

On the drive to Jim's house, Medea had told the Empusae what had happened on the twenty-seventh floor. Over breakfast she answered questions about it and filled in details.

When breakfast was over, Joe volunteered to wash the dishes after Jim mentioned his automatic dishwasher was in need of repair.

"I'll help you," said Bernice.

"Me, too," said Barbara.

"The kitchen's too small for more than two," Bernice responded, "especially with my wheels. Joe and I can handle it. Right, Joe?" She smiled at him.

"Sure."

When they were finished with the dishes, Joe and Bernice joined the others in the living room.

"I didn't know doing dishes could be such fun," Trudy said. "What was so funny?"

"Yeah. What's with all the laughing?" asked Barbara.

Joe and Bernice glanced at each other, then started laughing again. "You had to be there," Bernice said.

"Yeah," Joe agreed, "you *had* to be there." And they started laughing again.

"Tell us!" Barbara said.

"It was just something silly," Bernice answered. "Nothing to tell. Really. Okay?"

Joe looked at Medea and realized she would know without their telling. Resentment unexpectedly flared. "Or get Medea to tell you what we're thinking."

"I did not read your thoughts, Joe. I sensed they were private and did not intrude."

"That'd be the first time."

"You do not believe me?"

No one spoke for a moment, then Bernice took Joe's hand and gave it a squeeze. "Hey, I didn't want her to know all my thoughts at first either."

"Yeah," Jim agreed. "It's a natural reaction."

Nick laughed. "Absolutely. I had an especially hard time of it in that respect."

"You think *you* had a hard time of it?" Trudy asked. "You don't *know* private thoughts until you know some of mine. More than once I figured she would turn away in disgust."

Jim said, "No way could yours be any more disgusting than some of mine. But I think Joe's got the point. Right, Joe?"

Joe took a deep breath. "Yeah. Okay. Sorry, Medea."

"There is no need to apologize," said Medea. "You have had a stressful time and are very tired."

"I won't argue with you there. I could use some sleep."

"Me, too," Bernice said. She was still holding his hand. And *something* in her voice made Joe look at her. And he saw *something* . . . in her eyes . . . that made something happen, deep inside, the stirrings of a cozy warmth and the beginnings of a gentle . . . sexual response?

Into his mind came Jim's painting of Bernice . . . naked.

Shocked at the direction of his thoughts and feelings, Joe pulled his hand out of Bernice's and quickly looked away.

"I'm sleepy too," Barbara agreed. "Bernice and I talked a long time after we got home. We thought we'd have all morning to sleep."

Joe looked back at Bernice. She was looking the other direction. But the feelings he had felt for her were still there, and his thoughts turned to doing with Bernice some of the sexual things he had done with Medea . . . and then he remembered that Bernice had said she sometimes had telepathic flashes. She might discover what he was thinking. She might get a flash of his imagining they were lying naked together, making love, and—

She looked back at him. She smiled. He looked away again.

"A cold shower usually helps me," Trudy said, breaking into Joe's thoughts.

"What?" He remembered Trudy saying she sometimes got telepathic flashes, too. *You're getting seriously paranoid, fool,* he told himself. But Medea might know. And she could send images to others. *Seriously paranoid. And exhausted.*

"A cold shower helps me to wake up, I mean," Trudy continued. "Or more coffee."

Medea said, "I believe we could all use some more coffee while we discuss what we are going to do next. When we have decided, there should be time for those of you who want to sleep to do so before we return to the hotel."

"Let's you and me get the coffee, Joe," Trudy said. She stood up.

Barbara said, "I'd rather have a cold Dr Pepper. I saw some in the fridge."

Bernice held up a hand. "Me, too."

"Okay. Come on, Joe."

Yawning, Joe followed Trudy into the kitchen.

In the kitchen, Trudy started water running hard and fast in the sink, then suddenly grabbed Joe's arm and pulled him close. She leaned toward him and said, keeping her voice low, "I want to talk about Bernice."

He frowned at her. "What?"

"She was hurt very badly by men."

"I know that."

"I saw something in there just now you may not have noticed. The message was clear. She is *interested* in you. This is the first time, as far as I know, that she has been interested in a man in that way since what men did to her years ago. Don't give her false hopes just to be polite."

"Damn. And I was looking forward to playing her along, then having a good laugh at her expense."

She gripped his arm harder. It began to hurt. He grimaced with pain. She released his arm.

Rubbing his arm, he fought to control his anger. Struggling to keep his voice down so he could not be heard above the running water, except by Trudy, he said, "You don't know me very well. Your thinking I might be a piece of shit pisses me off, but I'm glad you care what happens to Bernice. Okay? I don't want her hurt again, either. She's been hurt more than enough. Medea showed me the painting in Jim's study."

The expression in Trudy's eyes changed, but not for the better. "How did that painting make you . . . *feel?*"

"What?"

"Did you find it . . . exciting? Sexually?"

"You've got to be kidding."

"Do I *look* like I'm kidding?"

"You think I'm some kind of—"

"Because that's the way it affected me, the first time I saw it. I was the Countess Bathory in a former life, remember? Bernice was a friend, but when I saw the picture it didn't matter. So, I'll ask you again, how did that picture make you feel?"

Her admission surprised Joe out of his anger. He had momentarily slipped back into the mundane worldview he had known before meeting Medea. The sudden expansion of viewpoints from the here and now to the vistas of reincarnation was more than a little disorienting. He said, "You were . . . *excited* by the sight of Bernice being *tortured?*"

She looked away, then back at him again. "I thought the *old* feelings would go away after all that happened to Phil and me, battling the Pain Eaters and all. But they didn't, and I've learned to deal with it. I have *never* in this life hurt anyone like that. Phil and I do fantasy things, of course, but the point is that I *know* about those kinds of feelings and how they can twist people who can't satisfy themselves with fantasies. I hope to specialize in stopping people who do those kinds of things for real, when Medea thinks my Empusa skills are up to it. Kind of a payback for all the monstrous things I did when I was Erzebet. So, if there's any chance you might be interested in Bernice for *that* reason, I want to know about it *now.*" She stared at him, hard. "Well?"

"Well, I was just thinking you must be the kind of person I would once have walked across the street to avoid. But now—"

"Don't give me that *I didn't know she was a freak* look. I've seen it often enough before, and I'll tell you what I tell others. No need to make you special. Stick it up your ass. I'm not proud of once being Erzebet Bathory, but I *am* proud of being Trudy McAllen."

"You didn't let me finish. I was going to say, but now I feel like we're kind of friends. And that's as shocking to me, after what you just admitted, as anything else that has happened in the last twenty-four hours. Okay? And anyway, don't you think Medea has policed my thoughts enough to know whether or not I have any dangerous inclinations?"

Giving him another hard stare, Trudy said, "She's not

infallible, as recent events show only too well. So, just don't forget how I feel about Bernice."

"I won't."

"And if you ever do anything to intentionally hurt her—"

"I *won't!*" He was still rubbing his arm. "You've more than made your point. Okay? I like my arm attached to my shoulders. Even if I *was* some kind of sadistic monster, I wouldn't hurt Bernice now. Next time, you'd probably rip my arm out by the roots."

"And beat you to death with it."

"Right."

She took a deep breath. "Sorry if I bruised your arm."

"I'll live. But look, well . . . thanks for caring about Bernice. And, uh . . . don't tell anyone else, okay? But just so you'll know, I think I feel something special for her, too. I noticed it just a little while ago. Surprised the hell out of me. I don't know if anything will come of it. But I sure don't intend to hurt her in any way."

Trudy nodded. Her expression finally softened somewhat. "I hope something does happen between you and Bernice. Something really good."

"Me too, I guess."

She gave him a mock punch on the arm. "Okay." She turned and opened a drawer. "I'll start some fresh coffee brewing. I know where things are from earlier. You get the Dr Peppers."

54
Bite

When Joe and Trudy rejoined the other Empusae in the living room, Medea led the discussion to decide how best to handle the aftermath of the slaughter on the twenty-seventh floor.

No one expected the convention to continue. Mr. Dacobocon might have planned to close it down anyway that morning. But after the second group of deaths was discovered, surely the convention would close, and perhaps even the hotel, temporarily. Medea would check telepathically later in the morning.

Jim was scheduled to be on a writers panel at noon, but he could not avoid going without looking suspicious unless he had other than telepathically acquired information. However, if the con did close, the news would probably be on an all-news radio station to which Jim planned to listen later. Or someone might call from the con to tell him. If neither of those things happened, Jim, and the rest of them, too, would return to the hotel and pretend surprise when they learned what had happened on floor twenty-seven.

Whether they had to act surprised or not, if they all returned to the hotel, Nick and Joe would arrive with Jim and, if needed, pretend they intended to have lunch together as planned, to develop the Toxique comic book proposal, even though neither of them wanted to do Toxique's comic now. The second attack had, understandably, killed any remaining enthusiasm for the project. But Nick left open his offer to do the art for some future comic Joe might write.

After further discussions, Medea said, "It is decided, then, yes? If we receive no news that the convention has been closed, I will enter the hotel with Jim and Nick and Joe, but I will walk unseen. No one saw Joe leave the hotel with me, and if anyone remembers seeing him go with me after the party, I will make them forget. So, we can claim Joe spent the night with Jim and Nick, and that all of you left the hotel at the same time, well before the trouble began, while I went to the room and there was slain."

"I don't like that last bit," Joe said, "not even as part of our alibi." He held Medea's gaze. "I know there's no choice, because they're going to find Toxique's body and she looks like you, but it feels, I don't know, like bad luck or something, to say you're dead. You know?"

Medea smiled. "This is not the first time I have pretended to be dead."

"Oh. Well, I probably wouldn't have liked the sound of it those other times, either." He yawned. "Excuse me. The coffee doesn't seem to be helping. Can't hardly keep my eyes open."

Jim said, "If we're done discussing things, go get some sleep. Use my bedroom. And Bernice, you and Barbara earlier said you needed some sleep, too, so take the guest room, if you want."

Bernice said, "Sounds wonderful. Barbara?"

"Yeah. It does."

Medea said, "Everyone here, including myself, could use more rest before we return to the hotel. Now that our decisions have been made, I suggest we all take advantage of the time available to relax and strengthen ourselves."

Jim said, "You take the guest bedroom then, Medea. Bernice and Barbara can have my bed, and Joe—"

Medea laughed and said, "Keep the arrangements as they were. I will be on your patio for a little while, making use of your Texas sunlight, yes?" She stood and stretched, hands over her head, arching her back, up on tiptoes. "Then, after the cleansing sun, I would like a long, hot bath." She slipped off her black gown and draped it over the back of the rocking chair in which she had been seated.

"Goddess. That must hurt like hell," Trudy said, seeing the burn on Medea's stomach. The wound was a dark, crusted streak surrounded by red and badly swollen skin.

"The pain is not unmanageable."

Joe said, "I still say you should do something about it."

Medea looked at him. "I *am.*"

"I mean, like a doctor. An emergency room. Something."

"I've seen her heal worse wounds, Joe," Nick said. "Trust her."

"I do, I guess. If I can trust anything anymore. It's like there's quicksand where there had been solid ground. Maybe when I've had some sleep . . ." His words trailed off into another yawn.

Naked, Medea walked across the living room to Joe. "Look at it, Joe. The wound. Does it not look better now than earlier?"

She was right. It did. It looked like it was well on the way to healing. But it had only been a few hours.

She smiled down at him. "I heal quickly, yes?"

"Yeah." He couldn't stop himself from looking at the rest of her nakedness, too.

She leaned down and kissed the top of his head. "Go and

rest now." She walked to the patio door. She opened it, then paused and looked back. "All of you, rest now. Please."

She went out and closed the door behind her.

Jim's patio consisted of a small redwood deck surrounded by a high, privacy fence. On the deck were two deck chairs, a chaise longue, and to one side a portable charcoal broiler for cookouts. Through the patio window they saw Medea stretch out, face up, on the chaise longue, offering herself to the bright sunlight.

Bernice yawned. "Come on, Barbara. I'll race you to bed. Want to join us, Joe? We won't bite. Unless you want us to."

Jim laughed. "Watch out, Joe. They might ravage you."

Bernice grinned. "He's so sleepy, I bet he wouldn't mind." She nudged Barbara. "We could have our way with him, while he got some sleep."

Joe blushed, then grinned. "I'm not *that* sleepy."

"That's what I was hoping," Bernice responded. "But Medea told us to *rest*. So . . . another time, then?"

Joe changed his grin into a smile. "Another time." He did not laugh after he'd said it.

Bernice held his gaze a moment, then looked away and said, "Come on, Barbara."

Bernice maneuvered her wheelchair around and headed out of the room, Barbara at her side. As they left, Barbara leaned close to Bernice and said something and glanced back at Joe and they laughed together.

Joe stood up. He noticed that Jim and Nick were still looking at him.

Nick said, "I'll be damned, but I don't think Bernice was joking!"

"I agree," Jim said. "Joe, she's a wonderful woman. But she's had a lot of . . . problems with her feelings about men since she was hurt so badly by them."

"Yeah," Nick agreed. "She hasn't shown any interest like she just showed in you as long as I've known her. So—"

Trudy said, "Shut up, you two. I don't think it's any of your business." She caught Joe's eye.

"I disagree," Jim said. "I think he should know that—"

"Oh, hell," Trudy said. "I might as well tell you. I already lectured him about Bernice in the kitchen."

"And bruised my arm doing it," Joe added. "I'm glad you all care about Bernice. And you might as well know what I told Trudy. I think I'm interested in her, too."

"That's *wonderful*, Joe," Jim said. "Just go easy is all. Okay?"

"You can count on it. If I don't, Trudy has promised to rip off my arm and beat me to death with it."

"She's not just *any* old Amazon," Nick said, looking at Trudy. He laughed. "She's *our* Amazon."

"Thank Goddess," Jim added.

Smiling, Trudy gave them a slight bow of her head.

"Yeah," Joe agreed. He looked out the patio window. Seeing Medea stretched nude in the sunlight, tired or not he immediately felt aroused. But a moment later he was thinking again of Bernice and of Jim's painting.

He said, "Jim, the men who hurt Bernice, were they caught and . . . punished?"

"Oh, yes," Jim said. "Quite thoroughly. One in particular, the one who hurt Bernice most. He was pulled apart by the reanimated corpses of the other women he had killed."

"By the what?"

"It's a long story. I'll tell you about it some other time."

Joe looked again out the window at Medea. Looked again at the burn on her stomach. Remembered the repulsion he had felt at the thought of the invisible beast-thing she had become during the battle, the savage things he had seen her do to her attackers. But he also remembered the closeness to her he had felt during the transfer of energy. And the sex he had experienced with her, the intense pleasure of flesh and spirit combined . . . and, thinking those things, his thoughts again turned to Bernice.

With another yawn, he said, "I'm going to get some sleep."

55

A Perfect Day

Lying naked in the sunlight, eyes closed, Medea sighed contentedly and focused her attention on the pleasures of the moment.

The rays of the Sun bathed her bare skin in wonderfully penetrating warmth. A soft, sea-scented breeze caressed her hair. Water lapped lazily against the shore. And in the distance, she could hear children laughing and playing.

A perfect afternoon.

A perfect day.

For a young woman pregnant with her first child.

She was so lucky, a woman in love with a wonderful, loving man who would be there soon, to take her in his arms and kiss her and show her how very much he loved her.

Medea again sighed with contentment and shifted her position on the Sun-warmed sand.

She felt her unborn child move. She touched her womb and said, "Goddess bless you, little one," as she said each time she felt the movement of the new life growing within her.

"Ah, Jason, my love," she murmured. "We are going to have such beautiful children. Beautiful and strong daughters.

And sons. Blessed by the Goddess, each and every one. Blessed by our love . . ."

She drifted back to sleep. And later awoke.

But something had gone terribly wrong.

The air stank.

A muffled roar surrounded her.

She was in pain.

And, opening her eyes, she saw not the beautiful vista of the sparkling blue sea but a wooden enclosure, imprisoning her on three sides, and on the fourth, a strange building—

Her surroundings twisted into familiarity with a nauseating suddenness.

The Sun overhead and the Earth below were many centuries older now than on that perfect day in her dream. In her memory. Hundreds upon hundreds of years . . .

Even if she returned to that shore on the Mediterranean Sea, as it was now called, she could never recreate that day from so long ago. The water and air and sand were no longer the same, polluted by poisons, as was the air she now breathed in a backyard in Dallas, surrounded by the muffled roar of rushing traffic and crowded city life.

Her body might appear that of a young woman, but her mind and soul had aged with the Sun and Earth and Moon . . . so many years, memories, responsibilities . . . separating her from the young woman she had been before the horror began, before her lover became a child-killing monster, before hate and revenge and duty became the focus of her existence, before . . .

So many things . . .

That were now lost . . .

Polluted . . .

Destroyed . . .

Sitting in the sunlight alone, Medea let flow her tears, for more things than she could count.

But only for a little while.

Then she wiped at her eyes and stood and examined the wound on her stomach. The burn's accelerated healing was continuing. The pain was not nearly as bad.

She thought about going back inside but decided to give herself a little more time alone with the cleansing and strengthening Sun.

She stretched out face down on the chaise longue and focused her thoughts on immortality's rewards instead of its burdens.

She thought about lying in the sunlight without having to worry about the hazards of prolonged solar radiation. Not for her a future in which her skin became leathery and dry. Not for her any worry about cancer.

And sex. Not for her any worry about sexually transmitted diseases.

Nor graying hair.

Dimming eyesight.

Faultering organs.

Brittle bones.

She breathed deeply. She let her thoughts drift. And then she smiled.

How wonderful that Bernice and Joe had tender feelings for each other. She had not anticipated it. Even after so many centuries, life still held pleasant surprises.

"Goddess, bless them," she whispered. "May they find happiness." She pictured them in her mind as she had seen them earlier, laughing together, and she remembered what she had discovered from their thoughts. "May you laugh and love long and well, children, and find many perfect days to remember."

Soon, the sunlight warming her back, Medea slept once more and slipped into another dream. Another memory.

Naked and alone in the night, she stood on a cliff facing east, overlooking the sea, waiting for moonrise.

She stood with legs slightly spread, fists clenched at her sides, head held high. Her lips whispered prayers to Hecate. Her cheeks were wet with tears.

Wind from the sea whipped her long, unbound hair. Above, countless stars glittered in a clear, black sky. And behind her yawned the entrance to a cave deep and dark. The Cavern of the Crone. The Lair of Ancient Dreams. The Womb of Mother Death. Wherein waited either Life's end, or physical immortality. If she proved strong enough. Worthy enough.

Foolish enough.

The moments crept by, but she stood as a statue in a temple stands. Watching. Waiting. Praying. Until at last rose the Moon, swimming up from the depths of the sea.

She continued her prayers but spoke loudly now as the Moon rose higher.

Her prayers did not stop until the Moon rode high overhead, an orb as white as old bones.

Tears glistening in the moonlight, she turned and walked into the cave.

The Moon's light illuminated the path within for only a short way. Then she walked in darkness, feeling her way as one blind.

The path narrowed as it descended deeper and deeper into the Earth. Naked, she shivered with the increasing cold. Her bare feet ached with the chill of the damp stones upon which she walked.

The path twisted this way and that, at times becoming so narrow and the ceiling so low that she had to go onto all fours like the beasts of Mother Earth. Then the ceiling lowered still more, and she crawled forward on her belly as crawl the serpents.

The air became warmer. Where there had been cold, now there was stifling heat.

She gasped for air, sweat streaming, as she crawled on through the darkness within the Earth.

The path changed, allowed her to stand and walk again as a human walks. Then ahead she heard a rustling sound, knew what it was, slowed her pace, began whispering a chant of protection.

Soon, she felt them slithering over and around her feet in the darkness, the path now alive with countless snakes. She moved slowly, sliding her feet forward without lifting them, careful not to step on any of the hissing serpents, her whispered chant keeping her from harm.

Then she was past them, the rustling fading away behind as she moved yet deeper into the Earth. The heat continued to increase. But now, flickering faintly ahead there was light.

Around the next turn she found fire.

In the center of a vast cavern flames leapt upward from a pool of dark liquid. Bright though the fire was, the high, domed ceiling of the cavern was still lost in shadows.

She walked toward the flames until she began to feel pain from the heat.

Knowing what came next, she fought fear and a desperate urge to turn and run. To flee from the thing she had decided to do. From the vow she had made.

Then she remembered her children, lying sprawled in their own blood, and their murderer, laughing at her horror.

Fighting her fear with hatred and a renewed determination to have revenge upon the slayer of her children, the monster whose soul had temporarily escaped her fury, she stood her ground and waited for the Crone to speak, stood without moving, sweating in the heat, waiting . . . waiting . . .

"Nearer, three steps, if strong enough you be!" commanded an aged voice. The sound echoed from the walls of the cavern.

Medea said, "I *am* strong. I am worthy." And took three steps forward. She gritted her teeth with pain.

"Nearer, three steps, if strong enough you be!"

"I am strong," she said, between her clenched teeth. "I am worthy."

She took three steps closer to the fire. She gasped with pain, each breath a panted moan.

"Nearer, three steps, if strong enough you be!"

"I . . . am strong." Another step. "I am worthy!" And another. Gritting her teeth. Clenching her fists. The soles of her feet feeling as if seared by hot coals. No longer able to keep open her eyes. Gasping with agony. Taking a third step.

"Nearer, three steps, if strong enough you be!"

She made herself remember her children. She made herself remember Jason and how his soul had escaped her revenge. She made herself remember her vow to track him through time, to walk immortal until all that remained of him had been found and destroyed.

"I am . . . strong! I . . . am worthy!" She took another step, then two more, quickly, smelled the scent of singed hair. Her hair. And felt her skin . . . begin to blister . . .

"Nearer, three steps, if strong enough you be!"

She could not step nearer. She knew it as certainly as she had ever known anything. It was going to be *impossible* for her to walk slowly into the fire. But might there not be another way?

She staggered back until the pain of the heat was not so great and stood gasping for air.

The laughter of the Crone rang out. From the shadows near the entrance of the cavern emerged a wrinkled hag. Naked. Clutching a gnarled stick in one hand, a black-bladed dagger in the other. At her side paced a great black hound with eyes red as fire.

Creeping step by step closer, the Crone said, "You are weak, child! But you are not a fool. You do not run. You know my Hound would catch you." She cackled another laugh as she slowly raised the black dagger. "Come to me, now. Offer to me your throat. And your sweet blood. The price of your defeat."

"I came here not to die, but to live forevermore. And live I shall! I doubt that anyone ever became immortal by following the rules." Then she turned and screamed a wordless cry of pain and horror and hope as she *ran* toward the fire—

"Medea?"

She came awake at once and this time was not disoriented. Jim was standing at the patio door. "Are you all right?"

"Yes."

"You were moaning in your sleep."

"Ah, well, it was just an old memory, yes?"

"Medea . . . something has . . . happened."

She touched his thoughts. "Goddess. Have I made another foolish mistake?" She stood up and hurried toward the door. "I must be getting old."

56
Trap

"Look," Joe said, "I know I'm the newest member of this group, and I don't know a hell of a lot about what's what and where's where with this Empusa stuff yet. But one damned thing is certain. If the hotel is a trap, you should *not* walk into it alone!"

Medea answered, "Nevertheless, that is what I must do."

He looked at the others seated in Jim's living room. "Talk sense to her, somebody!"

While the others were still asleep, Jim had awakened from a nap and tuned in the all-news station on the radio in his study to see what was being reported about the new deaths at the hotel and to discover if the convention had been closed. But though he had listened for almost an hour, nothing had been mentioned of the slaughter on the twenty-seventh floor. As far as the news media was concerned, Medea's battle had obviously not happened. Which was when he had awakened her.

Medea had then used her mental powers to probe from a distance the minds of people in the hotel, where she discovered that, indeed, her battle seemed not to have happened. Meaning, she assumed, that Toxique had not been as dead as it had appeared and had evidently, like in a scene from

Joe's comic book about her, used her powers of atomic mutation to put things back the way they had been before the attack.

"Joe," Medea said, "while I appreciate your desire to help, we are not dealing with a death disorder of any ordinary sort here, nor with a merely physical threat such as the child killer yesterday. My best chance of survival is to enter the hotel alone and unseen with all of my psychic and mental shields and protections in place, then track and destroy her once and for all, without any hindrance from you or any of the others in this group."

Joe said to her, "Okay. None of the others. But you have to take me." He said to the others, "None of you have seen what Toxique can do. I have! Not just in my comic book but *for real*. I know the most about Toxique. I might be able to help. You can't let Medea make me stay here!"

"Yes, we can," said Bernice.

Trudy said, "Hell, Joe, I don't like it any better than you do! But we *have* to do what she says."

"And if," said Barbara, "she says we would only be in her way, including you, like it or not we've *got* to trust her judgment."

Nick said, "Joe, for Goddess sake, Medea can shapeshift and probably do all kinds of other things we don't even know about to survive."

Jim said, "If we were there, handicapping her and slowing her down, we could cost her the battle. Don't you see?"

"No." Joe looked at Medea. "If you're right and it is Toxique again, then it's still *my* fault she even exists. So, make the others stay here, but let me try to find some way to help without getting in your way. You won't have to worry much about Toxique hurting me. She probably still wants to rescue me is all. Goddess! It *is* like a comic book or a clichéd horror movie. The villain is dead. No he's not. Yes he is. No he's not. Or her. And why not? I *created* Toxique *for* a comic book! So, maybe I can think of something to help you destroy her. But not if I'm here!"

Medea walked across the living room to Joe. She was again wearing her flowing black gown. She knelt down so that they would be eye to eye. "Joe, I know Toxique as well as you. I have been within her mind. You cannot come with me."

"Then don't you go either, okay? Call the police or something. I guess that sounds lame, but please, at least wait a little while. Maybe we'll think of something else. Another way. Couldn't you call in more experienced Empusae from out of town to help?"

"There is not time. And how many others would Toxique harm at the hotel or elsewhere while I wait? No, I must go and go now. But alone." She smiled. "Trust me not to die, Joe. I have to train you yet, yes? Do you think I have lived all these centuries, just to let a mutated thought form kill me?"

A deep fear suddenly possessed Joe, adding to his anxiety. He felt panic building within him, danger and death rapidly approaching. "Medea. I can't let you go alone!"

She reached up and touched his forehead.

"What are you—"

His eyes closed and he slumped sideways on the couch.

Medea stood. She turned to Bernice. "There was harmful panic building within him. I despise that word 'panic.' It originated from the name of the Great God Pan. Weak humans who felt Pan's power tended to become terrified instead of joyous. Pan was a wonderful deity. And still is. He deserves a better legacy. As does our Hecate. But, there you are." She shrugged. "Allow Joe to sleep until I return, yes?"

Bernice nodded. "We'll watch him."

"Priestess," Barbara said, standing and going to Medea.

They embraced.

Medea kissed her then hugged her tightly.

Clinging to Medea, Barbara said, "Be careful. That sounds stupid. I *know* you'll be careful."

Medea hugged her again. "I love you, too." She moved away from Barbara. "And all of you. Try not to worry. Rest as best you can until I return, because I may well need your strength to replenish my energy if the battle is a hard one."

She slipped her black gown off and handed it to Barbara. She walked naked to the patio door.

She went out and closed the door behind her.

Then, through the window they saw her stand for a moment with arms upraised, fists clenched, and in the instant before she became unseen, upon her shifting form appeared the shape of vast black wings.

57

Rescue

To take his mind off the frustration and tension of waiting for Medea to return, Jim had decided to wash up in the bathroom that opened off his bedroom. That done, he slipped on fresh undershorts and socks, then walked to his bedroom closet for a clean shirt and jeans.

Jim, a woman's voice suddenly said in his mind. He turned quickly. Sudden fear gripped him. It was *her,* glowing with golden light, looking as she looked in his paintings, except more incredibly strong and beautiful than his art could ever capture. His Valkyrie! But her unexpected presence inspired him with fear, because she only appeared when he was faced with life-threatening danger. In confirmation of his fear, into his mind then came the words, *Great danger is approaching. Make haste. Follow me.*

Trudy was in the kitchen, fixing fresh coffee for herself and any who might want it.

Bernice was in the guest bathroom.

Nick and Barbara were sitting in the living room where Joe was still asleep on the couch.

Barbara looked at Joe and said, "I almost wish she had put me to sleep, too. That doesn't sound right. You know what I mean."

Nick replied, "We're all worried about her."

"Goddess, how long do you think we'll have to wait? No, don't answer that. You don't know any better than I do. But she'll be all right. She *has* to be all right."

"She's survived a long time. I'm sure she'll still be around after we're in Hecate's Womb, preparing for our next lives."

"Yeah."

Nick looked at his watch. "Well, it's been five minutes since I last checked my watch. Time really flies."

Barbara glanced at her watch, too.

The front door opened.

Seeing who was there, Barbara stood up and excitedly started to say Medea's name. But suddenly it no longer looked like Medea. It looked like a glowing skeleton covered with transparent flesh.

Twin beams of poisonous green radiation shot from Toxique's hands and vaporized Barbara where she stood.

Before Nick could cry out a warning to the others a new blast of focused radiation disassociated the atoms in his body and he was gone.

Toxique looked down at Joe. "Rescue time, lover," she said, "but first, there's the matter of the Witch's other slaves."

58

Intruder

While Joe continued to sleep, Toxique resumed the appearance of Medea and walked across the living room toward the kitchen. Trudy, busy with the coffee, unaware of what had happened in the living room, stood with her back to the doorway.

Toxique saw Trudy and without a word became a glowing skeleton and raised her hands for the kill.

Hurrying from his bedroom behind his luminous protectress, Jim saw the Valkyrie hurl her spear of golden light at the back of a glowing skeleton in the kitchen doorway. He recognized the intruder from Medea's descriptions.

"Toxique!" he shouted just as the Valkyrie's spear struck Toxique in the back.

Toxique screamed in pain and whirled around. She vaporized the spear buried in her flesh and then beamed radiation at her attacker.

The Valkyrie absorbed the radiation without flinching, materialized another light-spear, and hurled it at Toxique's chest. It struck and buried itself deeply in her glowing flesh.

Crying out with new pain, Toxique vaporized the second spear and fled.

The Valkyrie screamed a chilling battle cry and gave pursuit, golden light streaming in her wake.

"Goddess!" Trudy cried, emerging from the kitchen as Jim raced past into the living room.

Out the open front door he saw Toxique running down the street faster than any two-legged thing should have been able to run. The sight made him feel like laughing. *Thank you,* he mentally said to the Valkyrie, of whom there was now no sign. *Again you have saved my life. And thanks to Freya for sending you!*

"Where's the other one?" Trudy asked, also looking out the door. "Was that your Valkyrie? She saved my life!"

"She saved *my* life. And now that it's saved, she's gone."

Jim closed the door. It didn't catch. "She must have done something to the lock to get in." He bent to examine the lock. "Yeah. Look at that. She melted it!"

"I'll look in a minute," Trudy said as she knelt beside Joe, still sleeping on the couch. "He seems okay. When Medea puts them out, they stay out." She went to the door and looked at the melted lock. Then she looked at Jim, wearing only socks and undershorts. "Cute outfit. You're not half bad."

Jim looked down at himself. "I was getting dressed when—"

"What's all the shouting about?" Bernice came into the living room. She too looked at Jim in his shorts and socks. She raised her eyebrows. "What *is* going on?"

"You missed some excitement," Trudy replied. "Where's Nick and Barbara?" Trudy asked. "Did they miss it, too? They were here with Joe when I went to the kitchen."

Feeling sick at what he was thinking, Jim walked across the living room and looked down at a dark stain on the carpet. There was another one a short distance away, partially on the carpet, partially on the chair where he had last seen Nick sitting. And he knew. But he did not want to believe. "Look." He pointed. "I think maybe, I don't know . . . I think maybe they're . . . gone."

"What are you talking about?" Bernice asked. "Gone where?"

Trudy said, "They can't be. I just left the room to make more coffee."

Jim said, "These dark spots weren't here before."

"They *can't* be gone. Not just like that!"

Bernice said, "Hey, you two are scaring the shit out of me. Someone had better explain."

Trudy said, "Toxique was here."

"Here?"

Jim walked to the open front door again. He said, his voice less than steady, "We'd better keep a watch in case she decides to come back."

Trudy said to Bernice, "Jim's protectress, his Valkyrie, chased Toxique off before she could kill me and Jim and probably you. But . . . Nick and Barbara . . ."

Trudy's voice failed her.

"What about them?" Bernice demanded. "Oh, Goddess. What about them?"

"All I know," Trudy replied, trying to control her emotions, "is that they were sitting in the living room with Joe, but now . . . they're not."

"She got . . . Barbara. No!"

From the front doorway Jim said, "Toxique waited until Medea went to the hotel. There was a trap, all right, *but it was here.* She didn't hurt Joe, so I guess that means she still wants him. But I think maybe we'd better get the hell out of here before she makes another try."

Trudy said, "We could use your Valkyrie's help again. *Medea* could use it. I've heard you say you can't control when the Valkyrie appears, but she might come if you were in danger again, say at Medea's side."

"And she might not. I've been in danger other times and she *didn't* show. Anyway, her spears only seemed to *hurt* Toxique. They didn't kill her."

Bernice fought tears. "I don't see . . . Barbara's ghost. Or Nick's. Did . . . either of you see them?"

Trudy looked at Jim. He slowly shook his head no.

"I didn't either," Trudy said.

"So," said Bernice, "maybe they're *not* dead. Maybe they got away somehow."

"Or maybe," Trudy said, "Toxique also . . . got their souls."

No one spoke for a moment, then the grief on Bernice's face changed to a look of hatred. "To hell with this! I'm going to the hotel!"

Jim said, "Bernice, Medea does not want us there."

Trudy said. "Maybe Bernice is right. Maybe we might as well go to the hotel. I doubt that we can hide from Toxique. Remember what Medea said? Toxique has mental powers, too. So, we can't hide from her for long, unless . . ." She looked down at Joe. "Our only chance to get away from her might be if she's focused on Joe and we leave him behind."

"We're not leaving him behind!" Bernice exclaimed. "How can you even suggest such a thing?"

"I wasn't," Trudy answered. "Really, I wasn't. Medea would never forgive me, right?"

"Nor would I. Get your clothes on, Jim, if you're coming with us to the hotel. And we'll take Joe along, but for two reasons: to protect him as best we can and to *make* Toxique come after us. Maybe it will be Medea who sets the trap this time."

Jim said, "You mean, use Joe as some kind of bait?"

Trudy said, "I kind of thought you . . . cared for him."

"I do. But he's one of us, now, and when we wake him up I bet it's what he would want to do, too. That thing killed Barbara! And Nick. And by Hecate I intend to watch Toxique die!"

59

Gone

Joe heard Bernice's voice crying out, "Goddess! *It's gone!* Oh, Goddess! Goddess!"

He struggled to shake off the clinging remnants of deep sleep.

He fought to open his eyes.

He succeeded.

His vision was blurred at first. Then it cleared.

He was lying on the back seat of the van. The engine was idling, but the van was not moving. How had he gotten there? The last thing he remembered was being in Jim's living room and Medea, touching his forehead—

"Goddess!" Bernice cried again.

Fighting lethargy, Joe sat up.

With Bernice behind the wheel, Jim was next to her in the front passenger seat, both of them staring straight ahead. Trudy sat behind Jim, hunched forward, leaning on the front seat, also staring out the front window.

Joe looked out the front window, too. What he saw made no sense. He glanced around. On each side of the van and behind he saw a familiar city street leading to the hotel where the comic book convention was being held. People were hurrying out of houses along the street, looking toward what Jim and Bernice and Trudy were looking at out the front window. Joe looked in that direction, too.

In front of the van there was desolation, a kind of crater, blackened, smoking, jagged spears of metal twisting here and there toward the smoke-filled sky. Then he remembered what he'd heard Bernice say. "It's all gone!"

The hotel? Is that what she'd meant. The hotel was gone?

Bernice saw him in the rearview mirror. "Joe!"

"Yeah? What the hell's going on?"

All three turned to look at him. Bernice said, "We tried to wake you but couldn't."

"Medea put me to sleep, right?"

"Yes," Trudy said, "and while you were asleep—"

"Barbara . . . she's dead, we think," Bernice said. Joe saw that her eyes were red, as if she had been crying. "And Nick."

"What?"

Jim said, "Toxique came to the house. My Valkyrie drove her away before she could kill all of us. But . . . it looks like Nick and Barbara didn't make it."

"I . . . where's Medea? She went to the hotel! And the hotel . . ."

Bernice wiped at her eyes. "We don't know. But . . . if she was in the hotel . . ."

"Ground zero," Trudy said. "More of Toxique's work. Goddess help us, it sure as hell looks like she got Medea, too."

Jim wiped at his eyes and cleared his throat. "Yeah. Toxique caused the crater for sure. If it had been a natural explosion, lots of the houses along this street would have been flattened, too. We didn't *hear* an explosion, and obviously there was no shock wave."

Joe said, "But . . . all those people . . . in the hotel, and Medea . . . oh, no . . . no . . ."

"The question is," Jim said, "what are *we* going to do? If Medea's . . . gone, we're the only ones still alive who know about Toxique. She'll come after us, even if Joe isn't with us."

"I *caused* all of this," Joe said. "Me!"

"Joe," said Bernice, "no one blames you. And I heard Medea tell you not to blame yourself."

"So what? My filthy little comic book creation has killed Medea, too!"

"We don't know that for certain," Trudy replied. "She *might* have telepathically picked up the threat or something and avoided it."

"Then where *is* she?" Joe demanded. "If she were still alive, she would have come to you, to us, and you know it. And you also know I'm responsible for her death."

"What I know," Trudy replied, "is that we don't have time for you to feel sorry for yourself. Okay?"

"Feel sorry for *myself?* What I feel sorry for is all the people Toxique has killed! And is going to kill." He looked at Bernice. "I'm not going to let that happen to you," he said, holding Bernice's gaze. "I'll stop her myself. Somehow. I'll trick her. Make her think I want to be with her. Then when I'm close enough—"

"She'll read your mind and know the truth!" said Bernice.

"And maybe she won't care. She thinks Medea twisted my thoughts around."

"If neither Medea nor my Valkyrie could kill her, it's damned unlikely you could," Jim said. "I admire your bravery, Joe, but—"

"Bravery! Bullshit. *Desperation.*" He slid along the seat toward the door. "Let me out."

"No," said Bernice. "Trudy, don't let him go."

Trudy and Joe locked eyes. "You know I'm the only chance we've got, Trudy. The only chance a lot of people have got. Let me out. I'll start walking. Toxique will find me somewhere away from you three. Then I'll see what I can do."

Trudy hesitated a moment longer, then she said, "Shit. I think he's right. It's probably our best chance of stopping her."

"No! said Bernice. "It's no chance at all!"

"Better take this," Jim said. From beside him he lifted a shotgun into view. "I brought it from the house."

Joe said, "If I'm going to trick her, I can't approach her with a weapon."

"You could, if you make her think Medea has twisted your mind so you want to kill her."

"Damn! I don't know."

Bernice threw the van into reverse and backed into a residential driveway.

"What are you doing?" Joe cried.

But Bernice did not answer. She simply put the van into drive and burned rubber back the way they had come.

60

Luck

"Stop, Bernice!" Joe shouted. "Damnit it to hell! Stop and let me out."

Bernice, hands gripping the wheel, knuckles white, laughed and said, "Make me."

"Bernice!"

"I don't believe in suicide. Not mine. Not yours. I almost tried it once after what happened to me, before Medea came along, and it sucked, big time. Okay?"

"Jim, Trudy, make her stop the damned van and let me out!"

"How?" Jim asked. "If I grab the wheel and wreck us it won't solve much."

"Bernice," Trudy said, "look, maybe you *should* stop. Can't you see that Joe—"

"Goddess!" Bernice threw on the brakes.

"That's more like it!" Joe said.

"I didn't stop for you."

Then he saw what she meant. A woman wearing a black flowing gown, tall and exotically beautiful, her hair long and dark and unbound, was standing in the middle of the street, smiling at them. A woman who looked like Medea.

"It's Toxique," Joe said. "Medea would know our

thoughts, know about Barbara and Nick and how scared we all are. She wouldn't be smiling. Give me the damned shotgun and let me out."

Jim passed the shotgun to Trudy who handed it to Joe. She opened the side door.

Bernice said, "Joe, think about this a minute."

"We don't have a minute."

"What I meant was, if you get out, she'll have no reason not to blast the van. Stay with us!"

"If I stay, she'll just walk up to the van and kill you one by one. She's already walking toward us. Wish me luck."

"No!"

"You don't wish me luck?"

"Luck," Trudy said and gripped his shoulder.

"Yeah," said Jim. "May Hecate and Freya protect you, because we sure as hell can't."

Joe got out and walked toward Toxique.

"I should have wished him luck," Bernice said as she watched him go. "I feel so damned helpless. I can't even run away!"

"None of us can," Trudy said. "Guys, if Joe doesn't get her, it's been fun, right?"

"Right," said Jim after a moment. "Lots of fun."

"I should have wished him luck," Bernice repeated. She released her grip on the wheel long enough to wipe at her eyes. "I should have wished him luck."

61

Fury

"What's the gun for, lover?"

"To kill you, of course." No point in trying to conceal anything from her. His only hope was if she kept thinking Medea had warped his mind, long enough for him to get close enough for a killing shot.

He was aware that people, from the homes along the street, who had come out to check on what had happened down the street were now, seeing his shotgun, shouting warnings to each other and scattering, but he did not look at them. He looked only at Toxique.

Toxique laughed. "Does this mean you don't love me anymore?"

Joe did not know much about guns. When he was a kid, he and his dad had gone pheasant hunting with an uncle, and he'd learned how to use a double-barrelled job similar to the one Jim had given him. So he knew how to cock it and pull the trigger and that he was supposed to hold it tightly against his shoulder to prevent getting a bruise from the recoil. And he could have loaded it with more shells, if he'd had any. But that was it.

This should be enough, though, he thought, *if only I can get close enough before she turns on her powers.*

When she was glowing, she was nearly invulnerable. At least that was how he had written it in his comic. His damned comic! He cocked both hammers of the shotgun and kept walking toward her.

"That's right, Toxique, I don't love you anymore. I love only Medea, now, and she wants me to shoot you. So, that's exactly what I am going to do!"

Toxique clapped her hands. "Bravo, Joe. A fine performance. But it won't work, lover. I know your plan. Truth is, I don't care if you love me anymore or not. I want you, because I still consider you to be mine. And I'm going to have you. How you feel about it doesn't matter. It might be fun, though, having you try and fail again and again to kill me. I'd enjoy finding new ways to punish you each time. What do you think? Sound like fun? But first, I hope you didn't leave anything of importance in that van, because it's about to go bye bye."

She raised her hands and began to glow as Joe raised the shotgun and fired first one barrel then the other.

He was not as close as he'd hoped to be, and buckshot from the first barrel went wide to the right, but the second blast caught Toxique in the chest.

Blood erupted. She staggered back. Her glowing dimmed. She went to her knees. She looked up at Joe. Blood dripped from her mouth. Then she laughed. And sprang back to her feet. And began glowing again, the wound in her chest vanishing as she again became a luminous skeleton wearing transparent skin.

And again she raised her hands, aiming at the van.

Joe screamed, "No!" and ran forward, holding the shotgun by its stock like a club. But he could see he was not going to be in time. She was going to kill Bernice and Trudy and Jim. "No!" Still running, he hurled the shotgun at her. It struck her left shoulder a glancing blow she all but ignored.

Running, running, trying to stay between her and the van, wanting only to get close enough to throw himself against her and get his hands around her throat. Touching her while she was glowing might kill him, if it worked like in his comic, but he didn't care. He had to stop her, get his hands around her neck, kill her—

A piercing cry from above made Toxique hesitate and look up. Joe, however, did not look up. He used the extra time to cover the remaining distance and threw himself at the glowing monstrosity he had helped to create. But he hurtled instead through empty space, because suddenly Toxique was no longer on the ground.

Joe impacted with the street, knocking the breath from him. Struggling to breathe, he rolled onto his back, saw a coal-black nightmare-thing with vast bat-like wings and red, glowing eyes lifting Toxique into the air, its ebony talons embedded in the flesh of Toxique's shoulders and upper arms.

Toxique screamed, thrashed, twisted, and jerked spasmodically as the winged thing lifted her higher and higher, black smoke erupting from the places where its taloned feet touched the glowing, radiation-burning flesh of Toxique.

Toxique raised her hands to aim a killing beam at the thing that was carrying her into the sky. But the winged monster struck first, arching its long neck and covering Toxique's head with its befanged maw.

Its jaws clamped down, stiletto teeth slicing through Toxique's chest and shoulders and skull even as it pierced Toxique's lower body with its talons and pulled, splitting open the belly of its glowing prey while its own flesh charred and smoked wherever it touched Toxique.

But even then Toxique refused to die. She spasmed and thrashed ever more frantically. Her muffled screams squeezed from within the thing's mouth. Until the winged monster closed its jaws all the way and there came a decisive crunching sound.

Followed by silence.

Toxique stopped glowing. Her body went limp. But the winged thing was not finished. As it flew ever higher, it shook its head and tore free what was within its jaws, then began ripping and tearing the rest of Toxique's flesh with its talons, pulling the dangling corpse apart.

Drops of blood spattered the pavement around Joe. He felt warm moisture splash onto his face. Chunks of crimson flesh fell here and there on all sides as the monster in the heavens continued jerking Toxique's corpse apart and, Joe now saw, sickened by the sight, *devouring* the pieces that it did not drop.

"Goddess," he heard someone say nearby. Trudy. Jim was with her. Bernice was driving the van nearer. He heard sirens in the distance getting louder. Jim offered him his hand.

"You okay?" Jim asked.

Joe took Jim's hand and got to his feet. "I guess."

Jim picked up his shotgun.

Joe gawked upward again. The winged thing was almost out of sight.

"Joe!" It was Bernice in the van, pulling to a stop near where they stood.

He hurried to the driver's side and she opened the door and they put their arms around each other. "Goddess, Joe. I thought you were going to die."

"I thought we were *all* going to die," Trudy said, climbing into the van. "You're my kind of hero, Joe."

"Yeah," Jim said as he climbed into the front passenger seat. "Thanks for helping Medea save our butts."

"Medea? That winged . . . thing?"

"Yes!" Bernice answered. "She's still alive!"

"But—"

"She showed us her winged form one time," Bernice continued. "It's the form of a Fury. You've heard of the three Furies, right?"

"Maybe."

"Winged avengers. Related to Hecate."

"Like us, Joe." Trudy said. "And you. Hurry up and get in. Those sirens are getting damned close, and we've got to be gone before the cops get here."

"But," Joe said, "people along the street *saw* what happened. Look. They're coming back out now. They'll tell the police. And the cops will be hunting for me, and you three, and this van, and—"

"Just get in!" Bernice said. "We'll worry about all that later. Trust us, damnit! We know where Medea will be coming to ground. She sent a mental image as she flew away. And after that battle, she'll need all the energy we can give her in order to heal her wounds and live. So, the most important thing right now is to reach her. Okay?"

62

Disguise

Bernice drove to an isolated, deserted farmhouse north and west of Dallas, near Denton.

The driveway leading up to the house was overgrown with weeds. Bernice pulled the van into a barn that looked ready to fall down. Once inside, the van could not be seen from the road or from the air.

"I didn't think I'd *ever* have to come back here," Trudy said. "It's a good choice, away from town and all, but Medea's got lots of nerve, coming here. I suppose it was the only place she knew but still—"

"What do you mean?" Joe asked.

"Medea knows this place because this is where Phil and I nearly died. Damn if it doesn't still give me the creeps. Just don't say barbed wire to me while we're here, okay?"

"Barbed wire?"

Trudy glared at him. "Is that supposed to be funny?"

"No! I—"

"Okay. Maybe I'll tell you about it sometime."

The front door of the abandoned farmhouse was standing half open. They went inside.

The floor of what had once been a living room was littered

with cigarette butts and empty beer cans and candy wrappers and bean dip cans and tortilla chip sacks.

"Not my idea of a good place to party," said Trudy. She wrinkled her nose at the smell. "Yuk."

Medea was in the backyard, lying on an old, stained mattress, naked in the sunlight. She raised her head as they came near.

"I am so . . . sorry," she said, her voice harsh and low, wounded, "about Barbara. And Nick. If I had not . . . left you alone—"

"Stop it," Bernice said, fighting new tears at the mention of her lost friends. "No one blames you. You did what you thought was best."

"But do not worry . . . for their souls. They . . . are why I am . . . still alive."

"They weren't . . . destroyed?" Bernice asked.

Medea answered, "They came to me immediately after Toxique destroyed their . . . bodies. They told me what had happened, and I . . . was returning . . . to help you when the hotel was . . . destroyed. It was indeed a trap . . ."

Tears streaked Bernice's cheeks. "She *didn't* get their souls!"

"They are with Hecate, now . . ."

It hurt Joe to look at the wounded Priestess. She was horribly burned. Her hands. Face. Chest. And her skin was stained with dried blood, Toxique's blood, especially the charred remains of her mouth.

She met Joe's gaze. "I will . . . heal . . . with your help," she grimaced and her body momentarily stiffened with a spasm of deep pain. "But, Joe . . . you need not give energy again, so soon."

Without stopping to think he said, "I want to, please."

"Thank . . . you," she said. "All of you."

They helped Bernice onto the mattress so she could touch

Medea, then they knelt on both sides of the wounded Priestess and began to transfer life-energy to her once more.

Again Joe felt his consciousness mingling with hers as he
willingly allowed her to draw life-energy from him. And he
felt an intense closeness to the others, too, especially Bernice,
as they mingled together to help Medea.

But because Joe's energy levels had not had time to build
back fully since that morning, the transfer pulled on deeper
layers of his consciousness this time, forcing him to open
himself more fully than before.

More and more of his essence did he allow to stream
toward Medea's center of being, pulling on deeper and
deeper layers of his soul. Memories of former lives flashed
faster and faster through his consciousness as he moved
farther and farther back in time, until suddenly he sensed
danger ahead and tried to stop his journey backward
through the layers of his being, but it was too late. He had
opened himself too fully and an image of a life long hidden,
an identity long disguised, erupted to loom over all the other
lives he had ever lived.

Horror too long denied.

Evil too long unpunished.

He tried to pull away before Medea and the others
learned his secret. But it was already too late for that. Mingled with Medea's consciousness and the others as he was,
they knew in an instant.

Her rage stabbed into the core of his soul. *You!*

He tried to get away, could not escape.

You! she repeated. *A disguise!* Then his consciousness was
flayed by the razored shards of her scream.

63

Empusa

When Joe awoke, he was lying on the mattress in the back-yard of the deserted farmhouse. He saw Jim and Trudy and Bernice, again in her wheelchair, nearby, staring at him. *They know,* he suddenly realized. *Goddess. They know.*

Joe sat up. His head hurt. He rubbed his temples. "Where is she? What is she going to do?"

"To you?" Trudy asked. "Scared?"

"What do you think? Look. I didn't *know.* I—"

"She's gone," Jim said. "As soon as the transfer was finished, she just got up and walked away. Told us not to follow."

"*Warned* us is more like it," Bernice said.

Joe asked, "How long has she been gone?"

Jim looked at his watch. "About an hour."

Joe stood up, swayed unsteadily on his feet. His head hammered with pain. "Why am I still alive? Why didn't she kill me? I felt as if I was being torn apart, my soul, I mean, by her rage and her screams. I *should* have been destroyed. I . . . *deserve* to be. She's wanted to destroy my soul for so long. Why didn't she?"

"She didn't share that with us," Trudy answered.

Joe looked at Bernice. He tried to think of something to say to her.

"How long do you think we should stay here?" Trudy asked Jim. "She may not come back."

Jim said, "With energy from the four of us, she healed a lot, but far from completely. And that's not the only reason I think she will be back. There are lots of loose ends that need tying up in Dallas. She wouldn't just leave all that in our laps. And then there's Joe. Oh, yes. I'm sure she'll be back."

There was a sound in the house. In the doorway, Medea appeared.

Joe faced her. He forced himself to meet her wounded gaze. He found no words to say. He remembered the first time he had ever seen her, on Colchis in Hecate's Temple, so long ago.

Medea was silent for a moment, then she said, her voice subdued, "It seems that the Goddess sometimes likes to play jokes, even on me. I projected myself into Her presence just now. She granted a response to my questions."

She walked closer to Joe. She stared at him in silence, then said, "I am not going to harm you. I am not going to punish you.

"I remember what you once were, and so now do you, a great man with a hero's soul that I loved more than life itself. And we both know what you are now, what you have become, and the petty lives you have lived since that night of horror and blood so long ago.

"Your hiding from your deepest truth has been a worse punishment than any I could have devised. In my rage, I once took your life and sought to destroy your soul. But you escaped me then and for all the years I have lived, and now I know how. Hecate finally deemed me worthy to be told.

"The Goddess Herself sheltered your soul and hid it from me! But not to be kind.

"She knew you would punish *yourself* by living horrible little lives of denial and guilt. And she knew my lust for revenge would keep me searching for you through the corridors of time, knew my undying fury would give me the strength I needed to acquire undying flesh with which to serve Her, immortal."

Silence.

Then suddenly Medea laughed. "But, little hero, not all of your old self has shriveled away. I saw you today from above, attacking Toxique, not so much for yourself as for your friends. Especially for Bernice. Yes?"

Joe remained silent.

Medea looked at the others. "It is time we returned to Dallas. There will be many souls adrift from the disaster at the hotel, souls we must help to the other side. And there are many minds I must touch, many witnesses of the battle I must confuse in order to protect us all." She stared at Joe. "Including you, old soul.

"You always did have a strong imagination, even in the days when our love was young. And since it seems I am going to allow you to live, I must make certain you have all the training necessary to prevent another Toxique from being formed."

Joe finally spoke. He glanced at Bernice, then back at Medea. "You mean . . . you *still* want me to be an Empusa?"

"You *are* an Empusa," Medea replied. "Hecate accepted you, remember?"

"Yeah. But, well . . ."

Medea turned and walked into the abandoned farmhouse.

Jim gave Joe a smile, then turned and followed the Priestess. So did Trudy. But Bernice did not move.

Joe walked slowly closer. "I'm : . . sorry, Bernice. Sorry

that I'm not what you thought. Sorry . . . oh, Goddess! So sorry for so many, many things . . ."

He struggled to keep from crying. He failed.

Bernice took his hands in hers. "You don't have anything to be sorry about. Not anything *recent*. Other than unknowingly creating Toxique. And this morning you *saved* lives. You did a horrible thing a long time ago, and probably in other lives, too, but not today you didn't. Hey, are you listening to me, Joe? *Not today.* Right?"

He didn't answer.

"Right?"

"Yeah. Right. I guess."

"You guess." She squeezed his hands, then lifted them to her face and kissed them. She looked up at him. She smiled. "Come on. They'll be waiting. And I'm the one with the keys."

* * *

About the Author

C. Dean Andersson is a critically acclaimed author whose Zebra novels, *I Am Dracula* and *Buried Screams,* were recommended for the Horror Writers Association Bram Stoker Award, as were his *Torture Tomb* and *Raw Pain Max.* Other works include five novels written under the pen name of Asa Drake, and short stories, one of which, "Horror Heaven," co-authored with Nina Romberg, appears in Zebra's *Dark Seductions* anthology. Dean holds degrees in physics, astronomy, and art. He has worked as a professional artist, musician, robotics programmer, and technical writer. He lives in the Dallas/Fort Worth Metroplex where he is at work on his next Zebra novel.